YO YO LOVE

YO YO LOVE

Daaimah S. Poole

KENSINGTON PUBLISHING CORP.

DAFINA BOOKS are published by

Kensington Publishing Corp.
850 Third Avenue
New York, NY 10022

ISBN 0-7394-2780-6

To Hamid Nasir Poole

Acknowledgments

First I would like to thank Allah for making this possible.

My son Hamid, I love you. Thank you to my mother, Robin Dandridge, and my father, Auzzie Poole, for all your love, support, and guidance. My sisters Daaiyah, Nadirah, and Najah Goldstein; grandmothers Delores Dandridge and Mary Ellen Hickson; my aunts Bertha Dandridge, Elaine Dandridge, Edith White, and Cynthia Cargill; my uncles Teddy and Aaron Dandridge, Herbie Kidd, Jr., Steven, Julius, Eric, and Leon Poole; my cousins, Keva, Iesha, Tiffany, Leno, Lamar, Arron; Khalif Mears and Al-Baseer Holly; all the kids, my first and second cousins. To my stepmother, Pulcheria Ricks Poole, thanks for treating me like your daughter.

Special Thanks
Alvin Cooke—thanks for having my back and being there for me. Keva Dandridge—thanks for listening. Aisha Murphy and Aida Allen, thanks. Thank you to Ethel Allens, Principal Mrs. Elizabeth Riley, and former principal Mr. Herbert Rodgers for encouraging me at an early age. Thanks soooo much to my first readers for taking the time to read my work and encouraging me to keep writing: Michele Gray, Sonja McCleary, Shonda Evans, Lisa Jones, Yvette Williams, Tai-neisha Bryant, Sheila Williams and Hope Poole.

Thanks
Helena Gibson, Deidra Potter, Maryam Abdus-Shahid, Darryl Fitzgerald, Miana White, Katrina Elliot, Tamika Wilson, Dena Riddick, Gina Delior, Carla Lewis, Tamika Floyd and Tyesha Fischer. My girls at Ebauche Envouge Hair Salon, Qolour Shynes Hair Salon, Candance Irvin, Knots And Tangle, Nisa McGough, April Williams, Shawna Grundy, Dinyelle Wertz, Leonna Maddox, Janice Creswell, Linda Womack, Tracy P. Davis, Rameeka Presberry, Ms. Judith William Wise, Jenise Armstrong, Sherlaine Freeman, Adrian Thomas, C. Carolyn Jones, Loraine Ballard Morrill, Jabari Higgs, Kia Morgan, Jonathan Tuleya, Cheryl Haines, and Carol Denker. Thank you Kensington and

Karen Thomas for this opportunity and PMA Literary and Film Management.

Literary World
Journey End Literary Club, Vanessa Woodward, Rhonda Gibson, Our Story of Plainfield, N.J., Nubian Bookstore of Atlanta, The Black Library of Boston, Basic Black Books of Philadelphia and The Circle of Sisterhood, Vera Leath.

Thank you to Karen E. Quinones Miller—thank you so very much for believing in me. Camille Miller, thanks for giving your mom the book.

R.I.P.
My cousins and friends, Shahid Dandridge, Anthony Poole, Lamar "Woo" Kidd, Nicole Poole, Nicole Potter, and George "Wink" Jackson.

Final Word
Thank you again to my family, friends, and everyone who has been by my side since the beginning. This book is just an example that with hard work and determination anything can be accomplished.

Thanx a mil,
Daaimah S. Poole

Chapter 1

Kayla Simone Johnson

My life is a complicated one. I used to go out a lot, meet a lot of people, but now I don't feel like meeting anyone. My ginger brown complexion, long brown hair, and nice shape definitely turn heads. But I don't care about heads turning anymore, because I'm content with life. I used to think I needed a man, but now I know better. Actually, now I see I don't need one at all. I wish other women would realize that, too! Getting on talk shows arguing over men who lie and cheat and writing books about men. Who needs a man anyway? I don't. I met a man who proved it to me. Here is my story.

First, I'll tell you all about the boah, Emar. I met him one cold, rainy Wednesday morning as I was walking across Temple University's campus. I know the exact time, 11:40, because I was coming from an anthropology class I had forced myself to attend. Once I arrived at the class, I was told my professor would not be in. Damn. I had gotten up for nothing. I was mad as hell. I can't believe I'm only a sophomore and still have two more years of this shit.

It was one of those days when you just wanted to stay under the covers. That day, the sun must have gone on vacation and a nasty gray sky was subbing for it. It had to be about twenty-seven degrees outside, with freezing rain. I had on a gray sweat suit with a white tee hanging out and my Nike jogging sneakers. I was wearing my big coat, but the cold air was still going through my layers. Besides my coat, the only thing that somewhat protected me was my umbrella.

In no way did I feel attractive. I knew everybody else was feeling the exact same way—except for this one girl who was coordinated to the tee. Now, how some women manage to look like runway models when it's pouring down raining, I will never understand.

She was carrying a green, navy, and maroon plaid umbrella and wearing a navy beret that was tilted to the side with her hair peeking out. She also had on a navy wool pea coat with a maroon scarf wrapped around her neck that set it off just right. I was impressed. Here it was, I almost couldn't wake up and sis was looking like she was about to pose for *Vogue* magazine. All she needed was a poodle to walk and she would have been picture-perfect.

Well, back to my story.

It was cold and I was heading back to my small dorm room at Hardwick Hall when out of nowhere this guy came and got under my umbrella. I gave him a look like, "What the fuck?"

He smiled, and all I saw was his perfect gleaming white teeth, slanted eyes, and oak brown skin. He was about 6-feet 4-inches tall, with jet black hair. He also had a goatee and a little bit of peach fuzz above his lip.

"What's up, sis, can I get under here with you?" he asked with a huge smile.

I didn't say yes or no. He didn't give me a chance. All I knew was somehow he had steered me around and I was now walking in the opposite direction of my dorm.

"Where we going? I don't know you. Getting all under my umbrella like that. I never saw you on campus. You could be a killer." I jerked my arm away from his grip. Who the hell did he think he was, anyway? He was cute, but he wasn't all that.

"My bad. I'm not no killer. I don't bite and you never saw me 'cause I'm always on the road. You don't know me? You like basketball?"

"Yeah, I like basketball. Just not college ball. Why?" I said, shrugging.

"Why not college ball?"

" 'Cause you don't know none of the guys who are playing. It's just a bunch of nobodies running up and down the court."

"I guess I'm one of those nobodies. I'm Emar Gerson and I play point guard for the Owls," he said, shaking his head as if he couldn't believe I didn't know who he was.

"Really," I said, embarrassed.

"Yes, really."

"Where you got me walking to anyway?" I asked, trying to change the subject.

"I don't know. You want to get some coffee or something?" he asked as he glanced at his watch.

"I don't drink coffee, but maybe I can get a tea or something."

So I walked with this cute stranger to the coffeehouse, which was in the middle of the campus student activity center. It was packed. Like us, everyone was trying to stay warm.

As we made our way in, it seemed as if everyone was speaking to Emar, who just nodded his head up like, "What's up?" and kept walking. It made sense that everyone knew him because he was a senior and had been at Temple four years, plus he was a star basketball player. Watching him, I was so intrigued with his coolness that I almost bumped into some airhead freshman girls who were just all in the way.

"Hey, E," they said, giggling.

He didn't respond. As a matter of fact, he acted as if he didn't know them. He kept me from colliding into the blushing girls by nudging me slightly out of the way. Emar ordered my tea and his coffee and found a table for us. I grabbed us some sugar and poured pack after pack into my hot, steaming tea. Then I leaned forward and inhaled the vapor of this man who stood before me. It was a long, deep breath. Whooph. Emar was the mar, short for marvelous—or was it just that I could marvel all day?

He told me he was an athlete, actor, and poet and about to get drafted into the NBA. He explained how he was going to be in the second round, 'cause he had hurt his leg his sophomore year and needed to prove himself. The scouts had been saying he got it but he wasn't cut out for the NBA. But Emar was sure somebody was going to grip him up. Plus, his coach had put the word out and a couple of teams had been inquiring about him. All he had to do now was prove himself.

I took another sip of my tea as my thoughts raced from today to to-morrow with Emar Gerson. I imagined myself being Emar's girl, being Mrs. Gerson and the perfect life we would live together. I could see myself watching from the sideline of one of E's games. Probably in Chicago somewhere, cheering him on. I would be a basketballer's wife. I would travel with my husband all over the country.

Or maybe I would just stay home, go shopping, and do rich things, like take my Pekinese dog to the hair salon with me and have my own personal fashion designer. I would get massaged, manicured, pedi-cured, facialed, and pampered all day. I would have a personal cook and a fitness trainer available twenty-four hours a day to get me into shape after I gave birth to Emar Jr.

To keep myself busy, I would find a favorite charity to dedicate my-self to. And I would hire an interior decorator just to decorate my car. Yeah, I would be rich and have nothing better to do than to spend E's money from his 56.9-million-dollar Nike contract.

When I start thinking E's been acting up, I'll go over to Mrs. Jordan's house for marital tips. I'll ask her how her marriage sur-vived. And she'll confide in me because I'll remind her so much of herself when she was younger. She'll tell me what to do to keep Emar in check, and even share some of her favorite recipes with me. We'd even call each other every now and then just to keep in touch.

It was meant for me to meet Emar. We were meant to be together. It was fate. How else would you explain my not even wanting to go to class, getting up anyway and throwing on my old gray sweat suit only to meet him in the middle of a rainstorm?

Anyway, it was still pouring down rain outside and the coffeehouse was becoming crowded. The manager asked us to leave. We had al-ready stayed past the time allowed, which was two hours, and he needed our table.

We tried to keep ordering food so we could stay, but I was full from cookies, tea, and a turkey sandwich. Emar had three coffees and a bagel. We had to face it: It was time to go.

I didn't want to leave Emar. He was so interesting. I mean, the only thing I said in those two hours was an occasional "Really?" He told me so many basketball stories—how he actually met Michael Jordan at a basketball camp and played with Kobe Bryant in a summer league. He said he used to bust Kobe's butt, and he couldn't wait to play against him again.

"Where to now?" I asked Emar as I gathered my things.

"To my room. Can you hang?" he asked as he picked up his book bag and turned toward the door.

I couldn't say no to my dream of happily ever after, could I? I had to seize the opportunity.

"Yeah, I can hang," I replied, trying to sound unimpressed.

I knew exactly what he was talking about. He wanted some of me and I wanted a piece of him. He licked his plump, juicy, bubble-gum-colored lips as he led me out of the coffeehouse and across campus to his dorm room. His roommate, Rodney, was there. With his short, fat body, light skin, and curly hair, he looked like a bad imitation Heavy D. But I didn't have to look at him long. He scattered in a matter of minutes, leaving Emar and me alone.

I thought Emar was going to rush me, but he didn't. He took his time. He sat down on his black-and-white striped sheets, then grabbed a pillow and put it behind his head and leaned against the wall. Then he turned the television on with his remote.

When Emar noticed I was still standing by the door, he patted the space next to him and said, "Come have a seat. You don't have to be scared." Once I sat down next to him on the bed, he started playing in my hair. Then he asked me if I wanted to watch a movie.

"Sure, what do you have?" I asked.

He jumped off the bed and pulled a box out of the closet that was full of VHS tapes. He joked and asked me if I wanted to watch a porno.

"Ill no, boy." I said in disgust.

"Psyche," he said, grinning.

We watched a comedy, then a gangster flick. Don't ask me what happened in either movie. I don't remember, because it was getting dark and the lights were out. I could feel Emar's hands going up and down my back. His touch sent waves of exciting energy into my system.

I knew I shouldn't have sex with a guy on the first date. Damn, it wasn't even a date. We had just met about five hours ago when it was so cold and now it was so unbearably hot where I was lying. But . . . but . . . there was no excuse.

Fuck it. I gave him some.

Fifteen minutes later, after the intensity and fire was over, I wanted him to hold me, snuggle with me, and cuddle me.

But Emar did the exact opposite. He went from burning hot to ice cold in a matter of minutes. He leaped up from the bed and said he had some running around to do and needed to take a shower.

I smiled and said "OK." I knew what time it was. He might as well have said, "get to steppin'" like Martin Lawrence on TV.

Yeah, I could catch a hint. Mr. Emar Gerson was throwing me out.

When he was in the shower, I wrote my number down and left it on his dresser next to his watch.

Nah, I wasn't going to act pressed, like what had just happened meant something when it didn't. It was just another blow to take on the chin, and not a very powerful one at that.

I should have been blocking myself, keeping my guard up. Instead, I had let my opponent into my zone and he hit me. It was my own fault. You can't be doing crazy stuff like meeting a man and having passionate sex with him when you don't know him. If he wanted me, he would have to call me. I threw on my coat and left.

On my way home, I began to feel like a slut. Bad thoughts started racing through my head. *What if he don't call me—or, even worse, how about if he knows somebody I know and disrespects me?* He could start going around telling everybody he "had me" like some nutty guys do. Emar could be a nut.

That would ruin everything. There were plenty of guys on campus who had been trying to get with me for the last two years. They would feel some type of way to know all it took was some smooth talk, a little tea, and a bunch of basketball stories to part these legs.

By now, I was walking so fast, I was almost jogging. I was sweating. My heart was pounding and tears were streaming down my face. I wiped my tears away as I noticed people getting off the bus coming home from work. It was only 6:30 in the evening, but all I wanted to do was go home and get in my bed.

But it was taking forever to get there. It had gotten colder—at least it felt that way. Finally, I reached my building, where I flashed my school ID at the security officer and ran up the steps to my room.

Damn. Who was there but my roommate Tuesday with her why-did-I-cut-my-hair-if-I'm-not-going-to-keep-it-up self, and her boyfriend, Sherman, with his reformed nerdy wannabe-bodybuilder self.

There they were, cuddling in front of the television, watching a rerun of "Married with Children."

Damn. I couldn't even cry in peace. They were the last people I needed to see. They were just so happy, so perfect, so fucking sickening. All that lovey-dovey bullshit depressed the hell out of me.

I must have had *get out* written all over my face, because suddenly Tuesday jumped up and said in her always happy tone, "Kayla, we were about to get something from the Chinese joint. Want us to get you something?"

"No," I responded sadly, dropping my book bag on our pine desk.

"OK, see you later then," Tuesday said as they left.

After I heard the door slam, I thought about how I wished I could tell Tuesday about what just happened. But she would never understand. No, she would just look at me with judgmental eyes and give her typical goody-two-shoes opinion. No thank-you.

She was so good. I was so bad. She had good grades and a good man. I wished I had a Sherm, a nice considerate man.

Well, I almost did. When we first started school, I met Sherm first. But I thought he was a corny young boah. He used to meet me after classes and help me do my laundry. He was nice, but I didn't like him romantically. So I dissed him. I thought he was a nut. He was too damn nice.

But Tuesday saw something in him. She worked with him and molded him. Shit! How was I supposed to know he was going to turn into such a good man? I know I will never have what they have. Never ever. Good things like that don't happen to me.

I thought about calling Yaz. She would understand. Yazmine is my best friend. She was in a good relationship for the most part. I mean, her boyfriend do be doing his thing, but they're happy. I could ask her for some advice.

Nah, I didn't feel like talking to her either. I didn't feel like talking to anyone. Sleep is more understanding. It doesn't ask any questions or criticize. So I dozed off around 7:30 P.M.

The rain tapping on my window woke me up. I got up out of the bed and looked at the alarm clock. It was 3 A.M. I couldn't believe I had been asleep for so long. Tuesday hadn't come home. She must have stayed with Sherman. I walked to the bathroom and then crawled back in the bed.

But this time, I had a hard time falling asleep. I kept thinking about Emar Gerson and how I had played myself. Well, at least I had enough sense to make him use a condom. It could have been worse.

A week passed and I still didn't hear anything from Emar. I waited by the phone for his call. Every time the phone rang, I stopped whatever I was doing to answer it. I hoped Emar would be on the other end but he wasn't.

By the next Thursday, I had given up hope he would ever call. I didn't have class that day, so I went to Paley Library to do some studying. I had to type a paper and check my e-mail.

As I was walking across 13th Street noticing how everyone was racing to get to their next class, out of the corner of my eye, I saw Emar. I almost died.

I just kept on walking. I kept my eyes focused on the ground like I didn't see him.

You know, it's funny how I had never seen him before last week. Then, as soon as I say to hell with him, I had run right into him. Damn my luck.

When I got back from the library, I called Yaz and told her about the whole situation. Her answer for my dilemma was, "Fuck him."

"You fucked up, Kay. You know better than to do that nut shit. So fuck him. If he wants to be an asshole, let him. You don't need him," Yaz yelled over the telephone. She was just as mad as I was.

"You right. Well, I got to call you back, 'cause I'm going to finish up this paper."

Yaz was right, fuck him. I fucked up, so now I'm fucked. I decided if I ever saw him again, I would do like I had done earlier and just ignore him. Fuck him.

By now, I was getting hungry, so I walked down the street to

McDonald's, ordered a grilled chicken sandwich and fries, and took it back to my room.

The phone was ringing as I stepped through the door, but whoever it was hung up before I grabbed the receiver. I dialed star sixty-nine. The phone rang and a deep voice answered.

"Hello. Yes, did someone call Kayla or Tuesday?" I said, stammering a little. I was surprised to hear a male voice other than Sherm's.

"Yeah, I called you."

"Who's this?"

"Emar."

Oh, my God. What did he want from me? Why was he calling me? About time he called. I didn't think he was going to.

"What's up?" he asked.

"Nothing."

"What are you doing?"

"Nothing."

There are a million words in the English language, and all I could think to say was "nothing."

Then he went, "I know you saw me today, Kayla. Why didn't you speak when you saw me?"

"I didn't see you."

"Yes, you did. You looked right in my face. Anyway, what are you doing?"

"Nothing." *Stop saying that, you crazy lady,* I told myself.

"I thought you and a friend might want to come to one of my games."

"Sure. When's the next one?" I asked, trying to sound nonchalant even though my heart was racing. I knew it was something there and it was meant to be.

"Tonight at six. At St. Joe's on City Line Avenue. You drive?"

"No."

"Well, how you going to get up there?"

"I don't know. But I'll be there."

"Your tickets will be at the door. After the game, we can check out a movie or something."

"A movie?"

"Yeah, a movie. What, you can't hang?"

Once again I said, "I can hang."

I had to call Yaz immediately and tell her I had finally heard from Emar. Here I was thinking he really didn't want me and he did. It was just me overreacting as usual.

But first, I had to decide what to do with my hair. I had just taken it out of braids, so it was kind of raggedy looking. I started striking different poses and positioning my hair in different ways.

My hair had really grown from the braids, but it was time for a perm. As I played in it some more, I decided to part it in the middle and wear it down. Usually trivial things like clothes and hair didn't get me all worked up like this. I like to look nice, but I've never let getting dressed make me late for anything. I hate perfect people like that. But tonight I had to look perfect for Emar.

I got Yaz to drop me off at the game. She couldn't stay 'cause she had to take her sister Carrey to the market. I was glad, 'cause all she had to talk about the whole ride was how I was playing myself by even going to Emar's game, and how he probably invited all his girls to his games.

Oh, what does she know? Yaz is my girl, but since she's in her little relationship, she's been getting too righteous. Don't she know there is a shortage of black men and you got to work with what you got?

I walked into the gym and spotted Emar immediately. Damn, he looked good. His body looked like he jogged, lifted weights, and did a thousand sit-ups a day. His body was da bomb.

And so was his game. He could shoot, steal, and jump. Temple lost, but I didn't even notice until Emar came over to me mad as hell 'cause his coach had got all in his world for being a showoff. He called Emar a gun and said he would never make it to the NBA with his poor attitude. But Emar said he wasn't paying the coach any attention because he had just had the best game of the season even if they had lost. All the scouts had seen him, and now he was more convinced than ever he was going to the NBA.

"You waiting for me?" he asked, as he wiped the sweat off of his face and gave me a hug.

"Yeah. I got dropped off," I responded.

"All right, I'll be ready in a few."

I waited for Emar with a bunch of other girls who were waiting for their boyfriends. We didn't go to the movies, because Emar was hungry. We went to the Chi-Chi's down the street. I really don't like Mexican, but that night whatever he wanted was fine with me. We talked and talked. We ate tacos and drank margaritas. I was so glad the waiter didn't ask me for ID. I would have been so embarrassed.

Emar told me how he was from Boston and had lived in foster homes his whole life. He said he'd never met his parents and wasn't sweating it now that he was grown and on his own. He was majoring in theater and planned to try to get into the movies when his basketball career ended. He even claimed to be a poet. To prove it, he whispered some lines to me: "The love I search for has not yet found me, but in time I will find thee."

My heart just went out to him. I wanted to pull him close and smother him with all the love he missed growing up. We went back to his room and made mad, crazy love.

Over the next couple of weeks, me and Emar kept in touch. And each time we got together, it was better than the first. Emar was a full package. I couldn't get enough of him. When he called me in the middle of the night and asked if he could come over, it didn't matter if I was sleepy or mad at him, I would still let him come over. I was falling in love with him. How couldn't I? He was the shit.

I knew he was probably seeing someone else, but I didn't care as long as he kept coming to see me. Still, it wasn't long before I started getting tired of the long intervals between his visits. Only seeing him two or three times a week was getting old. Yaz told me to tell him how I felt.

One night, while we where lying in his dorm bed, I gave him an ultimatum.

"Emar, I'm tired of seeing you only when you want to see me. I want a relationship. If you want me, you got to give me more respect. I want to be your girl, or we can't see each other anymore."

He looked surprised, but then he said, "You're right. But I can't give you an answer right away. Because I don't know. How about we chill tonight and when I get back from winter break we'll talk? I got this big game coming up and I don't need this extra stress."

Then he kissed my forehead and I thought about what he had said. It was OK. I could respect that. He would give me an answer when he came back. That night, I made love to him as passionately as I could so he would have no choice but to say yes.

Those three weeks of winter break went by so slowly. I didn't hear from Emar, but I figured it was because he was trying to make up his mind. I missed him so much I wanted to call him, but I didn't. Tuesday had gone home to introduce her parents to Sherm. They'd never met because Tuesday's parents were very religious and did not believe in dating.

One day over break, I came home to find my dorm-room door open and all my stuff gone. Somebody had stolen my VCR and television and Tuesday's leather jackets. All my CDs were gone and so was my word processor.

I called my mother, Leslie, to tell her what happened. After I finished all I heard was "I'm on my way," and then a click.

I called her back.

"Leslie, I'm OK. You don't need to come all the way up here," I said.

"It's no problem," she said. Then she covered her hand over the telephone, and I could hear her yelling to my little sister, "Nicole. Hurry up and get your coat on."

"Mom," I started to say, but it was too late. She hung up again. I called back again. This time Nikki picked up.

"Put Mommy on the phone," I told her.

"She's out in the car already. What's going on?" she asked.

"I'll tell you later. Just go get Mommy and tell her I want her on the phone."

Nikki put down the telephone and got my mother. "Leslie," I said when she finally got on the telephone. "Listen, I can take care of this myself. I'm going to call the police and fill out a report. Then I'll jump in a cab and come over there. So do not come up here."

She hesitated and then said, "Are you sure?"

She knew I was right and there was nothing she could do. She was just acting like I couldn't take care of myself.

"Yeah, I'm sure," I assured her.

"OK," she said finally. "But call me when the police get there. And call me when they leave. And call me when you're getting ready to get in the cab."

I couldn't believe it when the dumb-ass cops asked me if I had the serial numbers of the stolen items. I must have been hyped, because my mother was calling every ten minutes. She was acting like I got shot or something. Anyway, I snapped on that cop.

"Does your fucking mom write down the serial numbers of her CDs?"

The cop just looked at me and said, "Miss, I know you are upset, but we are only trying to help you. And you don't need to talk to me like that."

"Whatever," I shot back and rolled my eyes. "You done?" I said as I pointed toward the door. They left, and I left right after them.

The minute my cab pulled up, Nikki ran over. She looked me up and down.

"You OK? Mommy said somebody robbed you."

"Mommy be exaggerating. Someone stole my VCR and television," I said as I paid the driver.

My mom was in the door with her leather coat thrown over her housecoat, a purple scarf over her rollers. She had her pink rabbit slippers on, looking like a crazy little old lady. She gave me a hug, took my bag, and said she was glad I was safe and that she would go to Wal-Mart and buy me a new television. That was cool with me. I needed a new one anyway.

When it was time to return to school, I was happy and sad at the same time. I was happy I would be seeing Emar and sad because I had to explain to Tuesday that all our shit had gotten stolen. That's when she came in, acting way too happy, and announced she was leaving with Sherm next week for Arizona. They were getting married.

When I told her about the robbery, she wasn't even upset that her stuff got stolen. She said she wouldn't need a leather jacket in Arizona and she was going to sell all her stuff anyway.

"What? You can't leave me! Tuesday, are you crazy?"

Tuesday was my sanity. She was the one who said study when I wanted to party. She woke me up in the morning to go to class and cock-blocked a lot of nights when I wanted to get some but was scared of what she would say. She even gave me money when I was broke.

And to think that at first I didn't even like her. I used to think she was a silly country girl who talked too much. She was too perfect. All she would ever talk about was her Baptist-preaching father and sermon-giving mom. Tuesday had nine brothers and sisters and was so glad to leave Tupelo, Mississippi, she didn't know what to do with herself.

She had this real bad skin and wore deep brown makeup, two shades too dark for her light brown skin. Which was a shame, because she had a pretty face. She was kind of short and thin and wore long skirts that made her look extra skinny. Then on top of all that she would wear tan stockings and button-up silk blouses and goofy glasses. Basically she was a mess, but still a cute girl—just unfashionable and a little weird.

She would walk around carrying her Bible, saying how she was going to pray for me. Plus she would always be washing her hands, saying cleanliness is next to godliness or something crazy like that. Other times I would come in from class and she would be having church on the phone.

Tuesday actually was my second roommate. My first roommate had been this white girl who was crazy. She was a grungy, anti-depressant-taking, evil-worshipping, all-black-wearing, alternative-rock-loving insane bitch. Luckily she dropped out of school in the second week. I knew I wasn't going to be fortunate enough to get to keep a room by myself, since Temple was so overcrowded they actually had girls staying in local hotels. But then I remembered about Tuesday, who lived down the hall from me. She was always complaining about her roommate, who was always hosting get-high parties in their room. Tuesday was more than happy to move in with me, and I figured I could put up with her little strangeness.

So even though Tuesday was a little dippy, I welcomed her too sweet, too sanctified self. She was a breath of fresh air after living with Ms. Evil.

"Tuesday, you can't leave. What about school?" I asked.

"I'll finish in Arizona. Sherm got a job paying four jobs' salary. So we'll be OK."

"Have you thought about what you are doing? This is not like you, Tuesday. What's the deal?"

"Yes, I have. I've already made up my mind. I'm out."

"But what made you decide this so fast?"

"Nothing. I just did."

After Tuesday's bomb dropped, I had to talk to Emar. I kept calling that whole day, but nobody answered. Finally, I got a busy signal. At least that let me know he was home.

I rushed over to his room. I knew for sure he would be happy to see me, too. He probably realized how much he had missed me and was calling but couldn't get in touch with me because my answering machine had gotten stolen, too. I was sure he realized how much of a mistake it would be to let me get away.

As I made my way across campus, I began to have second thoughts. *What if he hadn't missed me? What if he had found someone else?* I knocked on his door with a knot of anxiety in my stomach. Then the door opened. It was Rodney, who was busy unpacking.

"Hi, Rodney. Did E get back in town yet?"

"You're kidding, right? Didn't you know his season ended?"

"What! Are you sure?" I said.

"Yeah. He got kicked off the team right before break. He said something about the coach had it in for him. Anyway, he went back home to Chicago."

"I thought he was from Boston," I said, confused.

"No, his mom came and got him."

"Mom? I thought he was an orphan. He said he didn't have a mom. He said he needed a little time to think about us and he would call me when he got back." I couldn't believe it. "I guess it's my fault anyway for listening to my girlfriend. She told me to tell him how I felt and not to stand for no dumb shit. Tell him how he couldn't have his cake and eat it too anymore, and how he was going to have to give me a title as his girl or I was out."

I was just running off at the mouth, but I couldn't stop. I felt so stupid, and it made it worse that Rodney was looking at me like I was all pitiful.

"Damn, I shouldn't have listened to Yaz. She don't know what she talking about anyway. She lucked up with a man. She wasn't a professional at love or the way a man's mind works. Damn." I felt like such a nut. Tears came to my eyes. I should have known better.

"Emar finished all his credits last semester," Rodney was saying. "His mother had to catch a red-eye to come get that boy. He thought he was winning that tournament and would get drafted by some NBA team. You know he's an actor, right? That's my man, but he's such a liar. What else did he lie about? I feel so bad for you."

"Well, I'm just glad you told me the truth," I said as I dried my eyes with a napkin he handed me.

"Yeah, no problem. 'Cause, see, I don't believe men should lie to females. I think y'all are treasures, especially my black queens."

Shaking my head in disbelief, I slowly walked toward the door.

"Thanks again," I mumbled.

Then I closed the door and left Rodney to his unpacking. That was it. First, my room was broken into. Then I found out Tuesday was leaving. Now I had just learned my only hope of love was out the door because he was a fucking liar.

I should have known better. Damn him and every man I knew or had ever come in contact with.

I thought the reason he hadn't asked me to be his girl was because he was shy or didn't want to show his true feelings. I thought I could make him want a relationship and change him. But I was wrong.

I went back to my room, just crushed. Tuesday was still packing what was left of her belongings. I laid on my bed, looked up at the ceiling, and tried to sort everything out.

"Tuesday, why are you suddenly ready to leave and go with Sherm?" I asked, still staring at the ceiling.

"Kayla, because I'm ready. One day when you settle down, you will understand." I hated when she tried to talk to me like I was a child

"So that's it? What's up? What happened when you went to visit your parents?"

Tuesday stared into space for a moment, then looked at the floor before looking back at me and said, "Nothing. Kayla, please just let me do what I have to do."

I was convinced something must have happened for Ms. Perfect to make an irresponsible move like this. Then I thought about how it would be if I got an apartment off campus. The four walls of our tiny room were holding me in. There were too many memories in this place. I thought again of Emar. I needed to start all over again. I was becoming really depressed.

I still couldn't believe Tuesday was eloping with Sherm. But they had been together every moment of the last two years. It was like they never separated. They always looked at each other lovingly, as if they couldn't live without the other. They never argued and saw each other every day.

Chapter 2

Once Tuesday left, nothing was the same. I hated school. I hated class. So I dropped out.

Well, not really. I just dropped all my classes and registered for four summer classes so I could start over and still be a junior next semester.

I called my mother, Leslie, and asked her opinion on my getting an off-campus apartment. Her response was, "How the hell are you going to pay the rent?"

I told her I would get a job and pay my own bills.

Then she surprised me by agreeing to pay half if I promised to get a job and enrolled in summer classes.

Actually, I figured having my own apartment would be cheaper than living on campus. I could save money by cooking instead of eating out all the time. And it had to be safer than staying on campus.

Those were some of the arguments I'd used on Leslie, even though I wasn't the least bit scared of anyone breaking in again. I had found out who had robbed me—some kid named Danny from New York who smoked meth. He got arrested and was expelled from school. But he had already sold my stuff by the time they caught up with him. He got twelve other rooms besides mine.

Now, all I had to do was find a place.

* * *

I awoke to the telephone ringing.

"You feel like going to get something to eat, Kayla?" Yazmine asked.

"What time is it?" I asked as I sat up.

"I don't care. Where you want to go?"

"Damn, I can't go with you. I have to go look at apartments."

"It don't matter. I'll take you. We don't have anywhere to go today. I just don't feel like fixing the kids lunch and Sam is out in the streets somewhere."

"All right. Well, I'm about to get up and get dressed."

"I'll be there to pick you up in a few."

"See you when you get here."

Yaz's "a few" ended up being more like an hour. I was waiting by the door when I finally heard her drive up and start beeping the horn. She is so impatient.

Anyhow, she had the kids with her. Her daughter, Mia, is the most adorable, intelligent four-year-old. With her freckles and light brown hair, she looks just like her mother. But Yaz's nine-month-old son, Sam Jr., looks nothing like her. With his dark brown skin and high cheekbones, he resembles his father. I got in the car and asked Yaz where we were going for lunch.

"I don't know. Where do you want to go to look at apartments?" she asked as she peeled off into the street.

"Oh, shit. Thanks for reminding me. I left the addresses in the house."

I could tell Yaz was upset by the way she U-turned in the middle of the street to get back to my dorm.

"How come you can't never remember anything?" she snapped.

"Girl, please. Don't start with me," I warned as we pulled in front of my building.

When I returned, we debated on where to eat. We finally decided to go to Friday's on City Line Avenue. Our waiter, Jay, was a cutie. Yaz was flirting with him. She had him blushing when she asked him what size shoes he wore.

He told her you can't judge what a man is working with by his feet. You have to look at their hands, he said.

We both looked at his hands, and they were huge. We cracked up.

We had to chill, though, 'cause the kids started getting curious as to what was going on.

Yaz and I started spelling words out, because Mia was at the age where she wanted to repeat everything she heard. When we finished eating, Yazmine handed me some money and the check and said, "I'm taking the kids to the bathroom. Here go my half. I'll meet you at the car." I got up from the table and looked for the waiter.

"Here you go," I said, placing the money and check in his hand. I turned to leave as he counted the money.

"I'll call you later."

I turned around and said, "Huh?"

"This is your number, right?"

I grabbed the check, and sure enough there was my phone number in Yazmine's handwriting. I had been set up. I looked at the waiter, who looked confused. I said, "I'm sorry, my girlfriend plays too much."

"So I can't call you?"

"No, you can call me," I said. What did I have to lose? I wasn't seeing anybody, and he was kind of cute.

"I guess I'll talk to you later," I said as I raced out of the restaurant to confront Yazmine, who was placing Sam Jr. in his car seat.

"What the hell you do that for? If I want somebody to have my number, I'll give it to them," I said, as I got in the car and slammed the door.

Yaz just got in the car and started laughing. She really plays too much. "Look, Kayla, you need to start meeting some good guys and stop fucking with those losers you pick. He was cute and he was on you. Plus, he don't seem like your type, so it may work."

"Well, next time at least let me know what you're doing, so I can know what's going on," I complained.

"All right, all right," Yaz said still laughing.

But I knew she wasn't paying me any mind.

The first apartment we went to was roach-infested and just trifling. The landlord was charging $450 for an efficiency. I don't think so. The two after that weren't any better. I was totally disgusted.

"I'm tired of looking at these messed-up apartments. I wished I owned a building. These people are getting over. Charging all that money for these nasty apartments," I complained to Yaz.

"You only got one apartment left. This might be the one. You never know," Yaz said, trying to be supportive.

She made a right on Broad Street and headed south to the next apartment on my list.

"Well, the lady who owns the building told me to call when I got down the street. Let me see your phone," I said reaching for Yaz's purse.

I called the woman. By the time we got to the apartment building, she was standing outside with her hand on her hip. She was heavyset, sixty-something with short black wavy hair.

"Hi, baby. I'm Mrs. Jackson," she all but screamed at me. "You the one who wants to look at the apartment? I was waiting for you to come. I'm sure glad you made it before *General Hospital* came on, 'cause if you waited fifteen more minutes, we would have had to meet tomorrow. I don't miss my stories for nobody. OK, let me get the keys."

Mrs. Jackson dug deep in her huge black shoulder bag and pulled out a key chain with about two hundred keys on it. I wondered how she could tell one from the other.

"Baby, you the college student, right?"

"Yes," I said impatiently.

Yaz and the kids sat in the car as I walked in the building and almost got trampled by these little boys as they ran down the steps. A pretty woman screaming to the top of her lungs was right behind them.

"Kevin, Mark, Michael get back in here!" she yelled, as loud music blasted out her open apartment door. "Hi, Mrs. Jackson," she said, quickly smiling at the owner.

"How are you, Mrs. Franklin?" Mrs. Jackson said, in an icy tone. "I thought I asked you to stop letting the boys run through my building. I don't want them to get hurt. And can you please turn down your music?"

"Sorry about my boys running over you. They're going to get it soon as their father gets home," Mrs. Franklin promised. "I'll turn my music down, too. Sorry about that."

"OK. Mrs. Franklin, have a nice day, and I'll see you Friday."

As we headed upstairs, Mrs. Jackson said, "That no-good man of hers is not going to do anything to those boys. He never do. Them boys just bad. They write on the wall, put holes in them. That's OK, though. They time is limited."

As we reached the apartment, Mrs. Jackson rolled her eyes and shuffled through her collection of keys.

"Child, please don't mind her. You can't hear her terrors on the second floor, and I'm about to kick her out anyway 'cause she always calling the cops on her husband and letting them bad-ass boys run around. She's the reason my last tenant moved out. I just feel sorry for her. Oh, well. Here's the apartment."

As soon as I entered, I knew it was the one I wanted. It wasn't that big, but it was perfect. The walls where all freshly painted white and the apartment had a huge front window. There was also a tiny little kitchen and a gigantic bedroom. I didn't hesitate.

"I'll take it," I said, looking around.

"You sure, sweetie?" she said, raising her eyebrows in surprise at my quick decision.

"Yes, ma'am."

"Well, since you such a nice young lady. I'm going to give you a break. I was looking for about $550 a month but I'll give it to you for $500. I try to help the young people that's doing the right thing because somebody helped me and my husband out when we was young. Plus, you get a discount for having to put up with Mrs. Franklin's little boys."

I hurried and wrote a check for $1,000 to cover the deposit and first month's rent as she was still speaking. My own apartment!

"Here's the key," she said as she placed it in my hand.

I gave her a big hug and ran to the car to get Yaz.

"Yaz, you got to come look at my new place."

"New apartment, already just like that?" Yaz said in disbelief.

"Yup, I have the key and everything. You got to see it."

"I'll see it later. I got to get home. The kids got to take a nap and Sam just called my phone arguing with me about not telling him where I went. He talking 'bout I'm out to lunch with my boyfriend with his kids. He be tripping."

Sometimes I hate Yaz's boyfriend. He's so jealous and always accusing her of cheating. He's probably the one cheating. Well, at least I had my very own place.

The first time I went out with Jay, I could look at him and see he had a little potential. He went to LaSalle University and was a junior studying to be an accountant. He was twenty-two, no kids, was in great shape, had a truck and an apartment.

But it wasn't long before I figured out he was a nut. I never thought a cute guy could be so corny.

First off, he called too much. As soon as I got home that day, I discovered he had already left two messages saying he missed me. Now, I had just met him two hours ago. I guess I could have been flattered, but I wasn't.

And when it came to race, the boy was tripping. Now, I'm not down with, "Yo baby, yo baby, yo," type of guys. But I can't stand to hear a black man down talk other blacks like he wasn't one, saying, "They need to find jobs and stop having kids and being on welfare." But at least he had a truck, so he could help me move into my new apartment.

Yeah, I know what you're thinking. Black women always complain about being dogged. They get a good man and don't know how to treat him, but I couldn't take it. He was just too nice. Jay was crazy. We only went out like five times. And one of those times he was helping me move in.

He was trying hard to be down with me, but it was more like he was getting on my fucking nerves. The last straw came when he professed his undying love to me, saying, "I've loved you since the first time I saw you, and I want to marry you." He couldn't be serious.

"What did you say? Marry you? I've only known you a month. I don't even like to kiss you. I got a caller ID box especially to avoid your calls," I told him.

I tried to explain to Yaz that Jay was a bugaboo. She suggested I get with him, get the ring, and then break the engagement.

No, I wasn't going to do that. Besides, I was afraid he would kill me. I made sure when I got a waitressing job at this seafood restaurant called Mikhi's that I didn't give him the telephone number. Wouldn't you know he called information and had me paged while I was wait-ing on tables?

He had me all scared. I thought it was an emergency or something, because no one had my number at work. I ran to the phone, only to hear him ask me why I hadn't called him that day and saying I didn't appreciate him.

That was it. I had enough. I screamed at him, "You know what, Jason, you're not my type. I'm not ready for someone like you."

"I thought you wanted to settle down."

"I do, but not get engaged."

"Well, we can slow it down some. We don't have to have sex."

"We weren't going to have sex anyway. Boy, what is wrong with you? You are tripping. You are not in love with me. You are in love with the idea of being in love."

"There's nothing wrong with me," Jay said as his voice began to sound angry.

"Look, I'm sorry. It's just not going to work out. OK?" I said.

I was about to bang on him. He was getting on my damn nerves. He was too serious, wanting to settle down already. Now, how about that? I couldn't believe the pot was calling the kettle black. I did want a re-lationship, but not with him. He was too nice. I hate nice guys.

"OK, Kayla. But you are making a big mistake." He sighed, then hung up.

I stood there, scared for a moment, and imagined what might hap-pen. What if he turned into a fatal attraction? Would I come home to find dead roses pinned to my door or a sharp knife standing straight up in the center of my bed? I was beginning to get scared, so I called my mom. She said I was overreacting. I still didn't take any chances. Instead of taking the subway home that day, I caught a cab.

And to my surprise, the red light on my answering machine was not blinking when I arrived home. I just knew he was going to leave mil-lions of messages. If I had known it would be that easy to get rid of him, I would have done it a long time ago. I was insulted. He could have at least left a message or two.

Chapter 3

I had just poured a big bowl of Captain Crunch when I realized I was out of milk. So I ran out the door just like I was, hoping nobody but the store lady saw me.

That's when I met Terry. I had a scarf on my head and slippers on my feet, and there he was trying to talk to me. I was like, "I look like a bum."

And he was like, "I don't care. I can see past the rabbit slippers and scarf. You got a pretty face. So what's up, can I take you to dinner later?"

"Maybe. How are you going to get in touch with me?" I said, trying to play hard to get.

"You're going to give me your number," he said, as he looked me up and down.

He was kind of husky, but not fat. He had on a white tee shirt, baggy black faded Polo jeans, and fresh tan Timberlands. His black baseball cap was turned to the side. He was a nice-looking guy.

So I gave him my number and I walked out of the store. *He probably won't call, but what if he does call me? We would go on a date and fall in love. Then we would get an apartment, get married, have three kids and grow old together. It would be great. Nah, I'm jumping to conclusions.*

I shook my head and came back to reality. *I may never see him again.* Oh well, it's always fun to fantasize. Nothing's wrong with what if.

Well, he did call me a couple of days later. And we went to dinner at Bertha's Soul Food Kitchen in southwest Philly. As we walked in the screen door, the raggedy thing almost fell off the hinges. And the smell of old grease and funky pigs' feet nearly knocked me back on the other side of the door.

The brownish orange-colored plastic in the booth we sat in was ripped, and the table was leaning on one side. The whole place reminded me of a diner down deep in Alabama or something.

When she finally got her fat butt to the table, the waitress called us "sugah" and began to tell us everything she didn't have on the menu. I asked her if she could please clean the table. She rolled her eyes, then wiped it with a smelly rag she probably wiped every other mess up with. Uhhh. I ordered barbecue chicken and Terry asked for ribs and potato salad.

Anyway, by the time the food got there it was nice and cold. Needless to say, I was not impressed with the restaurant or Terry until, out of nowhere, he asked me if I would like to house-sit over in New Jersey with him for the weekend.

I was like, "Jersey for the weekend?" I was shocked. I didn't know him like that.

But on the other hand, I hadn't had sex since Emar, or a kiss since Jay. So I was kind of tempted. I wanted to go, but I knew he was going to want some. And we had only known each other for a week. And there was no way I was going to make the same mistake with him I had made with Emar.

Then I thought, maybe I could just go and make it very clear to him I don't want just sex.

We left about 1 P.M. that Friday. It took us about an hour to get to Princeton. We talked a little on the way, but mostly we listened to the radio, flipping back and forth from station to station. I took that time to ask him about his relationship status. He said he didn't have a girl but was looking. I told him I didn't have a man and I was looking, too, but wanted to take my time. He said he could understand that.

This was the third time I had mentioned I wanted to take my time the next time I got in a relationship. I was trying to make sure he got the message.

After a while, we made a right off of the highway onto a deserted road. A few minutes later, we pulled up to a big white mini mansion. There was a four-car garage, a tennis court, pool, and even a basketball court. It was a nice area, but I couldn't even see the nearest neighbor. I wouldn't live in a place like this. Somebody might attack me. And who would be there to help me? I need my neighbors.

"So where did your aunt and uncle go, anyway?" I asked as he led me into the living room, which was all in white.

"To Hawaii. They paid. They own a lot of real estate. They're trying to get me to go to school to be a realtor, but that's not me."

After giving me a tour of the place, we ended up in the kitchen, where he cooked me a steak and some potatoes. Then we stretched out on a huge sofa in the family room and chilled just watching videos on BET. Then we went for a swim in the pool.

Afterward, when we got in the Jacuzzi, I started getting nervous because Terry began turning into some kind of freak. He started getting real touchy-feely. He was grabbing my leg and trying to touch my breast.

But I was thinking *nada*. I climbed out of the Jacuzzi and went to take a shower.

I thought I had locked the door, but I guess I didn't, because Mr. Terry tried to slip in with me.

If I was feeling him like that, it would have been cool, but I wasn't. Before I even got in his car to ride over there, I had stressed to him I was just coming on a friendship trip. It wasn't going to be nothing.

I couldn't believe that short bastard hadn't listened. Oh, did I mention he didn't have any clothes on and it wasn't a pretty sight? I didn't think they made them that small. He looked like a naked, hairy hunchback. Ill.

So there I was, scared as shit. I said, "Terry, I'm not ready for this. Can you get out, please?"

I thought he was going to rape me. But fortunately, he got right out. I was so relieved. *At least he knows no means no,* I thought. When I came out of the bathroom, Mr. Terry was on the phone talking, saying something about how he would be right there in about a half hour. Then he asked me if I was ready to go.

"Go where?"

"Home."

"Why we leaving?"

"Because I'm going to get someone that will appreciate this. I'm not no hustler. I work hard for money, and I took off this weekend to be with you," Terry said as he threw his clothes into his green backpack.

"That's bullshit. You were going to house-sit way before you met me. Plus it's only been a week. Terry, I like you, but I'm not ready for this. I told you I wasn't having sex with you before I came."

"I thought you was just talking. You know how you ho's talk. Well, that's OK. Like I said, I got other ho's I can bring here."

"Ho's? I'm no ho. Who do you think you're talking to?"

"Whatevah. Look, get your stuff, 'cause we're leaving," he said, shooting me an evil glance.

The first thing I thought about was that I was in Jersey and if I got smart, this nigga might up and leave me and I didn't know who I could call to come get me. This little nigga better not try no nut shit like not taking me home because I wouldn't fuck his nut ass. He had seemed so nice. Who knew he would turn into a straight-up asshole?

I couldn't believe what was going on. But I hurried up and packed my stuff. He went outside and warmed the car up. I didn't even bother putting on my clothes. Wearing just my nightgown, I walked up to the car and tried to get in.

The door was locked. I started jerking on the handle. I looked in the foggy window at Terry and noticed that he had this silly smirk on his face. I didn't know if he was going to pull off or open my door.

Thank God, he opened the door. I didn't say anything the whole ride home. All I knew was it was cold outside. I didn't want to be on the other side of that door.

When we reached my house, I got out and Terry didn't even wait for me to get inside before he pulled off. I wanted to cry. I wouldn't do it to him, and he had treated me like shit. I couldn't win for losing.

I picked up the phone and dialed Yaz's number. The phone rang and rang before she finally answered.

"Hello," she mumbled sleepily.

"You sleep?"

"Yeah, what's up?"

"I just came in from being with Terry. He tried to come in the shower with me. I wouldn't do it to him, so he almost left me in Jersey. Then he fixed the bed up so he could bring someone else there. He was so nice when I first met him. I never thought he could be so nasty and mean. He kept calling me a ho."

"First of all, who is Terry?"

"The guy I met in the market. I think I mentioned him to you."

"Why were you in Jersey with him?"

"Because his uncle got a house over in Jersey and wanted him to house-sit for the weekend. I told him I was going there just on the strength. He said cool, but when I got there he changed."

"Kayla, when are you going to learn men are liars? Better you found out now he was a nut than waiting until later like with the other boah, Emar, from your school. At least you didn't make the same mistake twice. You know what I'm saying? How long you knew this character?"

"A week or two."

"That's not a lot of time."

"I know, but we were spending a lot of time together. I thought I knew him."

"Kayla, a week is not nothing. I'm going back to bed. Call me in the morning."

"All right."

I hung up the phone and just thought about my life. *Why am I here? I must be cursed. Maybe I'll get a witch doctor to lift it. I don't know.*

All I knew was I was tired of starving for love. I couldn't keep going hungry. I needed a man I could taste, salivate, and eat up. That would be fulfilling and oh, so very delicious. I was so tired of shopping around, so very tired.

I wished I could just eat love for a year. Then I wouldn't care what happened. After that, I would be so full and happy and spend the rest of my life with the memories of my love for that one year. Just one year.

Fuck it! Give me six months of someone waiting for me to get home and always knowing I have a steady lover, confidant, friend. I would do anything to get out of this web of disasters. I deserved some happiness.

Chapter 4

Of course, I was talking shit. The very next day after Terry, I met Maurice.

Well, I was set up by my mother. She called early in the morning, asking me to go out on a date with a coworker's son. She said he was a Kappa at Delaware State and about to graduate from their engineering program.

Although I was really tired and didn't want to meet another man, I had to do it. My mother didn't ask very much of me. She arranged for us to meet for brunch at a restaurant on Fairmont Avenue.

I arrived first. I walked in, got a seat, and ordered a hot tea. A couple of minutes later, he came in and sat down at my table and introduced himself.

"I'm Maurice, but everyone calls me Reese," he said, as he extended his hand for me to shake.

He was pretty as hell, dark eyes and dark curly brown hair. I know you usually think of guys as handsome, not pretty. But he really was pretty. And as I gazed at him, the word *sweet* came to mind. Even his voice had a feminine quality.

"How did you know who I was?" I asked.

"Well, there's a couple over there and the rest are groups of people and you're the only one sitting alone."

I laughed, embarrassed for asking such an obvious question. "You ready to eat?" I asked.

"Sure."

I got up from the table and we walked over to the buffet. I loaded up my plate with bacon, toast, grapes, eggs Benedict, and cantaloupe. I sat back down and began eating. Before he even reached the table, Reese was already eating. We both ate, not saying anything, until Reese broke the ice and said, "And by the way, I'm not gay."

"Huh?"

"I know that's what you were thinking but were afraid to ask."

"No, I wasn't."

"Yes, you were. That's OK, because my girlfriend thought the same thing before she got to know me."

"Oh, you got a girl?"

Now that he had said that, he had become more interesting.

"Yeah, the only reason I'm here is because my mom doesn't like her because she is white. She always tries to set me up."

No he didn't go there, I thought, munching my toast.

"Oh, I see. You don't like black men and white women either," he continued. "I can tell. But it's not what you're thinking. I do have pride in my people, I love my black women, and I love black people. I just happened to fall in love with Jessie."

"I guess that's understandable," I said, not really convinced.

"So why is a pretty girl like you having her mother set them up on dates?"

"Because a pretty girl like me has the hardest time finding a good date."

"You've got to be kidding. Well, any man that passed you up has to be a fool. If I weren't already in a relationship, I would walk you down the aisle right now."

"Yeah, right," I said, laughing.

Reese was funny as hell. And after our two-hour brunch, he didn't look gay. He looked good. Too bad he was taken. The good ones always are. We exchanged numbers and promised to call and tell each other's parents we weren't each other's type. But that was the furthest thing from the truth.

When he called later that night, I was thinking, *What does he want? He got a girl.* His honesty shocked me.

"I have a girl and I'm happy. I love her, but she's two hundred miles away and I'm here. So I need somebody I can chill with while I'm down here," he said.

I responded by saying, "I don't get down like that. I mean, I'm not going to front. I was digging you at brunch this morning. But I don't step on nobody's toes or go around breaking up any happy homes."

"Do you think I would be coming to you if it was happy like that?"

"I respect your honesty, but . . ."

"But what? You don't know her. Think about it and call me. We can just be friends."

OK, listen. I'm not down with messing with anybody's man, but come on now. She was away at school and I was kind of lonely in my new apartment all by myself. I had never lived alone before.

Reese came over every day from Sunday through Thursday. We watched movies, played Uno, Monopoly, and my favorite game, Life. It was nice having company.

But I knew better than to allow myself to get too close to him. I understood the circumstances. I wasn't even sexually involved. As the weeks went by, we got to be really good friends. I mean, it was like we spent all our time together.

And the things that didn't matter before began to, like his saying her name, *Jessie.* Every weekend when he didn't call me 'cause she was in town, it hurt. At first, I kept telling myself he would leave her. But it didn't happen in three months. Then I began thinking it probably wasn't going to happen. So, slowly but surely, I pulled myself away from Maurice.

He was everything I ever wanted in a man. He was smart, handsome, funny. But if I couldn't have him whole, I didn't want him in Reese's Pieces.

He said I couldn't handle the truth and I would rather be lied to. The truth was, I hated hearing about her because she possessed something I couldn't have.

He kept saying, "Hang in there a little bit longer and stop catching feelings." I can't just be with someone and not care about them. I don't know why I looove love so much.

Maybe it's my environment. Maybe it's all the love songs I hear played 50,000 times a day or because all my friends are in relationships and I'm not. Or maybe it just seems better than being single. I don't know why. It could be the influence soap operas had on my life at an early age.

My baby-sitter, Tanya, used to turn off whatever cartoon I was watching and make me watch her favorite story, *The Young and the Restless*. At first, I didn't like the stories. I couldn't see why Tanya was so interested in somebody else's life.

That was until I saw Victor kiss Nikki for the first time. Oh, my God. It was magical. I was only four years old, and I can still remember it.

Nikki and Victor were the perfect couple. I mean, they had so much money and were in love. Tanya said she wanted to be kissed like that, and I told her me, too! Maybe that's why.

All I knew was I couldn't wait any longer for him. So I told him when he was ready for me and me only, to give me a call. Why pour milk in cereal when you're not ready to eat it? So I let him go.

At least I was finally waking up out of my coma of dumbness. I couldn't have him my way, so I wouldn't have him any way. I'd rather be by myself. I didn't need Maurice or anyone else.

So, that's the story. Three months went by and I, Kayla Simone Johnson, had sworn off men forever. This time, I was for real. I decided I would just grow old by myself. I didn't need to get married, have kids and a family. That's overrated anyway. Nope, no men.

And I was doing good, too. No man. No problems. No worries. If a man even looked like he wanted to talk to me, I rolled my eyes to let him know, "No, thank-you. I'm not interested."

But this doesn't work on all of them. You always get one guy that says, "It's not that bad. Why don't you smile?" Then I'd look at them again and cut my eyes. They'd get the hint: *Leave me alone.*

I decided all I needed in life was to go to school, then to work. Make money and get good grades. I took all the energy I used to use to deal with dogs, cheaters, liars, and asshole men and began putting it into myself.

I did everything I could think of to improve my life. I lost ten pounds. I got back in school, taking summer classes to make up for spring semester.

School was going great. I was going to every class. I bought a planner and even started sitting in the front row of my classes. And you know what that means. It means no sleeping. It means you're answering questions and basically paying attention. It also means the professor noticing when you're not there.

Most semesters the front row is a no-no for me because I usually make it to class maybe twice a week if it's a three-day-a-week class. I sit in the back with my book open and have my head tilted down while I got my nod on.

But over the summer I managed to take four classes. I took basic math and African-American literature the first session and geology and introduction to elementary education the second session. I was so proud of myself for going to both summer sessions. I was doing things the right way for a change.

Thanks to waitressing, I made enough to furnish my apartment with a powder blue loveseat and a brass, glass-topped coffee table. I also bought a new TV and CD player. Everything was going along great.

To hell with men, I thought. I was still working at Mikhi's in Center City. I loved it, until I was forced to work every day without a break for weeks after everyone started quitting.

The night I quit, I had two tables. Two middle-aged women who probably came out to talk about what their husbands hadn't been doing, and what they wished their kids would do, sat at one table. I asked them if they wanted anything to drink.

"Water, no ice," one of the ladies said.

OK, like that is so stupid, to get water without ice. People who ask for soda with no ice really get on my nerves, like they're going to get that much more soda. The other lady ordered Scotch on the rocks. I already knew this table was going to get on my nerves and I decided I wasn't going to give them good service. So I went and asked my other table if everything was OK. They had finished their food more than an hour earlier and were still sitting there talking.

They had to be on their first date. I could tell because the blonde-haired woman, with the pale complexion and pink lipstick that looked like crayon, was laughing too hard at the black-haired, very tanned, handsome guy's jokes.

While my second table was deciding what to order, I went to my manager, Scott, and said, "I need a vacation!" He looked at me and answered, "We all do." He wasn't having it.

Then he had the nerve to say I was the best waitress he had and he couldn't let me go right now.

What do you mean you can't let me go? I was mad as shit. I don't smoke cigarettes, but I was ready to smoke one now. I had a final in the morning. I walked over to the register where he was standing and told him about my final. I thought at least Scott would let me go for that. But being the asshole he was, he shouted, "Look, either you work or you go home!"

I needed the money, so I stayed. I had too many bills to quit. I had some money in the bank, but not enough to live off of. My summer consisted of work, school, work, then back to school. Oh, how I wished I had never dropped all my classes in the spring, 'cause I damn sure was paying for it now.

I just stood there thinking about my life and my goals. I knew I didn't want to be a waitress all my life, and I needed to pass African-American lit. If I didn't pass my final and turn my term paper in, I was going to fail and lose my grant money.

I walked back over to my second table and asked them what they were ordering. They ordered lobster tails and steak. I rang their order up, thinking all the while about my goals in life.

Then I noticed the two ladies were looking at me like, "Where's my food?" I walked to the kitchen and asked where my order was.

"Right here," the cook said, as he handed me the plates. I took the ladies their food and hoped they didn't ask me for anything else. But that would be too much like right.

One of the stupid ladies flagged me down. I wanted to say, "What do you want with all your stretch marks and cleavage hanging out?" Instead, I forced a smile on my face and said, "What can I do for you?"

"Can I have some steak sauce?"

"Would you like anything else?"

"No."

I snatched a bottle of steak sauce off another table and gave it to them. Then I saw the couple at the other table about to get up. I walked over and thanked them and told them to come back again. I didn't really care if they came back again or not. I was just making sure I didn't get stiffed for my money. You know how some people eat and run out without paying for their food.

I had gotten run out on once and only once. I was not having any more money taken out of my paycheck. Anyway, the couple that just left might as well have not left a tip, because they left me a lousy $2 on an $80 check. Don't they know you're supposed to tip at least 15 to 20 percent? People like that make me mad. I had been very nice to them.

"Fuck 'em," I thought as I cleared off their table. When the ladies asked me if I could wrap their food to go, I glanced at them like, "Why are you bothering me? Can't you see I'm busy?" Reluctantly, I wrapped their food, gave them their check, and waited for them to leave. They flagged me down again, to give me their money and check.

"I'll be right back with your change," I said.

"No, keep it."

Here it was, I had just treated these two ladies like shit and they had tipped me $20. That was nice. I thanked the ladies. I wanted to apologize for being shitty to them.

I walked over to the hostess and told her I was leaving and not to seat me anymore. But no sooner did I say, "Don't seat me," when April sat me not once but twice.

I walked back over to her and said, "I thought I told you not to seat me."

"I know, but Scott said don't listen to you," she said, organizing menus.

"Well, tell Scott he just lost another waitress."

I took my apron off and threw it in the corner. I emptied my locker and ignored all the *Kayla, what's wrongs? Where you goings?* as I stomped out the door.

I was tired as shit. Let him wait some tables and see how he feels.

Chapter 5

The next morning when I awoke, I just laid in the bed listening to my alarm clock going on and off for about an hour. I found myself pondering many of life's questions I knew I could not answer: Why was I here? What was my purpose? How did this all start and how will it end? Why did some people die at birth and others at seventy-seven? Whose God was the real one? Why were some people's deaths caused by cancer and others from coming home from work and being in a car accident and never knowing what hit them? I guess you never know when you are going to go.

Meanwhile, I am twenty years old and depressed because the man of my dreams had not yet entered my life. Some might say I was much too young to worry about such a trivial thing as a man. But see, that's what I always wanted, love. To say I was in love, to love.

What was love anyway? Who made it up? Who woke up one morning and said, "This is love?" You need it from the moment you enter this world until the day you die.

But there are different kinds of love. Brother and sister love. Man and woman love that people will make movies about. That's the kind of love that everyone wants. The only difference is some will mimic the movie screen love and some will actually really feel and breathe it.

Love, love, oh love. Love, why do you continue to hurt me? I asked myself as I turned over on my stomach and clutched the pillow to my face. What I didn't want most was to end up like my mother. Leslie hadn't had a man or love in the last decade. She was still feeling the pain from her last husband who had died in a tragic car accident. And I didn't want to end up like my aunt, whose only love in life was her cats.

When I finally started coming out of my daze, I decided to turn on the television and flick through the channels. I stopped at a commercial for a psychic hotline. I toyed with the idea of calling. Maybe they would know why I couldn't find love. Maybe they could tell me what I was doing wrong and how long it would be before someone special would enter my life.

After a few minutes of debating, I decided not to call the psychic people, but to reflect on my latest teases with love. The teases I equated with winning the lottery for a billion dollars, buying the dream house with the big pool, going shopping and not looking at the prices, buying whatever I wanted, taking exotic trips to Jamaica and Cancun, just sitting on the beach being tanned by the hot, blazing sun while the water met my feet—then waking up with nothing. Like working hard every day to come home to find someone has robbed you.

I felt this way every time I met a man who didn't work out. How could someone play games and say things they didn't mean? How could they tell lies and not feel guilty? Men were pigs and dogs. Even worse, they were cowards.

Still, I wanted one. Maybe one day I would wake up with a good man by my side and remember how it used to be and be so glad I wasn't in the rat race any longer. Would I ever meet that person who would be happy just being with Kayla and nobody else? Why was I given this miserable fate?

Would I be like an actor who auditioned for every role, but never got cast for anything, not even a commercial? A lawyer who never went to trial or a writer who had never been published? Is that how I would be? Why was such a miserable fate put upon me?

I know I'm not very nice sometimes. I'm way too pushy. But what did I do to deserve this? Was it because I lied occasionally or because I sometimes talked about people, or was it that time I stole that eyeliner pencil out of the pharmacy?

Whatever it was, I was paying for it. I was just so sick of meeting guys and talking to them on the phone and then going through all the bullshit going-out stages: "I like you." "I don't like you." "Don't call me." "Why didn't you call me?"

People saying the opposite of what they mean. For instance, "I'm looking for a girlfriend, but if I tell you I'm not you'll like me more." Then there's all that crap about should I call or shouldn't I call? I was tired of getting to know somebody's bad and good habits and asking them their favorite flavor of ice cream.

I just wanted to meet someone that I could call as soon as I got home, to tell about my day. Somebody to say to me, "Baby, it's going to be OK. It's going to be all right." I used to pray to God every night to please send me a man, and he sent me more than one. Just not the right one.

I don't get it. If I don't sweat guys, they sweat me. Either they call too much or not at all. It's just something about a challenge, I guess.

Why should I settle for less? I got it going on. I'm twenty. I don't have any kids and have my own place. I got a job and go to school. I want someone who has a job or is at least in school and has a future. I deserve to have somebody who doesn't have any kids, either, or baby moms, babies on the way or live-in girlfriends. I want someone who isn't married and who doesn't go both ways.

I deserve to be wined and dined. I want to have flowers sent to my job just because. I want somebody I can check out a '76ers game with, someone who won't smother me but give me just enough attention. I just want to meet my Darius and be his Nina and have someone jonezing for me. I just want someone to chill with, lay up under, and be around.

All I know is that no modern medicine can cure this man ache I have. I tried to convince myself I didn't want love anymore. Fuck love. Fuck men. Who needs them? But I was only lying to myself.

I hated to admit that as soon as I met another man I liked, even a little bit, a ray of hope would shine out saying, "Maybe this is The One." But then I would climb up on the carousel of hope only to get thrown back off. I couldn't win for losing.

I needed to buy summer clothes. I hadn't bought myself anything in a while and I needed everything. Plus I knew shopping would take my mind off my not having a job or a relationship. I decided to see if Yaz felt like going to the mall with me. I picked up the phone and dialed her number. Yaz answered on the first ring.

"Hello."

"What's up? You feel like taking me to the mall?"

"No, I can't. Sam has the car. Plus I'm tired and the kids are here. What you going to get?"

"Probably an outfit to wear tonight and a pair of shoes."

"Didn't you just buy some shoes?"

"Yeah, but they a mess."

"How you be dogging your shoes like that?"

"Well, if I had three hundred pairs in my closet like you, I wouldn't dog my shoes."

"Girl, I don't have three hundred pairs of shoes. Maybe a hundred."

"Psyche. I'm only playing. I'll see you later. I have to go jump on this bus."

I hate catching the bus. It's always crowded. I had to catch the subway to City Hall, walk to 13th and Market and wait for the bus to the King of Prussia Mall. It was thirty minutes outside of Philly by car. By bus, it was another story.

I walked to the back and sat next to the window. I thought I would have the opportunity to read my book and just maybe doze for a minute. This would not be the case.

Across the aisle was this short guy who was talking loud on his cell phone. How corny can you get? If you can afford a cell phone, you should not be on the bus. I could see if you had a car and was like, "I don't feel like driving." But it didn't look like that. He looked like he was accustomed to riding the bus. He had this big CD player and a large book bag. He looked like he was going to work.

That's all good. He can go to work. But he didn't have to be a nut talking loud on his phone saying, "Yeah man, you better have my money," and "Yeah, I'm about to go buy this Benz tomorrow."

I hope he didn't think I was impressed, 'cause I wasn't. Please.

Then he started looking in my direction, smiling with his crooked teeth and needing-a-haircut self. I wanted to say, "You can't do nothing for me. You don't even have a car, so stop torturing me." Please.

What am I going to do with a man that ain't doing any better than me? What's he going to do for me, carry me on his back?

Finally, the bus was almost at my stop. I got up, pulled the cord, and walked to the front of the bus. The guy said, "Bye, precious." Ill. Precious—could he have gotten any weaker?

I went straight to Macy's. They were having a sale, plus I had a credit card with them, so I probably wouldn't end up spending any of the money I had in my pocket. I really needed to pay my bills. But if I saw something I liked, I would buy it. My motto is, "Charge it."

I entered Macy's and took the escalator up to the first level. As soon as I walked to the shoe department, I fell in love with the first shoes I saw. They were these black, knee-high boots. They were so cute.

I turned the boot upside down to look at the price. They were $230. Shit! I had only brought $250, and I needed some jeans.

I brought the display boot over to the salesgirl. "Can I see this in a seven, please?"

"Sure."

The salesgirl went to the storage room to get my boots. When she came out with them, I sat down and started trying them on. Then I stood up and walked to the mirror to see how they looked. They looked right. I was buying them.

I got like $200 of credit on my card. I figured that I would put $130 on the card and then pay $100 in cash. That way, I could still get my two pairs of jeans I needed.

I looked up, because I felt someone looking at me. This tall, caramel-colored basketball-type guy was gazing at me. I pretended not to notice him. I had put my head down and started unzipping the boots, when dude and another guy walked over to me.

"How you doing? You want them shoes?"

"What?" I asked, looking up at him like I didn't understand what he had said.

I didn't want to stare into those pretty almond-shaped eyes, so I looked back down and finished pulling the boots off.

"I said, do you want me to buy the shoes for you?"

No, I don't. I'm an independent African-American woman who can take care of herself, is what I should have said. Instead I said, "Do you see me trying them on?" That way I didn't seem pressed. Plus what guy is crazy enough to buy two-hundred-thirty-dollar shoes for someone he doesn't know?

"See, if you wouldn't have got smart, I would have bought them for you," he said.

"That's game. If you were going to buy them, you still would," I shot back.

Then the salesgirl came over and inquired, "Would you like them?"

"Yes."

"Well, when you're ready, you can bring them to the register."

"I'm ready now." I put the boots back in the box and pulled out my wallet.

"I'm serious," the guy said as his friend walked away laughing. "Where you going, man?"

"To the phone booth. Give me 35 cents."

The basketball guy dug in his pocket and gave the guy some change. Then he turned back and began concentrating on me again. He raised the boot out of the box and said, "Girl, you got me in here buying you shoes and I don't even know your name."

"My name is Kayla. What's yours?"

"Wil."

I got up and started walking toward the register. I still didn't think he was serious. At least I didn't until the basketball guy, I mean Wil, handed me two crisp $100 bills.

I didn't want to be greedy, but he hadn't given me enough money. So I just told him, "Uhm, they cost $230."

"No problem," he said, pulling out a stack of bills.

He gave me another Benjamin and I paid for the shoes.

"Write your number on the back of this," he said, reaching for my receipt and tearing it in half.

I wrote down my number and he wrote down his.

"You going to call me?" he asked.

"Yeah, I'm going to call you."

"You promise?"

"Yeah, I promise."

I tried to give him his change, but he told me to keep it. Wil walked away and left me wondering what was his deal.

Chapter 6

I bought blue jeans and a tiny black dress with the back out. I was planning on wearing the dress when I went with Yazmine to this club called Karisma's. I was about to take a shower when the phone rang.

"Hello."

"Yes, may I speak to Kayla?"

"Who is this?"

"Wil, the guy from the mall."

"Which one? Psyche, nah. What's up?"

"Nothing much. Calling to see what was up with you. What you about to do?"

"Why?"

" 'Cause I want to see your pretty face once more today. You want to go out or something?"

"I can't. I'm about to go to Karisma's with my girlfriend."

"You be clubbin'?" he asked.

"No, not really."

"Good, 'cause I hate girls that go to the club every week."

"No, I be too busy to go out every week. I go to school, plus I work. Well, I used to work. I'm about to get another job."

"Where do you go to school at?"

"Temple."

"That's what's up. What's your major?"

"Secondary Education English."

"So what you gonna be, a English teacher?"

"Yes, I am. Why? Would you like a lesson?" I said, trying to sound professional.

"Nah, I went to college before. It just wasn't my thing. I went to Morehouse for three years and majored in parties, shopping, and trying to pledge Q dog. So my dad told me he wasn't wasting any more money on me."

"Really? Well, I got to go, so I'll probably call you tomorrow or something," I said as I turned on the water for my shower.

"How long before you leave?"

"Like an hour."

"Where you live at?"

"You know where Community College is?"

"Yeah."

"Down the street from there, 17th and Wallace. Why?"

" 'Cause I'm coming to see you. I want to see your pretty face once more before I go to bed. You don't mind, do you?"

"My address is 1752 Wallace Street," I said.

"I'll be there in twenty minutes."

"I'll be outside."

I got dressed in my new black dress and went outside. It was a breezy and clear night. I stood at the top of the steps taking in the last days of summer and waited for Wil.

It seemed everything pulled up in front of my door except for him. I was just glad he wasn't the guy in the old yellow Corolla, with the tires that were too big and the shiny rims that looked like they belonged on a Benz. That piece of shit was blasting Jamaican music as if people ten blocks away had to hear it. It was a relief when that guy kept going.

Now, I'm not materialistic. I just don't see the sense in hooking up an old car. Right after that, a silver Ford Expedition rolled up, flashing its lights at me.

OK, I thought, he got a couple of dollars. Then again, it doesn't have to be his. Wil got out of the car and hugged me.

I thought it was a little early for him to be touching me. But he smelled so good, I couldn't resist. I hugged him back. But at least I was the first to let go.

"Look at you. You look nice. I don't think I want you to go out."

Damn, he looked good, too. *Shit, I'll stay in with you if you ask me,* I thought.

"Psyche, I'm playing. I wouldn't hate on you like that," he said, still holding onto my hand.

Don't play with me, I thought, still toying with the idea of staying at home. But then I thought about how I had just met him a couple of hours ago. I hadn't even had a real conversation with him yet, and I was all ready to be a nut and cancel my plans to be with him.

"Well, I just wanted to see you again. I'm going to call you tomorrow. All right, baby?" he said, as he kissed me gently on the back of my hand.

"Baby," one point deducted, I thought. I hated baby, boo, boop, cookie, sweetie, love, bey, any of them corny lovey-dovey pet names.

"All right. I'll see you later," I said as I tried to ease my hand out of his.

Yaz was pulling up in her boyfriend's black Lexus when he finally let go of my hand. He got back into his truck and screeched off really fast. Yaz reached over and opened the passenger door for me. Being nosy, she asked, "Who's that?"

"This boah I had met at King of Prussia Mall earlier. He walked up to me out of nowhere, asking did I want these boots I got on. I said 'Yeah.' Then he bought them."

"Well, if he spending money on the first day, he's a keeper. Kay, I can see you pushing that truck, girl."

"I think so, too, but it's not about that truck or the boots. I think I could really like him like that."

"Please, I know you. You don't really like anyone. You'll get too happy too soon and start tripping and say something stupid like, 'He is too nice.'"

"No, I won't."

"We'll see. Next week you will be calling me saying, 'I hate him. He's a nut.'"

By now, me and Yaz had pulled up to the club on Delaware Avenue. It was about six other clubs along the same strip—black, Puerto Rican

and white clubs. It was a fashion and car show all in one. There were
six clubs, but all the cops were at the black one. Go figure. We circled
the block looking for a place to park, until I saw a parking space.

"Park right there," I said.

"No, they might give me a ticket."

"Girl, they don't give out tickets on Saturday. Plus, it's at night."

After hesitating a bit more, Yaz finally decided to park. We got out.
I pulled down my dress while Yaz checked her makeup in the
rearview mirror. As always, Yaz had gone all out and made sure everything matched perfectly.

She was wearing a hot pink snakeskin halter top with matching
Capri pants and sexy pink snakeskin sandals with an ankle strap that
wrapped up her leg. We had started walking toward the club when
this guy walked up to us shouting, "Hey, baby, ughn, ughn."

His voice was raspy and he was balding. I'd rather have a period,
breasts, and kids before I would want to go bald like a man does. He
had on a purple silk shorts set with sandals. He probably thought
what he had on was hot. I thought not.

We ignored him, but the guy must not have liked rejection, because he started trying to play us, calling us SWV—Sisters Without
Vehicles—as we stood in line to get in the club.

I came back at him with, "Stop hatin'."

"You not all that, you trick," he yelled back.

After that, I knew it wasn't no reasoning with that fool. Yaz felt dif-
ferently, because she shouted at him, "You're just mad we wouldn't
talk to you. You-so-broke-your-man-had-to-drop-you-off-you-don't-have-
a-job-playing-the-outside-'cause-you-can't-get-in, hatin'-nut-ass-nigga."

Everyone started laughing. He walked away, still talking shit. That's
when I remembered I didn't have my fake ID on me. I hated being
twenty.

"Yo, Yaz. I don't have no ID."

Yaz went in her bag and gave me her old driver's license.

"What am I going to do with this?"

"Use it."

"They going to know it's not me."

"No, they won't."

"I hope this works."

After waiting in line awhile, we got into Karisma's problem-free around 12:30 A.M. See, you couldn't get to the club any earlier, 'cause you wouldn't be able to make a grand entrance. We had about an hour to mingle, because the club closed at 2 A.M. After getting IDed—the bouncer didn't even card me, he just patted me down—we paid the $15 cover charge and had our hands stamped. It was worth it because the music was loud and the club was most definitely off the hook. My favorite club song, "Let Me Clear My Throat," was playing.

"Come on, girl. Walk me to the bathroom," Yaz said, leading the way through the crowd.

We walked through the crowded club filled with freaks, tricks and dicks. I had to say "excuse me" to every other person it was so packed.

Finally, we made it to the bathroom. Yaz went into the stall while I fixed my hair. My hair stayed tossed even when I was broke, which was often. The hairdressers' is where I met Yaz. We were under the dryers talking when I found out we both wanted to go to this comedy show. She didn't have anyone to go with and neither did I. So we went together and had been cool ever since. Yaz came out the stall and asked me the age-old girlfriend-to-girlfriend question, "Is there anything on the back of my pants?"

I told her to walk in front of me. "No, I don't see anything."

"Good."

We walked out of the bathroom toward the bar. The music was loud, the lights were flashing on and off, and everybody was dancing, having a good time. Guys started crowding us with reason. We looked good. These other girls didn't have nothing on us.

A couple of them were on our level, but we were always in the top ten when we went out. If we went to the club and guys weren't sweating us, there was a major problem. That night, there were three guys in our faces, but it was like they all wanted to talk to Yaz. It must be that I-got-a-boyfriend vibe, 'cause I was sitting there like, "Talk to me, I'll go out with you. She's almost married. She won't call you. I will." Then Yaz kicked me, telling me to move over 'cause she spotted her boyfriend's best friend, and she didn't want it to look like she was talking to those guys.

"Look, there go Darryl. I hope he don't see us, because I'm trying to get my dance on and I don't want him running back telling Sam shit."

That's when Darryl started walking toward us.

"What's up, Lil' Sam? Staying out of trouble?" Darryl asked, eyeing her tight Capri pants and halter top.

"Yeah, I'm chilling," she said innocently as she sipped her drink.

"Who you here with?"

"Dave and my little brother, Samir."

"I didn't know you had a brother."

"Yeah, he's away at school," he said as he slurped the last piece of ice from his drink. Then he turned around to leave and said, "All right, ladies. I ain't trying to fuck up y'all play. Be careful out here."

I was glad when he walked away. Quite frankly, I was tired of seeing Sam's friends or guys I already knew. When I went out, I would always be bumping into guys I went to school with or somebody I had played hide-and-seek with. Or I would see people I never called or who never called me.

The killers would be the guys I used to fuck with who thought they were taking me home after we left because we used to mess around. See, I have this philosophy that if I hadn't messed with you in the last six months, then you had to start over from scratch, not pick up where we left off.

Then there would be the guys I'd meet that Yaz would tell me not to talk to, because her sister used to talk to him. He'd tell me his name was Nasir or something, when his name is actually Nate but he had changed his name when he went to jail. Yaz would tell me he wasn't shit and not to fuck with him. I'd throw the bubble gum wrapper he wrote his number on onto the floor. As you can see, this dating shit gets very boring at times.

"Let's get a drink," Yaz said, interrupting my train of thought.

"I don't feel like drinking tonight."

"Why not? Well, I'm getting me something to drink."

She flagged down the bartender, saying, "Can I get a Long Island iced tea, please?"

"Damn, girl, why you got to go straight to the hard liquor? Order me a Sex on the Beach."

I lightly patted Yaz so she could see what this girl walking by was wearing. She had this fucked-up black and gold leopard print cowgirl hat with the outfit to match and some white sandals.

"No, she didn't play herself like that. That shit don't match," Yaz said under her breath.

"How could her friends let her do that to herself? If I ever look that whack, beat my ass."

We started laughing at the girl some more and drank our drinks. This guy came over to me and asked me if I wanted to dance. He was kind of cute. He had close-cut hair and molasses-colored skin.

"Yaz, watch my drink," I said as I stood up and tugged my dress down again.

The guy grabbed my hand and I followed him to the dance floor. We danced off one of Jay Z's songs. Then I noticed that the guy was trying to outdance me, but he wasn't doing nothing 'cause I was kicking it.

He then started asking me the usual questions—was I involved, did I have any kids, and could we go out-type questions. I answered his questions with "No, no, and yes."

He just started laughing and said, "I like your style."

I liked his, too. He was dressed real cute. He had on a cream-colored blazer and cream-colored linen pants with matching boots. His beard and hair had to have been cut with a knife, 'cause his shit was sharp. His smile was perfect, too, except for the extra tooth he had coming in on the side of his mouth. I kept looking at it. *Maybe he could get it pulled or something,* I thought. I had looked past much worse things like height, weight, money, education, and the fact that they were involved with somebody else. I didn't like that shit too much, 'cause you can only act like you don't care for so long. The song finished and the guy I was dancing with asked me to dance again. I told him no, because I couldn't leave my girlfriend by herself for too long. I wrote my number down and told him to give me a call.

"All right, I'm going to call you. My name is Samir."

"OK. I'll see you."

I walked back to the bar to find Yaz and my drink gone. Where did she go? I looked around and ran into some girl I had gone to high school with.

"What's up, Kayla?"

"Hey, Gina. Nothing. What you been up to?"

Ain't it funny how you can see someone and converse with them like you actually gave a fuck what was happening in their life?

"Going to school in Maryland."

While she was talking, I was thinking, *Damn, she got fat. Her dress is cheap. I need to give her a business card for my hairdresser,* 'cause her shit looked a mess. And why does this girl got the raps like I forgot what happened? She stole my first boyfriend away from me when I was in the eleventh grade.

"Where, Morgan State?"

"Yeah."

"How you like it?" I asked.

"It's all right. Where you at?" she questioned.

"Temple."

"Oh, all right. See you later."

Whatever, I thought as I flashed her my phoniest smile. I decided to go looking for Yaz, but she found me first.

"Girl, where you been at?"

"I was dancing with this guy."

"Oh."

"Where my drink at?"

"In the trash."

"Why you throw it in the trash?" I snapped back, annoyed.

" 'Cause I didn't feel like carrying it," she said casually.

By now, the lights were on and an announcement was made for anyone who wanted to enter the best body contest to come onto the stage. I was thinking, *Who would get on stage and degrade themselves like that?*

But there were plenty of would-be contestants. First, the guys went on, these bodybuilder types. Nobody even watched them.

When these hoochie mama ho's started getting on stage, everyone started looking. The sounds of bass, Luke, and chanting, "Don't stop. Get it. Get it. Pop that coochie. Do do brown. I want to rock," filled the air.

The girls were dancing, the guys clapping and hollering, "Go girl." The girls on stage gyrated and flexed their butts. Some got on the ground, while others just shook everything. One girl was a little too big, but she still was shaking it.

The deejay came back on stage to judge the freak show Apollo-style. He put his hand above each contestant's head. The fat girl got booed and two other girls didn't get enough claps.

It ended up being a tie between these two girls who looked like their names could be Fifi and Gigi. They were probably go-go girls anyway. They looked experienced.

To break the tie, the deejay made them face off. The music started up all over again.

I couldn't believe it. It was like I was at home watching a porn movie and not out at a club trying to get my dance on. The girls started stripping on stage. Fifi put her hand in her pants and Gigi took her shirt off. That's when people started booing them.

One guy screamed, "Put your clothes on, you trick."

Now they were tricks. A few minutes ago, they were the shit. Fifi jumped off the stage while Gigi went to put her shirt on, but some-body had taken it. She had to leave the stage in the deejay's jacket. After that she got propositioned by men.

I heard one guy ask to trick her for a thousand dollars. She said "No, I'm not that type of girl."

Shit, I can't tell, I thought. Well, that was on her.

Then the lights went down again and the music started back up. Yaz went to dance with this tall, lanky guy and never came back. It was 2 A.M., closing time. I figured I'd go outside and wait for Yaz by the car.

The first thing Sunday morning, I decided to beep Wil, but I couldn't find his number. I looked everywhere—in my pants pocket, in my room, I even dumped everything in my pocketbook out. I finally found his number in the trash. I beeped him. The phone started ring-ing—or at least it seemed that way—before I even hung up the phone.

"Yo, somebody call a beeper?" a deep masculine voice asked.

"Yes, I did. This is Kayla."

"What's up? Why you put 22 in my beeper?"

"Because that's my code."

"Oh. How was Karisma's?"

"It was cool. I was enjoying myself until I couldn't find my girl-friend. I thought she had left me, but she had to go and move her car because the cops were towing."

"Females kill me. Y'all always getting away with something."

"That's not true."

"Yes it is. Y'all never get stopped by the cops and if y'all do, y'all flirt with him and then get his number."

"What if it's a lady cop?"

"Then y'all be like, 'Hey girl, where you get your hair done at?' But see, that shit don't work for us. We get pulled over twenty times in one day."

"Whatever," I said as I laughed off his last comment. "Who you live with?"

"My mom and pop. I just moved back in. I used to have my own place, but I just decided to move back in with my peeps. What did you say happened to your job?"

"I thought I told you that story already."

"No, you didn't."

"I quit because I was burnt out. I was working and taking summer classes. I had a couple of dollars in the bank. So when I asked my supervisor for some vacation time and he said no, I decided to take an extended vacation. I haven't found another job yet, and my mom is going to be tripping if she finds out I'm not working. She wants me to get a car before it gets cold. Where you work at?"

"My dad and uncle's construction company. You ever hear of Carter Contracting?"

"No."

"Well, we do a lot of big jobs. We probably did somebody's house you know. My dad is really big. We even did some work on Patti LaBelle's house."

"Oh, that's nice. A family business."

"It is. Basically, I supervise things, maybe get a little dirty. So when are you going to let me take you out?"

"Well, I got to go to register for school tomorrow, so probably Tuesday. We can hook up. I'm going to let you go, all right?"

"All right, that's what's up, so I'll talk to you later then."

Wil called me on Tuesday and we chose to go to dinner over a movie. I really don't like going to the movies on a first date because you end up not knowing any more about the person than you did before you went in the movie. And I really wanted to get to know Wil.

I was glad I was going out with him that night, because registering for my classes had made me mad as hell. All the good classes had been taken. It was my own fault, 'cause every semester I waited until the last minute.

But I didn't need the academic counselor bringing it to my attention. She kept looking down at my transcript on her computer, saying shit like, "Sweetheart, do you realize you have put yourself back by dropping classes over the last two years?"

I wanted to say, "I'm very aware of that," but I was trying my best to smile. Maybe she could perform a miracle so I wouldn't have to go to school every day. But she couldn't.

Shit, I should have registered by phone. Finally, the bitch processed my classes. She got me in all the classes I needed, political science, psychology, biology and intellectual heritage. I had to be to school at 8:40 in the blankety-blank morning on Monday and Wednesday for that damn poli sci class. I wanted to kill her. I never get up before 10 A.M. and always get out of my classes before 3 P.M. I don't like all those breaks between classes. I like to go to class two days a week, on Tuesdays and Thursdays. But I guess beggars shouldn't be choosy. A good date would take my mind off the events of the day, I figured.

I straightened up my apartment. It was small, but I liked it, except for my neighbor, Maria Franklin. The only reason I knew what her first name was because her mail always somehow managed to get in my mailbox. Her and her kids got on my nerves something terrible. She was always kicking her husband out, then letting him right back in. She let her kids run up and down the stairs. I was so glad I lived on the second floor and not the first. Otherwise I never would have gotten any sleep.

I continued straightening my place up in case Wil wanted to come in after dinner. No, I wasn't planning to let him come up. But I figured I'd tidy up a bit just in case. I fixed the pillows on my sofa, which was powder blue and white. I had a white throw cover over it and my new brass coffee table in the corner. Not too much else could fit in there, except for my entertainment system and CD rack.

My apartment was small, but it was freedom. I could do whatever I wanted. I didn't have any stupid roommate I didn't get along with anymore and I was a couple of stops on the subway from campus.

This apartment was going to put a slight strain on Leslie's pockets, but my privacy was worth it. My mom always acted like she didn't have any money, but she still had a ton of insurance money from when my stepfather died.

I glanced at the clock. It was 7:15. If Wil was not there in another fifteen minutes, I was going to take my clothes off. I had already broken rule number one: Never get dressed until you hear your date's car pull up so you won't feel played if they don't show. Wash up, iron your clothes, but don't get dressed.

Finally, 7:30 came and my bell rang. *About time,* I mumbled under my breath as I grabbed my clutch bag and ran down the steps.

Wil took me to this nice Italian restaurant. We walked in and the hostess signed our name on a waiting list. As we sat on a tiny couch waiting for them to call us to our table, I looked around and admired the restaurant's authentic feel. It had Italian paintings on the walls and music playing. When our name was called, our waiter seated us in a booth right next to the window and gave us our menus. Then he gave us a little speech on what specials they had, told us his name, and left. The view was extraordinary. I could see all the streetlights starting to come on and the sun setting.

"So, Kayla, tell me some more about yourself."

"There's nothing to tell. I'm twenty and have one sister. How about you? Do you have any brothers and sisters?"

"No, I'm the only child. I'm the sole heir to the empire. When is your birthday?"

"March 23. When is yours?"

"Next month. September 16. I'll be twenty-six."

Damn, his birthday was in a couple of weeks. I hate when a guy's birthday comes before yours. That means you gotta spend money on them first. You don't want to be cheap, but then again you don't want to be spending on a man you don't know.

"What you going to do for your birthday?" I inquired.

"Probably chill with you."

"Sounds good," I smiled.

By now, our waiter had returned to our table and we hadn't even looked at our menus yet.

"Sorry, can you come back in a minute? And can I have a white zinfandel? Kayla, what are you having?" Wil asked.

"I'll take a virgin strawberry daiquiri with no whipped cream."

"She'll have a zinfandel, too," he told the waiter.

"No, don't listen to him." I said, laughing.

"You sure?" the tall skinny waiter asked. I could tell by the waiter's expression he was getting tired of us playing around.

"I'm sure."

"You're embarrassing me, ordering a virgin daiquiri. You might as well have ordered a soda," Wil complained after the waiter had left with our drink order.

"I just don't like to drink."

"I'm only kidding. I'm glad you don't drink. Most girls I know would be like, 'can I get a margarita with a twist of lime and salt rim?' " he said, imitating an around-the-way girl.

I laughed. He was funny and was looking real tempting in his black jeans and red Polo shirt.

"Wil, what are you getting?" I asked, as I noticed him dipping his silverware into the ice-cold water the waiter had brought out. *How are you going to sterilize silverware with cold water?* I thought.

"Uhm, I don't know, What about you?" Wil answered.

"I think I'm going to have the shrimp alfredo," I said, still looking over the menu.

Our waiter came back and placed our drinks on the table with an I'm-better-than-you-are attitude. We gave him our order. As he left the table I asked Wil, "Do you think he got an attitude?"

"Yeah, he's got an attitude. He didn't have to slam my glass down."

"I hate people like that."

"He fucked up on his tip. Me and my cousin Stevie don't tip unless the waiter is excellent. They got to work for their money."

"No, don't do that. Tip his tall racist ass so the next black person that comes in here will be treated with more respect. I know. I used to be a waitress and they would always try to sit all the black people at my table. The majority of the time they didn't tip well. So they came to the conclusion that all black people were bad tippers."

"They probably didn't know any better, but I know what you're talking about," he said, nodding in agreement.

"I'll be right back," I said as I got up to go to the rest room.

By the time I returned, the food was already there. I sat down and enjoyed my dinner. It was not hard, because Wil made me forget about my bad day. He was such a gentleman. He spoke to me like I was the only person that mattered. The whole evening, he hung onto everything I said, as if he didn't want to miss a single syllable.

After dinner we walked down on South Street, got some ice cream, and went back to my place. When Wil came in, he didn't try to kiss me or anything. He only stayed for about ten minutes before saying he had to take care of some business.

That had been three days ago. I had wanted to call him last night, but he didn't call me yet, so I figured I'd wait. After all, if he had had a nice time, he would call me.

I sat on the sofa with my blanket wrapped around me and started changing the TV channels. I couldn't find anything to watch. What was the purpose of cable?

Then the phone rang. Quickly, I pushed the mute button on the remote. Maybe it was Wil.

"Hello," I whispered in my most seductive voice.

"Kayla, who are you waiting to call you, sounding like that?" Yaz snapped.

"Shut up. I sound regular."

"Yeah, right. Anyway, did I tell you that guy you met named Samir is Darryl's brother?"

"Darryl did say that he was there with his little brother, but we didn't catch on."

"So I don't know if you should talk to him or not 'cause you know all of them West Philly guys is dogs, not excluding but including Sam. But Sam said he supposed to be different, because he's away at some school down Maryland."

"Well, I haven't talked to him yet. I didn't get his phone number. I gave him mine. When he calls me, I'll feel him out and see what he's about, but right now I'm tripping off the boah, Wil."

"Who?"

"The one who was here that night we went out."

"Oh, him."

"He took me out the other night. Girl, we went to this Italian restaurant, then we went to South Street, and after that he brought me home. We talked for a couple of minutes, but he had to go. He didn't even try to kiss me or nuttin'."

"He wasn't supposed to. You so used to messing with nuts, you forgot how it feels to be treated by a real man. You should be happy he didn't try to kiss you."

"So he still left me hanging. His lips looked good."

"Why are you tripping?"

"Because he didn't call me yet."

"Call him."

"No. He needs to call me first."

"Girl, you better pick up the phone and call him. There's no rules to this," Yaz said, starting to sound annoyed.

"You right. If he don't call me by tomorrow, I'm going to call him."

Before I could complete my sentence, Yaz interrupted, whispering, "I've got to call you right back. Sam just came in looking all evil."

Yazmine's perfect relationship was turning out to be not so perfect. I mean, it seemed like she had it all, but maybe she didn't. Sam did do for her and the kids, and Mia is not even his. She does have a nice apartment, she don't have to work, and they get a new car like every year. She got every pair of shoes and all the clothes you could want.

But on the flip side, Sam ain't shit. He's always cheating on her and making her miserable. Or maybe that's just how relationships work.

It was September, but it felt more like November. Outside it was dreary and raining. I was writing checks for all my bills, and there were a lot of them. I was tired of having all those dumb-ass credit cards. They were addictive as hell.

During my freshman year, credit cards were being thrown at me. I couldn't say no. That wouldn't have been polite. Besides, I needed shit back then that I couldn't afford—that I still can't afford. Now there I was with all these credit cards.

I continued watching television and signing my name when I heard a knock at my door. I was startled as hell.

"Who is it?"

"It's me."

"Me who?"

"Me, Wil."

I opened the door and there he was, standing in my doorway, drenched.

"What's up?" I asked, surprised to see him at my door.

"I was in the neighborhood and decided to stop by. I lost your number. When I got home the other night I realized I didn't have it. You gonna let me in or what?"

"I guess. You smell good. What do you have on?"

"Issey Miyake."

I kicked my shoes and checks under the sofa while pulling the blanket off and balling it up under my arm. I told Wil he could have a seat.

"Nice place. I didn't really notice it before."

"Thanks."

"Look at you, all independent with your little apartment."

"Well, I just moved here. I used to live on campus, but my roommate moved out, so I got this."

"That's what's up. It's cute like you. So tell me why you don't have a man. What's wrong with you?"

"What you mean, what's wrong with me?" I shot back.

"Not like that. It's just that you're pretty, you're in school, have a job, no kids, and your own place. I mean, why wouldn't someone already have snatched you up?"

What Wil was saying did make a lot of sense. Why didn't I have a man if I had all these things going on for me? I spaced out for a minute, then I told him I'd be right back. I walked out of the living room into my bedroom. I threw the blanket on the bed and checked myself out in the mirror, to see if there was anything on my face and if my hair was in place.

When I walked back out into the living room, Wil had made himself comfortable on my couch. He had turned the channel to ESPN Sports Center and was watching that guy that's always rhyming. Wil had taken his wet boots off and was sitting on the sofa looking through my CDs.

"Don't steal none of my CDs," I joked.

"Please. Everything you got, I got."

Then he asked me if I was expecting company.

"No. Why, what's up?"

"Good, because no guys are allowed over here no more. I'm your new man and you're my woman." Wil said, sounding all self-assured.

On the inside, I was ecstatic, but I tried to play it off. "I'm nobody's woman," I said, standing in front of him with my hands on my hips and my chin all up in the air.

"You know what I mean. Just tell all your little guy friends you got a man now and don't call anymore. You are a free agent, aren't you?"

"Yeah, but who said I wanted to get signed yet? The next time I sign with a team, I want fringe benefits and longevity."

"Yeah, I hear you. I got your fringe benefits. In all seriousness, I really want to be with you."

Could I be hearing him right? Did he really want me to be his woman? As bad as I wanted to say OK, I couldn't. I just told him we could work on that. Besides, we had only had one date. I can't build myself up for failure anymore. No one was going to hurt me again.

The next time I got involved with a man, I wanted to dot my i's and cross my t's. I didn't want to play games anymore. I want to meet a man, date him until I got out of college, and then get married on an island somewhere. I wanted to have Babyface or Luther Vandross sing at our wedding and have our picture in *Jet* magazine on the wedding page or something. I didn't really want kids, but if I had one I would want a boy so I could make him a junior.

I knew I was living in fantasy land, but that's what's wrong with me. The minute I meet a man I like, I'm writing my first name down with his last name. What I wouldn't do for a real sincere brother.

"Turn back to HBO. I hate ESPN. It's not Sixers season yet," I said, pushing his long legs out of the way and plopping down on the couch next to him.

"You like the Sixers?"

"Yeah, we might have a chance this season. We got Iverson and McKie, plus Ratliff."

"You like Iverson?"

"Yeah."

"You like him or the way he plays?" Wil said, looking down in my face.

"The way he plays. Come on, now. I'm no groupie. The boy's got skills."

"You never know. The Sixers got an all right squad. But I like San Antonio."

"Uhm, what's their name? The Spurs?"

"Yeah."

"I only watch Philly's team."

"You shouldn't limit ya . . ."

Wil stopped mid-sentence. He could hear my neighbors downstairs. Mrs. Franklin was arguing with Mr. Franklin You could hear someone hitting the floor and what sounded like a wrestling match.

"What's that noise?"

"Oh, that's the lady on the first floor. She's probably kicking her husband out again. In a few minutes he'll be banging on the door."

Wil was looking like, *What the fuck?*

"They're always fighting. She always kicks him out, then lets him right back in. The cops will be here soon."

"You got to be kidding."

"No, this is normal. Every other night. Stop changing the subject. Turn back to HBO," I said, trying to grab the remote out of his hand.

"Hold up, let me see this. It's only going to take a minute," Wil said, as he held it up out of my reach.

After struggling a bit to reach it, I sat back down for a minute or two. Then I jumped up and tried to grab the remote again. This time, I got it out of his hand. Wil grabbed me and took my arm, twisted it backward and said, "Put the remote down now."

I was laughing but I acted like it hurt. "Stop playing. Wil, you play too much," I whined.

I tried to get away, but the harder I tried, the tighter his grip became. Finally he eased up and the remote dropped to the floor. He turned me around and pushed me back onto the sofa. I fell on my back.

The next thing I knew he was kissing me. I didn't fight it. His tongue was soothing and very wet. He ran his hands up and down my back and hugged me so tight I wanted to burst. Then he slowly unhooked my bra, caressing and licking my breasts. He sent me into a world of erotic pleasure.

After a few minutes of it, I started feeling as if I couldn't take it anymore. I had to get up. A couple more minutes and I would be done for. As hard as I could, I pushed his head up off my chest.

He jumped up and said, "What's wrong, Boo?"

"Nothing. I just want to take my time. I'm trying not to rush into anything," I said, as I sat up and reached for my bra.

As Wil watched, I slipped it back over my shoulders. It wasn't that I didn't like Wil. I just didn't want to make a mistake again. But I didn't want him to get mad at me and never speak to me again.

Then he surprised me by saying, "No problem. I can wait."

He grabbed my hand and kissed it. He came closer again, then started massaging my neck with his tongue. In a few minutes, I was right back in the same position I had just gotten up from.

I couldn't help myself. He was doing all the right things. And he just wouldn't stop. God knows I shouldn't have been just letting him.

Our tongues met. They touched and licked each other. But somehow, I managed to catch myself and got up again.

"Wil, we've got to stop," I demanded in my I-ain't-playing-no-more voice.

He said, "OK. Let's just lay here then."

I leaned back and laid my head on his chest. I could feel his heart racing. He watched TV as I drifted off to sleep pressed against his body as his gentle breathing sang me a lullaby. When I woke up the next morning, I had forgotten Wil was there. Then I looked up and began tapping him on his arm.

"Wil, don't you have to go to work?" I asked.

"Yeah, what time is it?"

"Eight."

Wil gave me a kiss and said he would call me later. He had to hurry up so he wouldn't be late.

"You going to get up and lock your door?"

"Uhm, uhm just close it. I'll lock it later," I said sleepily as I pulled the cover over my head.

Then I went right back to sleep. When I got up, it was almost 1:00. There was a little note on my pillow that read "Beep me when you wake up." It was signed William Carter Jr.

I looked at the note and smiled. Then I got dressed and decided to go to my mother's house. I had nothing else planned until next week when school started back.

Chapter 7

I'm not one to knock anyone's hustle, but when I heard some girl on the train talking about some guy named Black Sam from 58th Street who was taking her out and taking her shopping, I had to turn around, hoping she wasn't talking about my girl Yaz's baby father. I realized I knew the girl from the hair salon, so I had to speak instead of getting up and slapping her.

"Hi, Kay," she said.

"Hey, Sonya."

Then she turned back around to her friend and kept talking. She couldn't have known Sam was Yaz's baby father, because she would have shut up when she saw me instead of going on and on about him.

"Yeah, he took me down Atlantic City. He ate this and I kissed him there. He got this girl, but she dumb. She got two kids."

Sonya's girlfriend was sitting there with her mouth wide open, like *For real?* Little did they know I was writing everything she said down in my head verbatim. I couldn't wait to get to my mom's house so I could call Yaz.

Then I decided to go to her house. I had to tell Yaz to her face. My mom would still be home later on. The next thing I knew, I was off the train and running up the subway stairs thinking, "I hate men."

I walked a couple of blocks until I reached Yaz's door. I knocked hard. Yaz opened the door with Sam Jr. on her hip. Her hair was all over her head with a comb sticking out of it. Yaz let me into her apartment, which was very stylish. Everything was gold and black. She had a black leather sofa, a matching loveseat, and black and gold vertical blinds that matched the borders on the wall.

"What are you doing here?" Yaz asked, as she used her free hand to pat down her hair a bit.

"Is Sam here?"

"No, why? What's up? He had to go out of town on some business."

"Well, let me tell you what kind of business he went on. I was on the subway on my way to Leslie's house when I heard this girl talking about how she fucked with this guy named Black Sam from 58th Street and how he got a dumb baby mom with two kids. She said he took her to Atlantic City last night and all this shit that he did to her and she did to him. So I turned around and it was Sonya from the shop. She must don't know you fuck with him, 'cause otherwise she would have shut up. But she didn't, she just kept rapping."

Yaz turned toward her bay-style windows and said, "I kinda knew he was fucking around. When I see that Sonya, I'm going to fuck her up."

"No, you need to be fucking up Sam. He's the one cheating on you."

"You right."

As soon as she agreed, Sam walked in the door.

"How you doing, Kayla?" Sam said, as he threw his keys on the table and grabbed Sam Jr. out of Yaz's arms.

"I'm fine," I said.

Sam turned to Yaz and asked her, "What's wrong with you?"

"Nothing. Where have you been?" Yaz said, eyeing him suspiciously.

"I told you, I had to take care of some business."

"Well, I need the car. Mia is in her room asleep. I'm taking Kayla to her mom's house. I'll be right back."

Yaz grabbed the keys and I followed her out the door. We got in the car and she turned the music on and blasted it. Then she sped off, causing her tires to shriek.

"What are you going to do?" I asked, turning down the music.

"I don't know."

"What you mean you don't know? You need to leave that nigga alone and move back with your mom. Go back to school and get a job."

"It's not that easy. You don't know how it is. You never really had a man and you don't got no kids."

"All I know is, you were doing a lot better before you met him. You were in school, you had only one child and you were about your education."

"Whatever. I'm not going to say anything. I'm going to wait and catch him in the act."

Yaz turned the music back up and we didn't talk for the rest of the ride. I couldn't solve her problems for her. She knew what she had to do, and that was to forget about the money, car, and clothes.

I mean Sam, he does take care of her and her kids, and Mia isn't even his. But come on, she don't have to go through all that just for money. I kept telling her that.

Before him, she was comfortable. She was going to nursing school and working at a hotel, but then she got pregnant with Sam Jr., and he told her she didn't have to work anymore. Because he was blowing up on the streets, he would throw her a couple of thousand every week like it was nothing. Almost overnight, Yaz went from wearing Gap to Gucci. They even took trips to Las Vegas to see the fights.

But it wasn't all good. I mean she almost caught a case once, picking up money for him down Hunting Park Avenue. That was not cool. I told her to leave him then.

And I told her again to leave him when he cheated the first, second, and third times. It was on her if she stayed with him. I guess she just didn't want to give up the glamorous life.

Yaz dropped me off at mom's house. As I got out of the car I told her, "Your hair looks a mess. When you getting it done?"

"Probably tomorrow," she said, squinting at herself in the rearview mirror.

"I see why he cheating on you. You can't even keep your hair done."

Yaz started laughing. I knew that would make her smile.

"Well, if you get an appointment, make me one too! See you. Thanks for the ride," I said as I slammed the door.

I stood outside for a moment or two watching Yaz speed off down the street. Then I noticed Leslie's car wasn't outside. I pulled out my keys and walked in. I heard faint noises in the kitchen.

"Leslie, is that you?"

"No, it's me."

I walked into the kitchen, and it was my sister Nicole cooking. I hadn't seen her almost all summer. She had just turned seventeen and had let her hair grow into a chin-length bob with a bang. She was petite—only 5-feet tall—just like my mother. She was wearing an oversized pajama top with a pair of faded blue jeans and stirring something in a pot on the stove.

"What's up? Where Leslie?" I said as I opened the refrigerator door.

"Out with her boyfriend."

"What boyfriend?" I said, shocked, almost dropping the water bottle I had pulled out of the refrigerator.

"Mr. Charlie, the same one she had for the last couple of months. He works at her job."

"What?" I asked.

Then I starting hearing noises coming from upstairs.

"Who's that upstairs?"

"Karim."

"Mommy know you got company when she's not home?" I asked as I pulled out a chair and sat down at the same table my mother had had since I was ten.

"Yeah, 'cause she's hardly home anymore. She don't care. She spends the night over her boyfriend house all the time."

"Why didn't anyone tell me she had a boyfriend?"

"Because you were so busy with summer school and working. I guess she forgot to tell you."

Karim came in the kitchen and shyly nodded hello. He sat down at the table, I turned and took a good look at him. He was kind of short, with braids going back. He had on a two-sizes-too-big aqua-and-black-plaid shirt that hung open over a white T-shirt. He was a cute little boy.

"Well, you could have called me, Nicole. I mean, who is this guy? How long she been seeing him?" I said, turning my attention back to

Nikki, who by now was chopping up onions and tossing them into a pan.

I couldn't believe my mother, Leslie, had a boyfriend. I mean, she never had a boyfriend. She was married to my dad. Then they got divorced and we hadn't seen him since I was like four. She married Nicole's dad, David, but he was killed in a car accident.

That's when Leslie stopped dealing with men. She was so lonely. Some nights I would be awakened by her crying, saying "Why me? Why me?" Then I would start crying because Leslie was sad.

I used to beg her to go out. I'd even bring my friends' fathers over so she could be happy, but she said she'd rather just stay in the house with us. In all these years, I had never seen my mom even look twice at a man. Now she got a boyfriend.

"What are you making, Nicole?" I asked.

"Spaghetti."

"You making it the good way or nasty way?"

"The good way. I don't mix the noodles and sauce."

"That's the nasty way."

"Karim, which way do you like it?"

"I like it the way she make it."

"Well, don't make mine like that. I like mine mixed."

I got comfortable in my chair and talked to my little sister and her boyfriend. She seemed like she had everything together. She knew what she wanted to do with her life. She told me how she was going to apply next year to attend Spelman College and wants to study law, and how Karim had already gotten an early admission to Clark Atlanta. After dinner was over, Karim started the dishes while me and Nikki continued talking in the living room.

"I didn't know you wanted to go to Spelman."

"Yeah, I want to see the rest of the world."

"What you going to do about Karim?"

"Karim will be there. That boy already asked me to marry him."

We were interrupted by the phone ringing. I started to get it, but Nicole had already asked Karim to answer it.

"Karim, who is it?"

"It's for your sister."

I got up and answered the telephone. It was Yaz.

"Did you make the appointments?"

"Yeah, we got to be there tomorrow at 10."

"Can you come and get me?"

"Where you going to be at?"

"Probably here. As a matter of fact, I will be here. I'm going to spend the night. How Sam acting?"

"He know I know something,'cause he tried to kiss me and I turned away. Well, I got to go. Be ready tomorrow."

"All right and remember what I said. You don't need him."

"I hear you. Bye."

While I was on the phone, Karim and Nicole tiptoed upstairs. I laid there on the sofa thinking about Wil. I wanted to call him, but decided not to. I knew he thought I was rude for not getting up and walking him to the door. I knew he turned me on. I was going to love messing with him.

"Nikki, throw down a blanket. Karim, leave by 11:30," I yelled, as I turned off the light.

It was Friday night, and I fell asleep watching television.

The next morning, Yaz's loud horn blowing woke me up, as well as half the neighbors. I jumped up off the sofa and saw Karim walking down the steps with Nicole.

"Mommy ever come home, Nikki?" I asked, stretching and rubbing the sleep out of my eyes.

"No," she responded.

"Karim, what are you still doing here? I thought I told you to leave by 11:30. You better be glad I don't have time to get you now." I ran upstairs to brush my teeth and wash my face. "Tell Yaz here I come."

Nikki ran outside and told Yaz. Then she came back in the house and said "Kay, Yaz said hurry up."

"Tell her I'm coming."

I could hear Nikki screaming, "Here she come" as I raced back down the stairs, almost tripping. Yaz was sitting in the car impatiently.

"I told you to be ready. I'm not trying to be late."

"Shut up. You're going to get your hair done."

Yaz's hair was the opposite of mine. Hers was short and jet black while mine was medium brown and hung a little past my shoulders. I changed the radio station, because a song I hated was on. That got Ms. Grumpy even more upset. She said, "Don't get in my car turning the station."

"Look, shut up and get me to the hairdresser."

"What number is Biggie's CD?"

"It's number eight."

I reached up and changed the CD selector and we listened to "Ready to Die" for the rest of the ride. When we pulled up at the salon, I could tell by all the cars it was crowded inside.

"Shit, we going to be here all day."

"I know. Let me out so I can put our name on the shampoo list."

I walked into the salon and all I heard was blow dryers. The smell of burnt hair and hair spray were strong. Michelle shouted, "What's up, girl? I thought Yaz was coming with you."

"She outside parking the car."

When I sat down, Michelle said, "What, you lose some weight?"

"A little."

"Don't you feel good?"

I didn't answer Michelle's stupid question. Like I didn't feel good about myself before. Anyhow, she was just happy because she was extra skinny. How, I don't know. That girl got like four kids and not one stretch mark and she always had something tight on with her belly button out, showing off her navel ring and butterfly tattoos.

After I told the receptionist our name, I sat down and grabbed a *Solid Gold* magazine. I was looking at a hairstyle I thought I might look good in when out of the corner of my eye, I saw a girl walk up and sit next to me. I couldn't believe it was Sonya. She picked up a magazine, too, and started thumbing through it. I was thinking, *Oh, shit.*

Then Yaz came walking through the door. I jumped up off the sofa. I had to warn Yaz to keep her composure, to handle that shit with Sam and not to play herself in front of millions.

Too late.

"What's up, Shelly Shell?" she said, slightly waving her hand at the hairdresser.

"Yaz, come here." I started pulling on Yaz's arm.

"What?"

"Don't look, but there go Sonya. Promise me you going to act civilized and not start nothing."

"Where at?" She spun around, wildly looking around the shop.

"Right there." I pointed at the seat where Sonya sat flipping through a magazine.

Before I could say anything else, Yaz pulled away from me and walked over to Sonya and said, "Excuse me, can I talk to you for a minute?"

"About what?" Sonya responded, looking up from the *Jet* magazine she was reading.

"About you fucking with my man."

"Who's your man?"

"Black Sam from 58th Street."

"I don't know no Sam from 58th Street," Sonya said, and began flipping through the magazine again.

"Oh, you don't? Oh, OK. You don't know no Sam?" Yaz was muttering on about, "I'm a fucking nut. You don't know no Sam. Oh, OK."

She fumbled around in her bag and grabbed something out. By this time everybody was looking. I knew Yaz was going to do something stupid, but what she did was uncalled for. She grabbed Sonya by the hair—or should I say the weave—and just started punching sis all in her face. Then she maced her.

I tried to break it up, but there was nothing I could do. I was coughing from the mace. Yaz proceeded to beat the shit out of Sonya, until the girl managed to break free and run out of the shop.

Everybody had a *that ain't right* look on their faces and was coughing and gagging. They had to open the window and turn the fans on to get the mace out. I asked Yaz if she was OK. She answered, "Yeah, but I broke a couple of nails."

Yaz went into the bathroom and in a few minutes returned like nothing had ever happened. After Michelle cussed her out for spraying mace, she teased Yaz, saying Sonya was going to come back with a squad of thirty to give her a beat down.

Nobody was even hyped about the fight. They were used to seeing somebody's crazy boyfriend running up in there looking for them, or a mad wife trying to figure out which stylist was messing with her husband. They just wanted to know what was going on. They were nosy, like hairdressers tend to be. But Yaz wouldn't tell them nothing. She had had enough drama for one day.

Meanwhile, I was thirsty from all the excitement. I asked if anybody wanted anything. Immediately, I found myself wishing I hadn't asked. Everybody wanted something. After I collected everyone's money, I made a list and went to the Wawa around the corner. Then I came back and distributed everybody's stuff. I thought I would have to wait, but Michelle had Yaz already in the chair and told me I was next. She said she didn't want no more drama in her shop.

I guess she thought Sonya really might make it back with her crew. We got out earlier than we'd expected to, because Michelle had put us in front of everybody. As soon as Yaz dropped me off at my apartment, I beeped Wil. He called right back.

"What's up, Kayla?"

"Nothing."

"You want to go out?"

"Where?"

"Me and my cousin Stevie and his girl are going out for my birthday."

"Birthday?"

"It's not today. It's Monday, but my cousin wants to take me out tonight."

"All right. I'll go. What time you coming to pick me up?"

"I'll be there around 8. Be ready."

"OK."

I needed to take a shower and change my clothes, but I didn't want to mess my hair up since I had just gotten it done. So I quickly washed up in the sink and then straightened things up a little bit. Wil arrived around 7:45. They beeped the horn.

I got in and spoke to Wil, his cousin Stevie, and girlfriend, Kia. She was pretty and tall, about 5 feet, 11 inches, with a short Halle Berry-style haircut. She kept going on and on about how she goes to New York and models, and how she was going to be famous one day. She said she couldn't wait to get picked up by a major agency, because she was going to be the next Tyra Banks.

I didn't think so. Even models need to have some brains. She made me think of bells ringing ding dong. I kept wishing she'd shut up.

Stevie made the mistake of letting her drive while me and Wil were in the backseat.

"Make a left," Stevie said.

She made a right and almost swerved into a pole.

"Pull over. Pull over. Get out. Get out," Stevie screamed at her.

The car came to a stop with us all jerking forward. Stevie's platinum-colored Lexus was going to be trashed if Ding Dong continued driving. Stevie got out of the car and Kia moved over to the passenger side.

"I thought you said you knew how to drive," he said as he pulled off.

"I do," she said, trying to catch an attitude.

Wil busted out and said, "Not like that you don't."

We all started laughing. Then Wil asked, "Where you taking me and my new girl at anyway after we go bowling?"

"I didn't say anything about taking her. And we going bowling. That's it. What you think this is?" Stevie responded.

I was blushing, but trying not to smile because Wil had referred to me as his girl.

When we got to the bowling alley, it was crowded. A league of old gray-haired ladies were playing. We had to wait for them to finish up before we got our own lane.

"How many games we need?" Stevie asked Wil.

I interrupted and said, "Get two games. That's all we need to kick y'all asses."

"You want to put some money on the shit your girl talking, William?"

"Yeah, I got five on it that we beat."

"Y'all petty betting $5." I said.

"Nah, baby, $500," Stevie said, waving a fat-ass knot of money.

"Oh, my fault. Y'all Big Willies," I said, laughing.

"Yeah, your fault. Stay out of grown folks' business." Stevie laughed as he tucked the money inside his jeans pocket.

Me and Kia went to get some bowling shoes while the guys went to the bathroom. Kia chose that time to start getting in my business. She asked me how long I had known Wil.

"A couple of weeks."

"You lying. He must really like you, 'cause all he kept saying was 'His girl this' and 'My girl that,' the whole way to your house."

"For real? Uhm. Well, how long you and Stevie been seeing each other?"

"Like a day. I met him last night at this club over in Jersey. Then we just spent the night together."

I'm thinking this girl not only didn't know how to drive, she was also a freak johne'. We walked back over to where the guys were standing. They had their shoes on and Wil had already rolled a strike.

"Tie your shoe up," he said.

"No, you tie it up for me," I demanded.

Wil got on his knees and tied it. I hadn't expected him to actually do it. He is so sweet.

"You next," Stevie said.

I grabbed the ball and rolled a strike.

"You might as well give me my money now," Wil said.

"I ain't giving you nothing," Stevie snapped.

Kia went to bowl and slammed the ball down hard. It went straight to the outer lane. She didn't knock down one pin.

"Wil, your turn again," Kia said, not even looking embarrassed.

Wil rolled another strike. Stevie knocked down about three. We were winning. Wil asked me if I was hungry.

"No."

"Well, could you get me a beer? I'm getting thirsty from beating him."

"All right."

"Tanisha, walk her," Stevie said.

"What did you call me?"

"I called you by your name."

Stevie knew he called that girl Tanisha, 'cause I heard him and so did Wil. We were both laughing.

I walked away and Kia followed. I approached the beer counter and a girl who didn't look twenty-one her own self asked to see some identification. I couldn't wait until I turned twenty-one. Then there would be no more borrowing somebody's ID and getting played. I walked back over to Wil and told him I couldn't get his beer for him.

"Why not?" he asked.

"Because I'm not twenty-one."

"Oh, I forgot I was messing with a baby. Don't worry about it. I'll get it later. Have a seat."

I was a little embarrassed. I was twenty and still getting carded at a bowling alley. I looked at Kia out the corner of my eye. Now that she had mentioned meeting Stevie last night, her clothes did look kind of last-nightish—stained, creased, and out of shape. She must not have gotten a chance to go home and change.

How could she meet a guy at a club, then go home with him the same night and think he was still going to want her in the morning? She was a cute girl. I don't know why she played herself like that. If she had waited, she probably could have had Stevie for more than one night.

The score was 45 to 260. Wil and I won. After Wil collected his $500, we all went to this 24-hour diner in the Italian part of town in South Philly on Passyunk Avenue. It was late, but the place was packed. I guess the clubs had just let out or something.

I felt funny, us being one of the only black couples in the restaurant. It was like every nonblack person in there was thinking about a lynching—like they were going to turn the lights off, drag us in the back, and torture us. Not that they said anything or looked at us any type of way. I just don't like to be outnumbered. Luckily, we were saved when some reinforcements walked through the door.

Meanwhile, it was obvious Stevie was not liking his date anymore. He kept using the pay phone when his beeper went off, even though he had a cellular phone in his shirt pocket. He was sitting like ten feet away from her when the booth was only three feet long.

But me and Wil were chillin'. I was resting my head on his shoulder 'cause I was loving him. *I hope this one works out,* I thought.

Since I had only known Wil a little while, I didn't know what to get him for his birthday. It was time to call my ride again. Yazmine.

"Hello."

"Yo, Yaz. Don't you need some stuff from the mall?"

"Why? You got to go?"

"Yeah, I got to find a birthday present for Wil."

"You must be in love, because you don't buy nobody nothing."

"Are you going to take me to Cherry Hill Mall?"

"I'm tired of that mall. Let's go to King of Prussia."

"That's cool."

"Be ready. I'm going to beep the horn."

"All right."

"Be ready. I'm not playing. I'm not getting out and ringing the bell."

"I'm going to be ready. I'll see you when you get here."

The mall was busy. People must have been doing their back-to-school shopping. We went into Gap Kids first so Yaz could pick up some things for the kids. Then we went to Nieman Marcus, where Yaz was looking at these green, purple, orange, and yellow pants.

"Ain't they cute?"

"No, they are ugly."

"They Prada and they cost $460."

"I don't care who they are. They are a mess. Ugly is ugly no matter whose name is on it. I told you. You need to learn how to shop. Name don't mean everything."

Our conversation was interrupted by a short, white saleslady with a lavender and white polka dot dress and a strand of obviously fake pearls.

"May I help you?" she said.

"No, we were just looking," I responded.

"Looking for what?" she inquired nosily.

"When we need your assistance, we'll come and get you, all right?" Yaz snapped at her.

The lady walked away in a nervous fit.

"Come on. Let's get out of this department before I give sis a beat down North Philly-style. I hate when they keep following you around the damn store like you going to steal."

Yaz pushed Sam Jr. in the stroller and Mia tried to help her.

"They always think somebody going to steal," she yelled as we walked out of the store. We decided to go to Macy's in the other part of the mall. We went straight to the men's department, where I found a red and green short-sleeve Polo shirt I was thinking of getting. That's when Yaz held up a blue and white FUBU shirt and said, "This is cute. Buy him this."

"That's cute. How much is it?"

"Eighty-three," she replied.

"I planned to spend a $150 on him. I'm going to use my charge card. All right, I'm going to get it. Those colors are pretty. I can see him in this shirt and some Timbs."

"Why don't you get him some cologne to go with it? Damn, he look good as shit."

"Who?" I asked as I turned around and spotted the poster she was salivating over. It was the male model Tyson Beckford.

"He do look good," I agreed.

"Who you telling? I'll leave Sam for him."

"Ooh, I'm telling my daddy," Mia said as she laughed and held her little hand over her mouth.

"Mia, didn't I tell you you were too grown and to stop repeating what I said? You better start acting like the four-year-old you are before I beat your butt."

Mia looked down at the floor.

"Stop yelling at that girl. She's not grown. Come here, Mia," I said, pulling her toward me.

"Stop babying my child. She's going to get it when she get home."

Yaz went to swing at her, but I blocked her hand. Mia flinched and grabbed my leg tightly. Yaz tried to hit her again and I blocked her again. When she tired of my turning and blocking her punches, she started to laugh.

"She only get that grown stuff from all your sisters' grown kids. What do you expect?" I said as I walked over to the register and the salesman began ringing the shirt up.

"Will this be all?" he said as he folded the shirt.

"Yes."

"Your total is $65."

I thought, *Damn, this shirt must be on sale or he made a mistake. Either way, I'm not going to open my mouth.*

"Cash or credit?"

"Credit."

I pulled out my credit card and handed it to the salesman. He handed it back to me a few seconds later and said my account was over the limit and I needed to contact the business office.

"What? I sent my payment off weeks ago," I said, surprised.

At first the salesman gave me this look like, "Girl, you know you don't pay your bills and ain't got no money in your account." Then he tried to act professional and said sometimes the accounts don't get processed right away.

"If I were you, I would call the accounting department tomorrow," he said.

Then he took the shirt out of the bag and started putting it back on the hanger.

"Wait. I still want it."

"You got enough money, Kay?" Yaz asked as she came up behind me.

"Yeah."

The sales guy rang it up all over again, handed me my bag along with the receipt, and thanked me. We headed over to the perfume and cologne department. I got Wil some Tommy Hilfiger cologne and shower gel.

After we exited the department store, I began to look in this small lingerie shop. I saw a sheer black nightgown on display I just had to have. Because the store was having a sale, I bought some new bra-and-panty sets just in case things got steamy between me and Wil. I didn't think they would, but I bought them anyway just in case. It's funny how a man can make you want everything new.

Yaz, of all people, said I was spending too much on underwear. I know somebody who was about to spend $460 on some pants wasn't even talking. She said can't nobody see your underwear but you and your man, and your man don't care if it comes from Victoria's Secret or Kmart, as long as it's tight and fits right.

Back at home, I beeped Wil and left a message that I had a gift for him. He didn't call me back, so I didn't call him again.

As I waited for him to return my call, I started getting mad. I was ready to get my money back from his shirt. He don't let nobody beep him and not call them back. He need a damn cell phone. I was tired

of beeping him and waiting for him to call back. He told me he didn't
like cell phones 'cause he didn't need anybody trying to keep track of
him, but he needed to do something because beeping him was getting real old.

I figured I should go ahead and study for the political science test I
had the next day. I should have been doing that anyway. I don't know
why I always wait until the last minute. I'd known about this damn test
for like two weeks, and this was going to be the first time I opened up
the book.

I tried skimming through the chapters, but I finally gave up and
went back and read the whole thing. I wouldn't have had to if I had
been paying more attention in class, but that professor was just too
boring. A couple of times I even fell asleep in class.

I thought taking political science as my early morning class would
be OK, just talking about politics, but it was more challenging than
what I expected. And the biggest challenge was getting to class and
then staying awake. But I needed to get a good grade on this test if I
wanted to maintain a good GPA.

The phone finally rang.

"Hello."

"Hey baby, can I come over?" an unfamiliar voice sang in my ear.

"Excuse me. Who is this?"

"How soon we forget, huh?"

"I'm going to ask you again, then I'm going to hang up. Now who
the hell is this?"

"Come on, Kayla, it's me. Reese. Should I come over and refresh
your memory?"

"Reese who?"

"Maurice, Kayla. Has it really been that long?" he said with an attitude.

"Oh, Maurice! I am so sorry. What you been up to?" I couldn't believe he was on my phone. I wondered where his white girlfriend was.

"Thinking about you."

"Really? How is your girl Jessie doing?"

"We broke up."

"Sorry to hear that," I said as I tried not to laugh. What makes him think I care if they broke up? It would be different if he would have called a couple of months ago, but now I have my Wil.

"Yeah, well I'll tell you everything when I get there."

"Reese, you can't do that. My boyfriend is on his way, and I don't think he wants to meet you."

"So you went out and got a boyfriend on me?"

"Reese, please," I said as I sucked my teeth in disgust. "I haven't talked to you in months. I can't really talk now. Good-bye." I hung up the phone.

I could not believe Reese. No, he didn't think I was going to be still sitting around waiting on him. Well, that's what he gets. Talking to his ass made me appreciate Wil even more. Why would I give up a sweet guy who is all mine to go back to someone who is caught up in that jungle fever shit? I looked up at the clock. Damn, why hadn't Wil called yet?

By the time he finally did call, an hour had gone by and I had a big attitude, so I just let the answering machine pick up. He left a couple of messages, but I didn't return them.

I was trying to teach him a lesson. He had to learn to call right when I beeped him. I didn't care if he was on the expressway. I wanted him to get off at the nearest exit or beep his horn at a car where somebody had a car phone and say, "May I please use your phone?" I wasn't playing with him. After another half hour or so, the phone rang again. This time I decided to answer it.

"Hello," I said, trying to sound casual.

I heard a faint voice. "Kayla, can you hear me? Hello, can you hear me?"

I could barely hear, but I said, "Who's this?"

"It's Wil. This phone is messed up. Can you hear me? What are you doing?"

"Nothing really. Just reading this book for class."

"Do you want to go to the movies?"

"When?"

"Now."

"What do you want to see?"

"*The Best Man.*"

"What time does it start?"

"Around eight. Be downstairs in fifteen."

"All right, I'll see you."

I didn't know how I was going to be ready in fifteen minutes. I didn't know what to wear. I looked through my closet. Everything was either dirty or at the cleaners.

I decided to just throw on my black jeans, a white button-down shirt, and some black shoe boots. I looked at the clock. It had been twenty minutes since he had called. I brushed my teeth, put on some lip liner and lip gloss, and was out the door. By the time I got downstairs, Wil was waiting outside. He got out and opened my door. I handed him his gift bag as he tried to hug me.

"What's this for?"

"Your birthday."

"Thank-you."

He smiled, then put the bag behind his seat. He didn't even look inside it. How rude. But I didn't want to say anything, so I chilled. Then he asked me why I hadn't been calling him back and I made the mistake of telling him the truth.

" 'Cause you didn't call me back when I beeped you."

"Oh, I'm sorry. I promise I'll call you back every time you call from here on out. It's just that I was out with my parents and cousin."

"If you say so. What movie theater we going to anyway?"

"Down Delaware Avenue."

Ten minutes later, we arrived at the movies. The only thing I could think of was at last I was at the movies with a man and not my girlfriends. Usually I would be the jealous girl sitting there with Yaz, being loud and talking to the screen, but not tonight. Tonight someone could be jealous of me. Wil grabbed my hand and we walked down the aisle of the theater as the previews were playing.

"Why you walking to the front?" I wanted to know.

"I can't see back there."

"Well, let's just sit right here."

We sat down in the middle of a row next to another couple. Wil asked if I wanted some popcorn or anything. I declined. We sat for the next hour and fifteen minutes watching the movie. It was funny. We laughed and had a good time.

After the movie was over, Wil drove me home and parked his car. I guess that meant he was coming in. I didn't ask him up, but I hoped my apartment was presentable. As I walked up the steps, I felt Wil's hands caressing my legs.

When I tried to pull out my keys, Wil grabbed me from behind and leaned me against the door of my apartment. He began stroking my breasts up and down, left and right. He was kissing my neck, grasping me tight. I couldn't take it anymore. I turned and faced him, letting him kiss me wildly. I managed to open the door. Then we walked straight into my bedroom.

He pushed me on the bed, lifting my shirt and shoving my breast in his mouth at the same time. He caressed, slobbered, and grabbed every part of my body. He undressed me from head to toe.

Then he spread my legs apart and allowed them to rest on his shoulders as he gently proceeded to lick. His tongue was warm and gentle. It went deep inside of me, tracing every opening and crack of my cave until it began to rain—or shall I say a hurricane emerged. Then he undressed and I saw every part of his perfect body. I asked him if he had a condom.

"No, I left them in the car. We don't need one," he replied.

"Huh? Yes, we do. Grab one out of my top dresser, the tall one," I said with a slight attitude.

I don't play that try-to-fuck-me-without-a-condom bullshit. Little did he know, he had just turned me off.

He got up off the bed and went to get the condom. By the time he came back, the condom was on. He got back in the bed and the next thing I knew he was inside of me. Immediately, I was turned back on again. Damn, he felt so good. The pleasure, the pain. "Ugh, ugh, uhm. Damn, damn, ugh."

There were no words to describe how good Wil made me feel. I had to clasp his sides and hold on for support, because the earthquake he was creating was shaking the shit out of me. Everything bad I ever said about not wanting a boyfriend, a man, a relationship, went out the door.

Then he asked me, "Whose is it?"

"Yours, yours," I moaned.

I had to tell him that. If he could make me feel like this, he could most certainly have it. He was making me quiver, shiver, and cry all at the same time. The bed frame shook, the world spun around, and then it was over. I didn't want to be the first to move, but I had to. His body was crushing me.

I wanted to grab him and just fall asleep in his arms. I wanted to tell him I thought I was falling in love with him, but what if he didn't like cuddling or if he had to go? Or what if he didn't feel the same way?

So I chilled. I wouldn't be the first to show my feelings. I had been there before. This time, I wouldn't let anyone hurt me. Wil gently raised up, wiped the sweat off my forehead, and asked, "Are you all right, Boo?"

"I'm fine," I said as he kissed me again.

"What do you have to drink?" he asked.

"There's grape juice in the refrigerator."

Wil walked out of the room with nothing on, and in less than a minute he returned with a full glass of grape juice. We talked about nothing for a while. You know, pillow talk. Then we talked about our future, our plans, *our life*. Then I drifted off to the warmest, most beautiful sleep ever.

The next morning I woke up on the other side of the golden gates of heaven. And I was definitely in heaven. I couldn't believe I had finally found someone. I looked over at Wil as he slept. He looked perfect. Everything was perfect.

Until I looked at the alarm clock. Eight o'clock. I jumped out of bed. The political science test was starting in forty minutes.

I ran in the bathroom and showered and brushed my teeth, then ran back in the bedroom and threw some clothes on and I was out the door. I started to wake Wil up, but I figured I'd be back before he woke up anyway, since I only had that one class, and I was going to leave as soon as I finished my test.

The test was mostly multiple choice, and I couldn't believe how easy it was. Thank God. I got back home before 10, and just as I thought, Wil was still asleep. I was hungry by now.

I walked into the kitchen and decided I was going to cook my boo some breakfast. But when I looked in the refrigerator, I saw it was pretty much empty. I didn't have anything but some beef sausage links, and Wil didn't eat pork or beef. So I had to run to the corner store.

I hated wasting my money there, but I had no other choice. The supermarket was too far to walk to and there weren't any other stores in the area except for the black-owned store two blocks down that didn't have anything on the shelves. I wanted to support my people, but first they had to stock up.

When I got back home, I emptied the plastic bag carrying my eggs, turkey bacon, grits, and orange juice. It had all come to $13.11. I turned the stove on and began preparing the food. Then the phone rang.

"Hello."

"Hi, Kayla. I heard you stopped past," Leslie said.

"I did. Where were you? And when were you going to tell me you had a boyfriend?" I asked as I placed strips of bacon into the pan.

"I'm grown. You don't tell me when you have a boyfriend. So I didn't know I had to FedEx you the message that I met somebody," she said sarcastically.

"No, Leslie, for real. This is serious. You leave Nicole there by herself to be with a man? I mean, who is this guy? What does he do? Where did you meet him? When can I meet him?"

"Kayla, hold up. Am I your mother or are you my mother? First off, I met Charlie at my job. We started having lunch together and he made me laugh. One day, he asked me out on a date and he has been making me very happy ever since. I'll introduce you to him. You should be happy for me. Second, Nicole is almost grown. She is about to be seventeen. She can stay in the house by herself."

"Well, do you know Karim be over there with her?"

"Yes, I know. Well, that's what I wanted to talk to you about."

"What's wrong?"

"Well, since she didn't tell you, I'll tell you. Nicole was pregnant."

"Pregnant? What the hell is she going to do with a baby?"

"I convinced her to get an abortion. I didn't want to be a grandparent, and more than likely I would have been the one to raise that baby."

"Well, when I was over there she seemed like everything was fine."

"Don't get me wrong. She took it well. She didn't cry or anything, and Karim has been there comforting her every night. So I want her to go on some birth control. She won't listen to me. She said she's not taking no pills because her girlfriend said they are going to make her fat. She doesn't want any shots or needles, either, and I don't trust her enough to use a condom every time."

I heard Wil calling my name from the bedroom, so I rushed Leslie off the phone.

"I'll be down there today. I have to put some applications in."

"Applications for what?"

"Mom, I didn't feel like waitressing anymore. Besides, I got a little money left."

"You better have something, 'cause your rent is due and I'm not paying all of it this month. And you got to get yourself a little car."

"Mom, I'm going to get another job. Why you always acting like you don't have any money? You make me sick with that. I know my rent is due."

"You are not supposed to just spend money 'cause you got it. And you sure shouldn't be spending my money because you think I got it like that."

"Uhm hmm, well. Are you cooking tonight?"

"Yeah."

"All right. I'll see you around six. Make sure Nikki's there."

Wil walked into the kitchen wearing just his boxers and hugged me from behind.

"What's for breakfast?" he asked, lifting the lid on the pot of grits that was bubbling on the stove.

Suddenly, I remembered Leslie was still on the phone.

"Kayla, who's that?" she demanded.

"A friend. I'll see you later."

"Kayla, who's your boyfriend this month? I don't recall you telling me about him, but I got to tell you about my friend."

"Leslie, it's not like that. This is different. When I get a good one, I'll let you know. Now I will see you later. Bye," I said as I hung up the telephone.

"A good what and who is Leslie?"

"A good none of your business and Leslie is my mother. Don't you have to go to work or something?"

"No, not today. See, that's the good thing about working for your family. You go to work when you want. Plus I don't really be getting dirty. I mainly be supervising our workers."

By then, the food was ready and I started fixing our plates. I asked Wil if he wanted some orange juice.

"Nah, I'll take some water. Uhm, why you call your mother by her first name? That is so disrespectful."

"To you, it's disrespectful. My mom let me do it since I started talking. I guess so people wouldn't know I was her daughter, 'cause she was so young. She was a child bride. She married at seventeen, was divorced by nineteen and married again at twenty. When I was four, she had my little sister and her husband got killed. So did I answer your question?"

"Damn, I know that shit must have been hard on your mother."

"Hell yeah, it was. I remember rubbing her stomach telling her everything was going to be OK and one day I would be rich and take care of her. She's never been exactly the same. I mean, she never had any fun after that. She never had a boyfriend or friends really. She just started reading a lot and went back to school and became a nurse."

"Where's your dad?"

"I don't know. The last time I saw him was at my third birthday party."

Changing the subject, I said, "You want to eat in here or in the bedroom?" We ended up in the living room just as *The Jerry Springer Show* came on.

"How come he only has 'Surprise I'm a Transsexual, Gay or Cheating on You' shows?" Wil asked through a mouthful of turkey bacon.

"I don't know, but I'm going to Chicago so I can say at the end of the show, 'Jerry, I came all the way from Philly to see you.' Plus those fights be the bomb. Every day it's a fight."

"You crazy. If you want to see a fight, go outside your door and walk downstairs to your neighbors'."

"What you trying to say? I live in a bad neighborhood?"

"Nah, nothing like that. But your neighbors be tripping."

I had to laugh 'cause he was right. The Franklins were five Jerry Springer shows alone.

"So you going to look for a job today?"

"Yeah."

"You were saying something about needing a car. Get a little job and I'll help you out and take you to the auction, 'cause I can't have my woman walking. Can you get my pants out the room?"

"No, I'm eating just like you."

"Please."

"All right," I said as I got up off the sofa. I walked in my room and grabbed his pants. I passed them to him and sat back on the sofa. He pulled out this big knot of money and started counting it.

"Here you go," he said, placing a stack of twenties in my hand.

"What's this for?" I said looking at the money.

"I overheard you talking to your mom. So put it toward your rent and the rest is for you."

"Thanks."

He paused and then said, "I got a woman that can cook and is cute. Too bad I can't spend the whole day with her, because I got to go and make some moves. Maybe if she's not busy, I'll see her later."

"I won't be busy, but I'm going to mom's house. You think you can come and pick me up from there?"

"Where she live at?"

"Sixty-first and Pine."

"Yeah, I can do that. Just page me, OK?"

Then he stood up and asked me to get him a towel and a wash-cloth. I walked in to the hall and grabbed one. While he showered, I cleaned up the kitchen. By the time I was finished with the dishes, he was dressed. I walked him to the door and gave him a long I-really-don't-want-to-let-you-go-let's-get-back-in-the-bed kiss. I almost lost my balance kissing Wil. The sweet smell of his cologne was still on his shirt from the day before. It evoked beautiful memories. Reluctantly, our tongues let go and we said good-bye for real.

"I'll call you later," he said as he walked out the door blowing kisses at me.

Uhm uhm, I thought and closed the door. I stood in awe for a moment, leaning against the door. *Finally! About time! I finally met somebody I like who's interested in me,* I thought. I couldn't wait to call Yaz and tell her about Wil. She picked up on the fist ring.

"Yo, Yaz, guess what?"

"What?"

"The boah, Wil, is the bomb."

"What you mean, he the bomb?"

"Well, we went to the movies last night. Then he came over and we did it. Oh my God, he had it goin' on. Then he just left. He kissed me, girl, and gave me some money toward my rent, and I didn't even ask him. Plus, we're getting together later tonight."

"Really? Uhm, that's what's up. See, that's a real man. So that's your dude now?"

"No, my friend, but you never know. I'm not going to rush it. Oh, did I tell you he did everything there was to do to me?"

"Stop it."

"No, I'm serious. I'm talking toes and everything. He is such a sweetheart, and we have so much fun together. I mean he just is the bomb."

"That is so good, girl. Now that you got a man that's doing right by you, Sam is over here tripping. I just about had enough of that nigga. He stayed out again last night. I don't want to move back with my mom, but he is stressing me and I'm not putting up with his shit."

"Fuck him. Start saving your money and I'll help you look for a place."

"You right. I just can't take it anymore. You know what, I don't even want to talk about it. So what you doing today?"

"I got to put some applications in and then I'm going to go down my mom's house. I'll call you from there. All right?"

"All right, bye."

I put on a pair of black dress slacks and a cream-colored sweater and headed to Center City to look for a job. It was a Friday during lunch hour. I picked the best time and day to look for a job. Everywhere was so crowded.

I went into every department store, boutique, clothing, perfume, and children's store. Everywhere I went, it was the same story. I'd walk up to the service desk and say "Hi. Do you currently have any positions available?"

"No," the salesperson would say. "But you can fill out an application and we will hold it on file for sixty days."

I sat down at the food court in the Gallery Mall after many hours of pounding the pavement. I was hungry. My shape said I should eat a salad but my stomach said feed me some Kentucky Fried Chicken.

The aroma hit me the moment I walked up to the counter. I ordered an original recipe breast and wing meal, with macaroni and cheese and mashed potatoes topped off with a Pepsi and a biscuit drenched in honey. After eating all of that, I felt weighted down. Why did I eat that much? But it was so good.

I was full and tired, so I decided to get ready to go home. I went to wait for the number 21 bus when I saw a sign in a bank window:

NOW HIRING TELLERS, DATA ENTRY, COLLECTORS. DAY & EVENING HOURS, WILL TRAIN. APPLY TODAY.

I ran across the street on a yellow light. I opened the door, almost knocking down the people coming out. I walked over to the service desk and said, "Hi, I would like to fill out an application."

"For which position, honey?"

"What position is available at night?"

"Data entry and collection. Can you type?"

"Yes."

"How fast?"

"I don't know. I never timed myself. I have my resume with me. Would you like to see it?"

"Fill out this application and I will give your resume to my supervisor."

I sat down and filled out the application. People were walking back and forth, interrupting my concentration. Every time I went into a bank I always thought of *Set It Off* or *Natural Born Killers* or some other Bonnie-and-Clyde-type movie. If I see anyone looking really nervous or pacing, I always start thinking, *Oh shit, they're going to stick this place up and I'm going to pass out.*

I could never be a teller. The robber would be like, "Give me the loot" and I would start crying and get shot for being too slow.

"Excuse me," someone said.

I looked up and saw a tall blonde in a nice navy-blue suit, maybe Donna Karan—or then again, maybe Fashion Bug.

"Hi," she said. "I'm Kathleen Markowitz. I'm head of the human re-sources department here. Tiffany told me you might be interested in working for us."

"Yes, I would."

"OK, so do you have time for an interview today?"

"Sure."

"Follow me," she said.

I grabbed my belongings and mouthed *thank-you* to Tiffany as we walked past the service desk toward the elevator. That was real nice of her. She didn't even know me and was looking out for me.

Kathleen walked on the elevator and held the door open until I en-tered. She pushed the button to close the elevator door, then pressed for the sixth floor. She flashed a fake smile at me, but I gave her a real smile back. Why not? She was about to give me a job.

We reached the floor and the elevator sprang open. Ding dong. A bell rang letting us know it was OK to exit the elevator.

As we walked to her office, she spoke and joked with coworkers we passed in the hall. I saw a couple of black faces. They gave me a *How you doing? Hope you get that job* nod.

Her office was bright and colorful. She had a mahogany desk adorned with a computer. On it were pictures of what must be her children and husband.

"You can have a seat," she said.

She closed her office door and looked down at my application and said, "Kaalae. Am I saying that right?"

I corrected her. "It's Kayla." I said, trying not to sound annoyed.

"I'm sorry about that. Tell me about your background."

In my most phony-professional-I-really-need-a-job voice, I said, "Well, right now, I'm in school majoring in education. I just started back at school. But before that I was working at a restaurant and going to summer classes, but I got burnt out so I had to take a break. I need to find a job, honestly, so I can help my mom pay rent for my apartment."

"Do you think you will be good in our customer service depart-ment?"

"Yes."

What else was I supposed to say?

"Well, we have a position open for a collector. It's part-time Monday through Thursday from four to nine. The pay starts at $9 an hour and we will train you."

"So I'm hired?"

"Of course. Tiffany is a valued employee. I know she wouldn't recommend any one who wasn't reliable. So I'll see you Monday in this office at 4 P.M. Bring your Social Security card and a photo ID with you. Oh, and we have to conduct a drug test. Will that be a problem?"

"No, not at all," I responded.

"Well, that's it. Enjoy the rest of your day," she said with a real smile on her face this time, like she had just crowned me Miss America or something.

I stood up and shook her hand, thanked her, and left. I went back downstairs and thanked Tiffany as soon as I came off the elevator.

She said, "you're welcome," and then added, "But please don't quit until I get my referral fee. You got to stay at least three months, all right girl?" She laughed.

"All right." I laughed as I walked back outside to wait for the bus again. It was getting cold. I looked across the street and saw the FOR HIRE sign out of the corner of my eye. I was so glad I had walked across the street. I sat down and waited for my bus. It was nowhere in sight. The bright sunny September day had turned into a windy November-feeling night. Finally, I saw the bus coming. When I got on it was crowded as shit.

Wil and Leslie were right. I needed a car.

My mom's row house in West Philly was huge compared to my little apartment. My mother had every award I ever received either hanging on the wall or saved in plastic, from perfect attendance in the first grade to my twelfth-grade report card. My mom was very proud of me. Yet I wished she would take all those old papers down. Just like the plastic on the furniture. Leslie had put that plastic on when I was five and it's still there. But it's no longer clear. It's brownish and has cracks and splits in it.

"Leslie, what you cooking?" I hollered into the kitchen.

"Turkey wings, string beans, and rice. Nikki didn't get here yet, but she will be here soon. She just called me from Karim's house," she said, entering the living room and giving me a hug and kiss.

"I found a job."

"That's good, baby. Where?"

"At Federal Bank as a collector."

"Well, don't call here, 'cause all those loans you got me takin' out I can hardly pay attention."

"Leslie, please stop exaggerating. You got a new car parked outside. You only pay my tuition and books and half my rent. I buy my own food and clothes."

"You're supposed to. You're twenty years old."

"I go to school with a lot of people who don't work at all," I continued as I followed Leslie back into the kitchen.

Then she said, "Child, you are not my only child, and I'm not them other kids' parents. Nikki be wanting all these expensive designers, Verbache, and I got to buy it for her or she'll say you got everything and she got nothing."

"Leslie, it's Versace."

"Whatever. I don't know. I don't buy no jeans that cost over $15."

"Why she always got to compare us? I didn't get no more than she did."

"Compare what?" Nikki said as she walked in.

"You and me. You know how you always said I got more than you."

"Cause mommy did always give you more," she said as she rolled her eyes.

"Whatever. You know that's not true."

"Mom, didn't you always give Kayla more than you give me," Nikki yelled to my mother, who was trying to stay out of it.

"Neither one of you got more than the other did," she said as the doorbell rang. "I'm going to get the door. Both of you stop being childish."

"Yeah, Kayla, stop being childish. Aren't you like twenty or something? Sitting here arguing with a sixteen-year-old." Before I got a chance to comment on Nikki's last remark, Leslie had already walked back in the kitchen, arm-in-arm with a man who she introduced as Charlie.

"This is Kayla."

"How you doing?" I said skeptically as I looked him over.

He was a nice looking older man. He had a dark complexion with salt and pepper hair. Leslie was all smiles while she fixed his plate and walked into the living room. Me and Nicole washed our hands and began loading food onto our plates. Instead of joining Leslie and Charlie in the living room, we sat and ate in the kitchen. Halfway through dinner, I asked Nicole about her abortion. She looked up at me like she had seen a ghost.

"Leslie," she screamed. "I thought I told you not to say anything."

Leslie didn't respond. Nicole just muttered "bitch" under her breath and began picking at her turkey wing.

"How you gonna get mad at Leslie? You should have told me yourself."

"I was scared to tell anybody."

"Well, what's up with this birth control? Why won't you get on the pill?"

" 'Cause it's going to make me fat."

"Nikki, if you get pregnant again, you're going to be fat for real. The other night when I was here, you were talking about going to school. How you going to do that if you get pregnant or get AIDS?"

"No, I'm not going to get no AIDS, because I've only been with one person."

"Please, Nik, you don't know who else that boy been with before he got with you."

"He hasn't been with anybody else."

"How you know? What, have you been with him every day of his life?"

"You right. I guess I could get on some pills and start using some condoms. Are you on anything?"

"Yeah, mostly condoms and the pill. I don't want any kids. I'm going to make you an appointment tomorrow, all right? Pass me the phone."

She passed the phone over to me and I beeped Wil and put in my 22 code behind the number. I was hoping he would come and pick me up. I couldn't wait to see him. I'd been thinking about him all day long.

Leslie came back into the kitchen and scraped her plate into the trash. Over Nikki's head, she mouthed the words, *Did you talk to her?* I nodded yes.

Leslie smiled and walked back into the living room with Charlie. My beeper went off. I thought it might be Wil, but it was Yaz.

"Pass me the phone again, Nikki," I said and began to dial Yaz's number. "What's up?"

"Nothing. Where you at?"

"My mom's house."

"Oh, I started to call you there."

"What you doing?"

"Nothing. I beeped Wil. He's supposed to come and get me. Hold on the other line."

I clicked over and heard this I-think-I'm-a-man voice ask for my sister. "Who is this?"

"Karim."

"Can you call her back?"

Nikki screamed, "No, I want to talk to him."

She ran over and tried to snatch the phone from me.

"Hold up, wait, I'll give you the phone," I said, pushing away her hand.

I clicked back over to the other line and told Yaz I'd call her back. Then I gave the phone to Nikki. I hoped Wil would hurry up and call me back.

"Nikki, if anybody calls, you better click over," I warned.

To help pass the time, I did the dishes. After I was done I looked down at my watch and back up at Nikki. It had been twenty minutes and he hadn't called me back. If he did call back, Nikki probably wouldn't have known, because she was steady yapping.

I folded the dishcloth and placed it on the side of the sink and walked into the living room with Leslie and Charlie. Leslie was still smiling and laughing at everything that man said.

"Leslie, here is your rent money."

I handed her $250, my half of the rent. She took it and tucked it into her bra.

"You got a ride home, Kayla?"

"No, my ride didn't call me back yet."

Then Charlie volunteered to take me home. Leslie hollered to Nikki that they were taking me home and would be right back.

When I got inside my apartment, the first thing I did was check my answering machine. Then I called Nikki to see if anyone had called there for me. She said no.

I was beginning to get angry, but then my anger started turning into fear. What if he didn't call me ever again? What if last night didn't mean anything to him? What if it was a one-night stand? I dialed Yaz's number.

"Yaz there?" I asked hopefully.

"Who's dis?"

"This is Kay, Sam."

"What's up? I heard you met my man Darryl's brother."

"Who? Samir? Oh yeah, but I didn't get with him. As a matta of fact, I gave him my number."

"Well, he asked Darryl what was up with you, 'cause he seen you with Yazmine. I'm going to tell him to call you."

"No, Sam, don't do that. I don't want to seem pressed. Plus, I got a boyfriend now."

"Nah, he ain't like that. I'm going to still give him your number. He's a good guy. I'm going to have him call you. Here go Yazmine."

"Hello."

"Yo, what's up with your boyfriend? Why is he acting so nice?"

She began whispering. "He right in the other room, so I got to talk low. He know that I know. I told him my uncle seen him in Atlantic City with a girl. Plus, he probably heard how I fucked up Sonya. He's been acting real nice. He said how he is going to buy me my car next month and he said it wasn't him and we about to go out to dinner."

"Where the kids?"

"At my mom's house. We about to leave now, so I'm going to call you back later."

"Oh, he acting really nice. Uhm, hold up. It's three things I got to tell you. One, I got a job at Federal Bank as a collector. Two, Nikki was pregnant and my mom didn't tell me she got an abortion. I got to make an appointment for her so she can get some pills and condoms 'cause she don't like to use them. And three, Wil didn't call me back at my mom's house and I checked my caller ID and my answering machine and he didn't even call me. What if it didn't mean nuttin' to him or he thinks it was a one-night stand or something?"

"Kay, listen to yourself. I don't think so. Y'all been together like a month."

"Five weeks."

"Whatever. He ain't going to do that to you. Why would he be throwing you out like that? Stop jumping to conclusions. You fall in love too fast, you know that?"

"You right."

"That's good you got a job and, last, Nikki ain't dumb. She be all right. Just talk to her."

"I did," I said.

"I'll call you tomorrow. Stop tripping, OK? Bye."

I sat down and stared at the ceiling. Yaz's pep talk hadn't done much to calm me down. The phone rang. My heart skipped. I hoped it was Wil.

"Hello, Kayla there?"

"Yeah, this is Kayla."

"This is Samir. I met you about a month ago at Karisma's. Darryl brother."

"Yeah, I remember."

"I'm just getting around to calling you because I just came home from school. Sam told my brother you were waiting for me to call you."

"No, that's not what I told him. But anyway, how you doing?"

"Fine."

"What school you go to?"

"Morgan State."

"For real? You know some girl name Gina? Brown skin, kinda thick, from Philly?"

"Do I know her? I just broke up with her four months ago. I had seen her at Karisma's that night I met you. She was looking like a straight freak."

"So I take it y'all didn't leave on good terms."

"We didn't. She was cheating on me with this guy in her class. He fucked her and left her. Then she wanted to get back together. I was like, 'Hell, no.' Everybody on campus was laughing at me. Enough about that. What's up with me and you getting together? You mess with anyone? You know what? Don't even answer that, because once you start messing with me you'll forget about who it is you deal with. So when we going out?"

"I don't know," I said, avoiding the question and asking when he was going back to school.

"Probably Sunday. But I be down here every weekend. Why don't you write my number down?"

"I got a pen. What is it?"

"You don't have any reason not to get in touch with me. So call me later when you got time, all right?"

"All right, I'll call you."

I hung up the phone, and it began to ring again.

"Kayla, it's Wil. Sorry I couldn't come and get you. I had something to do and left my beeper in the car. So what you doing? Can I come over?" he asked in an apologetic voice.

"Yes."

"I'll be there in a half hour. Bye."

Wil knocked on the door and I let him in.

"What's up, Boo?" he said, kissing me on the cheek.

He had on some black Timberlands and the shirt I had bought him.

"Your shirt is cute," I said.

"Well, thank-you. This girl I know bought it for me."

"Hey, I found a job."

"That's good. So now you can get a little car."

He sat down and asked me to sit next to him.

"No, I'm not sitting down with you. I'm mad at you. You don't tell me you're going to do something and don't do it."

"I told you what happened. Sorry. You hungry?"

"A little."

"Let's go get something to eat. We can go down South Philly to get some buffalo wings."

I grabbed my jacket. Wil opened the door and as we were leaving, we ran into Mrs. Franklin and her family coming into the building.

"How you doing? Sorry about all the noise. If we ever get too loud down here, just stomp on the floor. OK?" she said.

"Yeah, OK."

What I really wanted to say was, *Bitch, stop letting your blockhead little boys run up and down the stairs when I'm trying to sleep*. But I just smiled.

We rode to "Wing It" in South Philly near Snyder Avenue. Their wings are bangin' and people come from everywhere just to buy them.

"You want to eat in or out?"

"It don't matter. We can eat in."

We stood there staring at the menu like a couple of kids at McDonald's.

"What are you getting? I don't know if I want wings or fingers."

"Get a combo," Wil suggested.

"Can I help you?" the girl at the register asked, smacking gum and talking at the same time.

She was a classic example of a played-out, around-the-way girl. She had on two pairs of big gold earrings, gold chains, a ring on every finger, bright red lipstick, and extremely long nails covered with electric blue fingernail polish. Her hair was in waves and a pump tall as a tree with gold and silver glitter spray in it. Didn't she know all that gold had played out years ago?

"I'll take wings and fingers with honey mustard and she'll have the same," Wil said.

We sat down until our number was called. When it was ready, Wil picked up our food then came back to the table and sat down. I dipped my finger and saw that I had gotten barbecue sauce instead of honey mustard. I was irritated as hell walking back to the counter.

"Can I get a honey mustard?" I asked.

"Did you ask for honey mustard or did you ask for barbecue?" she said with an attitude.

"I asked for honey mustard. Can I have an extra one?"

"The extra one will be fifty cents," she said with even more attitude.

"Whatever. Can I just get a honey mustard?" I said, placing my hand on my hip.

She gave one finally after all the word-for-word.

"Can I have a bag, too?"

"Sure," she said.

Pissed, I walked back over to the table. Wil was almost finished eating and my food was getting cold.

"You ready to go?" I asked him.

"Uhm hum," he said as he stuffed another chicken finger in his mouth. "I want to stop past Stevie's house."

"I really don't feel like it, but OK."

Stevie's house was your typical bachelor pad. He had the usual black leather furniture, a big-screen television, mirrors everywhere, a huge CD stereo, a Sega Dreamcast. There were Polaroid pictures of him and his squad out clubbing.

I was afraid I was going to run into Ding Dong Dippy, but she wasn't there. She had been replaced by Stevie's new girl, whose name was Lan'ique. OK, what's a five letter word that begins with f and rhymes with Lan'ique? Yeah, that's right. Freak. From the door, I could tell she was a dancer. She just had that freaked-out look.

I couldn't believe this girl had on fake-looking green contact lenses and a long rusty brown hair weave. I could see all her tracks. She was wearing these tight white plastic pants and a lime green halter top showing all her bare essentials and plastic white-ass boots. Let me tell you, if I ever danced for a living I would not be wearing cheesey boots. Dancers get paid, so I don't know why she had to look like that.

"How you doing?" she asked.

"Hi," I said, not at all impressed.

Stevie looked down at my boots that Wil bought me and said, "How you like your boots?"

"I like them fine."

Stevie turned toward Wil and said, "You soft, man. You soft."

Wil said, "Whatever. I got her now."

I turned around and looked at him to let him know I knew what he was talking about.

"Psyche, baby, I was only kidding." Wil laughed and grabbed me around my waist to show me he was just playing.

"No, he ain't. He for real," Stevie said, still trying to instigate.

"Man, where's my jacket? I left it over here the other night."

"In my room."

"Kayla, walk me in there so I can show you some pictures."

As I followed Wil, I saw Stevie making his moves on tonight's not-so-innocent victim.

I knew his type. He had his own place, a nice car and looked all right. He was built and his haircut was always perfect. He had a standard pretty boy look. Stevie was a bona fide player. He would probably bring his dates to his house and once they walked in, they would fall in love and not want to go. Especially when they saw his room.

His bedroom was like nothing I had ever seen before. It screamed leave-your-panties-at-the-door. Everything was white—white satin sheets on his king-sized water bed, a cream-colored rug on the floor, and white candles everywhere. After getting all his needs met, he would probably get tired, receive a so-called important call or get damn right rude and show his date the door. Then he would wait until they weren't mad anymore and call them again like nothing had ever happened. The dumb ones would fall for the game. The smart ones would hang up on him.

Thinking about Stevie made me look at Wil in a whole new light. If Stevie was a Romeo-mack-player-of-the-year, was Wil one, too? Nah, not my Wil.

When we arrived home, I stretched out on the bed. Wil walked in and sat down, too. He took his Timbs off and laid down beside me.

"Turn the light out," I said.

"Why you wait for me to lay down?" he said as he jumped up to flick the switch.

We fell asleep in each other's arms, clothes on and all. I had to have been tripping to think he wasn't going to call me back. He was feeling me as bad as I was feeling him. The next morning, Wil woke me up with a kiss. As he was getting dressed, he asked what I was doing later, after I got out of school.

"Nothing."

"You want to take a ride?"

"Where?"

"Either New York or A.C. for dinner."

"That's what up."

"Well, I'll call you about seven," he said as he put on his baseball hat.

He gave me another kiss, and seconds later I heard my door shut. I stayed in the bed, thinking how me and Wil probably were going to get married and how he was The One. I was so happy and excited to have found him. God knows I needed a man like him in my life, thank-you.

I got out of the bed and walked into the kitchen for something to drink. I reached for a plastic cup out of the cabinet. When I grasped it, it fell from the cabinet and rolled over by the sofa. I bent to pick it up and noticed some envelopes. I picked the envelopes up and saw they were the bills I had never mailed. They had been here for a month, ever since Wil first came over.

Damn, that boy had me losing my mind. I couldn't even pay bills— or attention, for that matter.

I waited for the phone to ring at seven. It didn't. It didn't ring at eight or nine, either.

Then I beeped him. I didn't want to seem pressed, but come on, he had better call me and tell me something. Shit, I had been dressed since 6:30 waiting for him. I had even called the operator to make sure my phone was working right.

Eleven o'clock, no Wil. Just messed up hair and wrinkled clothes from lying around in them, waiting for him to call. Everybody but him called—Yaz, Leslie, and that boy Samir. I told everybody I was trying to sleep. I didn't want to talk to them. I wanted to talk to Wil, even though he had stood me up.

Then at 1 o'clock in the fucking morning, I heard a horn beep. I walked to the window to hear Wil say, "You ready?"

"Ready for what? To go to sleep?"

"I'm so sorry, Boo. I had to take care of something for my Dad. You going to hold that against me?"

"No, I won't hold it against you. I'll be down."

I was mad at him, but happy he had showed up.

As soon as I got in the car, I started nodding off. I tried to keep my eyes open, but next thing I knew, I went straight to sleep. I didn't care where we were going, as long as I was with him.

When Wil woke me up, all I saw were bright, shiny colorful lights blinking on and off. The skyline was beautiful. Wil had taken me to Atlantic City. I had never been to Atlantic City before. Well, yes, I had, but not with a guy on a date. First, we had to park, so we went straight to the valet at Trump Taj Mahal. As soon as we walked in, wouldn't you know it, I got carded by security. I was so embarrassed. Three dates and I'd gotten carded twice. I looked at the security guard as if to say, "What gives?"

"Here you go," I said, handing him Yaz's old driver's license. Luckily, I had never taken it out of my wallet. I wasn't going to give him a college ID 'cause it didn't have a birth date.

I held my breath. It worked. He gave me my ID back and let us enter. Once we were inside, I heard change jingling and bells ringing nonstop. Everybody was winning—or at least it seemed that way.

I wanted to play, but I didn't know what to do. The only time I had ever played blackjack had been with Reese, so I was totally clueless.

Wil walked over to the roulette table and gave the dealer $100. He asked me to pick a number. The first number that came to mind was my birth date, March 23rd. He put a few chips down on twenty-three and said, "I believe you are my luck."

The lady spun the wheel and, sure enough, the pointer landed on my birth date. I didn't know what he had just won. He had to explain the odds.

He had just won $1,000. He told me the number, and suddenly I felt like we were Sharon Stone and Robert DeNiro in the movie *Casino*. He gave me my own money to play with.

I walked over to the blackjack table like a high roller. The minimum bet was $10. Lady luck was on my side, so I bet $10. I won. I was on a roll.

The dealer asked me if I wanted to play another hand. I said "Yeah," so she dealt. I stood at 19 and the dealer had blackjack. She had a king and an ace. That meant she had won and I had lost.

Eventually, I lost all the money Wil had given me. *Oh, shit. I got to get some more money so I can get our money back.*

I walked back over to Wil, who was winning at the roulette table. He didn't notice when I took a $100's worth of chips from his stash and headed back over to the blackjack table. Lady luck came back for a couple of hands. Then I lost again.

I walked over to the table where Wil had been, but he was gone. I asked this lady if she had seen Wil.

She said he lost all his money and left the table about fifteen minutes ago. I looked everywhere, but still no Wil. I had to go to the ladies' room. When I came out, still no Wil.

Suddenly everything looked different. Everywhere I looked, I saw people with looks of despair on their faces. Nobody seemed to be winning anymore. When I'd entered the casino, I had thought everybody was winning. That's how it had seemed.

I kept walking around—broke, mad, and looking for Wil. Then I saw this man win really big. Everybody was surrounding him. He had won $25,000 off the quarter machine.

Now I understood why Leslie and my grandmom would go on bus excursions on Sundays to Atlantic City while we stayed with Uncle Bubbie and watched football. They had the itch. Everybody in the casino had the itch. Everybody was trying to get something for nothing.

Seeing that man win, I remembered that I had $10 in my pocket. I took that $10, cashed it in for quarters, and pulled down on the lever.

"Give me luck, big bucks, big bucks," I said to myself. Two minutes later, all my quarters were gone. No quarters, no money, and I still couldn't find Wil. So I just sat there until I heard the intercom announce, "Kayla Johnson, your party is waiting for you. Dial 8-2-3 if you're in the building." I looked around for a courtesy phone and dialed the number. It was Wil.

"Where are you?" he asked.

"I don't know. By the quarter machines."

"Stay right there."

"OK."

Eventually, he found me. He asked if I wanted to stay overnight or go home. I wanted to go. I was broke and I could tell Wil was, too. He just casually mentioned he had blown like $2,000. But he still asked me if I wanted to stay overnight.

I said no because I didn't want him to spend the last of his money on a room. We walked out to the valet and gave him our ticket. We got in the car and Wil tipped the valet guy. The next thing I knew, we were back on the highway. I turned around and looked for the bright lights—but they were gone, and so was all my money.

* * *

A couple of days later, I was sitting on the steps waiting for Wil to come to take me to the market. (Yup, he got me cooking for him now.) As I sat impatiently staring down the block for his car to pull up, Mrs. Franklin came and sat next to me.

"How you doing today?" she asked as she puffed on her cigarette.

"I'm fine."

"Want one?" she said, offering me the pack.

I told her no, as I did every other time she offered me one. She was a real nice lady, but she was too damn nosy. Anytime anybody beeped a horn or closed a door on our block, she would peep out of her blinds to see who it was.

Oh, and her chain smoking was ridiculous. She was always puffing away. It probably was one of the reasons she looked like she did.

Mrs. Franklin looked like she used to be real pretty—not that she wasn't still pretty. She just always looked so worn out. I guess I would probably look that way, too, if I had three bad-ass sons and a pervert for a husband.

Her husband was forever staring at somebody like they were a piece of meat. And as for her, she would always ask me the same questions whenever I ran into her: Was my job hiring and could I bring an application home for her?

"Yes, Mrs. Franklin," I would always say. But I never did. I didn't want that crazy lady working at my job with me. That night, I was saved when Wil pulled up just as she was about to go there again.

"Bye, Kayla," she said as she somehow managed to wave and light another cigarette at the same time.

After we returned from Pathmark, I unloaded the groceries as Wil took off his work boots and clothes. Then I started preparing lasagna and garlic bread for our dinner. I made our plates and we sat and watched a little television. I thought Wil was in for the night 'cause he had just gotten out of the shower and was wearing nothing but his boxers. I was lying all cozy on Wil's chest when his beeper went off. It was Stevie.

Wil called him back right away. I could piece together what Stevie was saying by the way Wil responded.

"Nothing. Just chilling with my wifey." He listened again for a few seconds then said, "Really, yeah. That's what's up. All right, I be there."

I'm thinking, *He'll be where, when, what? I don't think so,* I thought. I had gotten so used to me and Wil's little routine together. When we were together, we would always get something to eat, watch TV or a movie, have extremely good sex, and then go to sleep. With Wil about to change our schedule, I was more than a little upset.

I couldn't believe it when Wil jumped up and began putting his clothes on. I wanted to say something so bad, but I couldn't. I hated it when Wil hung out with Stevie. Stevie is such a dog. But if I had said something, then I would have looked like a hater.

"Wiiilll," I said, whining.

"What?"

"Nothing."

"What was you going to say, Kayla?"

"Never mind, forget it. It's just that . . ."

"It's just what?"

"It's just why you got to go out with Stevie? I mean why don't you stay in with me?" I said.

"You know Stevie thinks I have been neglecting him since I got with you."

"Well, I don't care what he thinks. I don't see why you got to go," I pouted.

"Boo, I'll be back. OK?" Wil said as he put his belt in his pants loop and bent down and gave me a kiss.

Chapter 8

By now, Wil and I were practically living together. He had under-wear in the hamper and his deodorant and cologne on my dresser. I was loving it. Money was not an issue with Wil. Whatever I needed, I got. He made me feel as if I were the best thing he had ever had and would do anything to make me happy. He really cherished me.

I had never had anyone worship me like he did. I mean, I was going to the mall so much there was practically nothing left there that I wanted. My prayers had been answered.

Finally, I had found the relationship I had longed for. Wil was the perfect man for me—well, except for his bad habit of leaving the toi-let seat up and going out with Stevie all the time. He was so romantic and such a gentleman.

I was good to him, too. I shampooed his hair, cooked for him every now and then, and washed his clothes. We did everything together from going to the movies to bowling. He was my baaabyyy! I used to hate that baby, boo, cookie, sweetie stuff, but I guess things change when you find the right person.

One night, we went to Karl's, a restaurant in Olde City that serves Southern-style food. It was about 6 P.M., happy hour. We were just sit-ting having drinks and listening to a jazz band when two women walked up. One was thick with naturally red hair and freckles. The other one was skinny as a pole, had brown skin and a bad overbite like she had been sucking her thumb since she was in the womb. The one with the messed up teeth kissed Wil on his cheek.

"How you doing?" she damn near yelled to me over the music.

"Fine," I answered.

"I'm Wil's cousin," she said, as she and her girlfriend sat down with us.

I didn't mind, but Wil obviously did.

"So what's up, cuz? Can I get a couple of dollars?" she asked.

"I knew you was going to ask me that shit. How much you need?"

"What can you spare?"

"Here, Tracy," Wil said, handing her some money.

"Cuz, where's my brother at? I want to introduce him to my girl-friend."

"Who?"

"Her," she said, pointing at her girlfriend, who was sitting there looking all eager.

Wil busted out laughing. Then he looked at her and said, "You really must not be her friend, 'cause you know he's a dog and don't talk to any girls over a buck thirty five."

Then he looked at the girl and asked her if she had any kids.

"Yeah, I got two," she replied somewhat defensively.

"Tracy, you know he don't mess with no girls with kids. No disrespect, sis, but my cousin Stevie is not a nice person for someone like you. Tracy is trying to play you. You don't want to meet him. Trust me."

Then we all started laughing. Wil was just letting the girl know the truth, even if he was being a little mean doing it like that. But even considering all that, the girl still wanted his number. After they left, Wil and I just sat back and listened to the band play. Snuggling against his shoulder, I sighed and thought about how I couldn't have asked for a better relationship. I loved me some Wil.

Because I was spending so much time with him, I had been slipping up on some things. For instance, a whole week had gone by and I hadn't spoken with Yaz. And I hadn't gotten around to taking Nikki to the doctor's office yet. When I realized how lax I'd been and that I couldn't prolong Nikki's appointment any longer, I decided to call my doctor's office as soon as I got to work.

I loved my job. It was easy and comical. When I got there that afternoon, Carole was sitting at my desk talking to Deborah. They were always complaining about nothing. They basically drank coffee and smoked cigarettes all evening long.

I was the youngest person at my job. The other ladies I worked with had this as their second job or were between jobs. They made me laugh, telling me stories about their grandkids and childhood.

I liked my job a lot, except for the fact that I got cussed out quite a bit by the people who owed the bank money. They would say things like, "I got caller ID. Don't call my house no more, you damn bill collector." Then they would hang up in my ear.

Or I would get a guy telling me how his wife had left him for his brother and he didn't have any money to pay his bills. Besides that, being a bill collector was easy. I could daydream, read, and eat while still doing my job. After taxes, my take-home pay wasn't that much, but luckily Wil was paying my rent. All I had to do was pay the phone and electric bills, which were nothing.

"Can I sit at my desk?" I said to Carole, who had made herself all comfortable.

"Sure, baby."

I sat down while Deborah and Carole talked on. It's a wonder they ever got any work done. I pulled out my phone book and called Planned Parenthood.

"Planned Parenthood. How may I help you?"

"Hi. I would like to schedule two appointments."

"What type of an appointment would you like for the first patient?"

"The first appointment will be an annual exam. The second will be a first visit."

"What's the first patient's name?"

"My name is Kayla Johnson and the second appointment is for my sister, Nicole Clarke."

"Has your sister ever been here before?"

"No." Hadn't I just said it would be a first visit?

"You can both come on November 6 at 5:00 and 5:30."

After I made the appointments, I began to talk to Tina, our temporary supervisor. Tina had twins—at least that's what she called them. But they really were nine months apart. She dressed them the same, as if they were twins, and they were in the same grade. Tina's husband is black and she thought she was, too, even though she was Vietnamese.

Deborah was a heavyset older woman who had to be about fifty, with dark skin and a short mixed gray bush. She was retired and worked because she didn't have anything else to do.

For Carole, this was her second job. She needed to help pay for her granddaughter's tuition at Catholic school. She was one of the only white collectors. All the rest of the white people at the company were in management.

"What's today's topic, ladies?" I asked.

"Welfare reform," Deb said.

"I was telling Debbie, I see those girls having all those babies and don't want to work," Carole said.

"Carole, you can't say they don't want to work. You're not one of those girls. You don't know if they want to work and can't find a job. How about if one of those girls was your granddaughter?" Debbie questioned Carole.

"My granddaughter wouldn't be pregnant. If she was, she would get an abortion or put the baby up for adoption," Carole said.

"That's all y'all ever do is get abortions," Debbie responded.

"Y'all meaning who? Do you mean white people, Debbie? 'Cause I know you not referring to me as y'all. See, y'all have a double standard. Y'all can classify white people all in one group but the minute somebody classifies blacks in one group, y'all on the phone calling Jessie Jackson."

I laughed, then butted in, saying, "What she's trying to say is it's more accepted in the black community to have a baby out of wedlock than it is if you're white. It's not right, but it's that way. Whites tend to have more abortions and put their babies up for adoption more so than blacks. We keep our baby and struggle."

"Kayla, do you have statistics to support that claim?" Carole turned her eyebrow up at me.

"No," I admitted.

"Well, I don't want to hear it."

Tina stepped in. "Ladies, let's do some work and debate later."

Debbie was so mad she was red even through her dark skin. And Carole was purple. But dozens of calls and a half hour later it was as if nothing had ever happened. Deb and Carole were speaking to each other again. Tina and I just laughed at them.

Most evenings went pretty much the same. Carole would talk about her perfect granddaughter and Deb about current events. Tina talked about her husband, Joey, and their twins, and I talked about Wil.

I got tired of Tina some nights, though, rambling on about how Joey was the best man she had ever had and how all her boyfriends before him would beat her, but Joey was different. He hadn't made her get an abortion when he found out she was pregnant. Instead he had proposed to her and they had been together ever since.

Don't get me wrong. Tina was my girl. But she always disclosed a bit more information than what was needed.

Before long, it was 9 P.M. and time to go home. I was tired as hell. I needed to study for my intellectual heritage test the next day, but I didn't really have the energy. I went straight home and pulled my books out and tried to get started studying when the phone began ringing.

"Boo, what are you doing?" Wil said.

"Nothing, I'm just getting home from work."

"I know. I've been calling there. I couldn't get in. I needed my other jacket and couldn't even get it. I need a key."

"Boo, I'm sorry you couldn't get your jacket. I was at work. What was I supposed to do? You could have come to my job and gotten the key."

"Why don't you just make me a key tomorrow morning? OK, Boo?"

"You can use mine until I get another one. You can get it tonight when you come over."

"Kayla, I don't know. I got business to take care of."

"What do you mean you don't know?"

"Kayla, I don't feel like arguing with you. I'm out."

"Wil, don't hang up on me. I just want to know why."

"Look, I got to go. I'll see you later."

Then I heard the phone go dead. No, he didn't hang up on me. I started not to call him back. Who did he think he was? But then I decided I was being petty, so I beeped him. He called right back.

"Are you coming to get the key?"

"Yeah, but I'm only going to be there a minute 'cause I got to meet up with Stevie. I be there just about every night with you, Kayla. So you got to understand if I have to do something."

"I understand. I'm just used to you being with me. I got a test I need to study for anyway."

"All right."

"Boo . . ."

"What, Kayla?"

"Can you stop and get me some ice cream?"

"Strawberry, right?"

"Yes."

"See you when I get there."

"OK."

What did Wil mean when he said that he wasn't staying with me? Didn't he know I was used to him staying here with me? If he wasn't staying here, then where was he going to stay? The phone rang again.

"Hello, may I speak to Kayla, please?"

"This is she. Who's this?"

"Samir. How you been? Long time no hear from. What you been up to?"

"Nuttin."

"Why haven't you been getting with me?"

"I been real busy, plus I got a boyfriend now."

"I kind of figured you had a man. But when you get tired of him, hit me up, OK?"

"All right."

"And if I call and a nigga pick up, I'm going to hang up."

We talked for fifteen minutes or so about mostly nothing, until I heard Wil at the door and told Samir I had to go.

Wil walked in looking upset.

"What's wrong with you?"

"Nothing. Where's the key?"

"Right here," I said, unhooking it from my key chain. "Where you going?"

"I told you. To do something with Stevie."

"Like what?"

"Why you third degreeing me? I might be back. When I get to Stevie's house, I'll call you," he said. He started toward the door, then turned back and gave me a kiss on the cheek.

"Hold up, Wil. How am I going to lock my door?"

"Put the bottom lock on and I'll pick you up from work. Beep me to remind me. How much you got saved up for your car?"

"Like $1,500."

"We goin' to the used-car dealer Saturday. You should be able to find a cute little car for like $3,500."

"All right, bye," I said as I closed the door and stood next to it for a minute. What was going on? What did he have to do that was so important? He was beginning to stress me. I was always worrying about him. It was affecting everything.

My thoughts were interrupted by the phone ringing. I hoped it wasn't that dumb guy, Samir, sweating me again.

"Hello."

"Kayla, about time I caught up with you," Yaz said, sniffing. It was obvious she had been crying.

"What's wrong, Yaz?"

"I left Sam."

"What! What happened? What made you do it? Where are you at?" I asked her all at once.

"Outside at a pay phone. The kids are at my mom house. She's acting crazy, too! You know it's crowded there. I don't know how much longer I can take my mom."

"Well, why don't you just get the kids and come and spend a couple of days over here?"

"He took the car, too! So I got to catch a cab and I don't have any money on me."

"Yaz, just come on. You know I got you."

It took Yaz a half hour to get to my place. When her cab pulled up, I ran downstairs to help her. Sam Jr. was asleep in her arms and Mia was barely awake. I grabbed her bags out of the trunk and followed her and Mia up the stairs.

"The door is open," I yelled as they reached my apartment.

Yaz walked in and put Sam Jr. on the sofa. I took Mia's clothes off and laid her in my bed. I walked back into the living room and found Yaz looking as if she were about to start crying again.

"So what happened?" I asked as I handed her a tissue.

Yaz began to speak, stuttering a bit.

"I heard him on the phone. I picked the phone up and he was practically having phone sex while me and his kids was right in the other room. He was like, 'Yeah, she almost sleep. I'll be right there and I'm going to fuck the shit out of you like this and like that.'"

"He's so stupid. Trying to be a player. So what you gonna do?"

"I don't know. I got some cash saved up so I can live off of that until I find a job and a place. Then I guess I can go back to nursing school."

"You know my mom can help you find a job when you finish school."

"I know. I left him like a week ago. I was trying to call you, but the phone just kept ringing."

"I know. I was here. I was turning the ringer off sometimes. You know Wil be here all the time and he hates for the phone to be ringing off the hook."

"Where is he at now?"

"He had something to do."

"What's up with y'all, anyway?"

I sighed "Yaz, I'm really feeling him and I see this going somewhere. Granted it's only been a minute, but he is just so right for me. I mean he is so sweet. He just left a little before you called me. He came to pick up the key."

"What key? You giving him a key already?"

"Yeah, what's wrong with that?"

"Are you crazy? Don't you see what predicament I'm in?"

"Yeah, but this is different. Wil said it doesn't matter how long you been together. It's how you feel."

"Wil said this. Wil said that. Kayla, you starting to sound like one of those girls."

"One of what girls?"

"You know one of those girls whose whole life revolves around their man and what he says. I'm trying to tell you. All that living together shit ain't cool."

"Girl, please. You and Sam just got finished living together for three years. Now you're going to tell me it ain't cool. He don't live here, anyway. He just stays here sometimes and I gave him a key," I said as I grabbed some sheets out of the closet.

"I hope you be using condoms so your ass don't get pregnant."

"Come on now. What I look like?" I said as I handed her the sheets to make the sofa.

"I don't know. Right now, you better get some birth control."

"I take my pills. Yaz, I got this. You need some rest. Go to sleep and we'll talk tomorrow. Turn the light off when you finish, 'cause you are tripping."

I went back into the bedroom and began taking off my clothes. As I pulled the covers up on Mia, I wondered if Yaz was right. Was I one of those girls who all they had to talk about was my "hussssband" or "boyyyfriend"? Was I taking Wil too serious too soon? I mean, we had only been together for two months, but if you spent every day and night with someone, a day seems like a week and a week seems like a month.

The next day when Wil came and picked me up from work, I gave him a kiss and asked him if he could drop Tina off.

"Where is she going?" he asked.

"South Philly."

"Tell her to come on."

I waved to Tina that he had said "Yeah." She got in the car and said, "Thank-you for the ride. I live at 19th and Catherine. I hope Joey got the car out of the shop, Kayla, 'cause I'm tired of catching the bus."

"Where are the girls?" I asked, even though I'd already heard enough about Tina's life for one night.

"With Joey's father."

Moments later, we pulled in front of the door of her row home.

"Thanks again," she said as she got out and walked up her steps. After we dropped Tina off, we headed home, but I forgot to warn Wil that Yaz was staying with me. I opened the door and saw immediately that the kids were running around wild. Clothes were all over the floor and Yaz was on the phone while wearing my nightclothes. I took a deep breath to get myself together. I wasn't used to this kind of chaos.

"Yaz, what's up?" I said as we walked in.

"Nothing. I cooked."

"I see."

My kitchen was a mess. Wil just looked on in disbelief.

"Hey, Wil."

"Hey," Wil responded.

Then he nodded for me to follow him into my bedroom. He shut the door and said, "What are your girlfriend and her kids doing here?"

"Her and her boyfriend broke up and she and her mother weren't getting along, so I told her she could stay here."

"Well, I'm not staying here with bey beys running around. I'm going home. If you want, you can get your stuff and come with me," he said with an attitude.

We'd been going out three months, but I had never been inside Wil's house. I never had a reason to. We chilled at my house all the time or at Stevie's. I knew where he lived, because sometimes he would stop in and get something while I sat in the car.

So when he asked me to go with him, I decided to go. I was curious to see how my man lived. Was he a neat freak or sloppy? I got my clothes together and told Yaz I was spending the night over at Wil's house and that I would see her tomorrow.

Wil was quiet the whole ride to his house in Mount Airy. As I walked up the steps, I could see what looked like a million and one plants pushing up against the window. Walking in, I smelled the fresh smell of mothballs. The furniture was very elegant. You could tell everything was antique.

Wil grabbed my bag and told me to follow him upstairs. I wasn't paying him any mind. I was too busy looking at his graduation, prom, and other family photos that were all hung up on a wall. Then I saw a picture of a pretty little girl who looked just like Wil, about five years old.

"Wil, who's this little girl that looks just like you?" I asked, stepping in for a closer look.

"That's my cousin Carmen's daughter, Ashley. Stop being nosy and come upstairs."

Upstairs in his room, there was a blue light shining from a tall floor lamp that illuminated a king-sized, black iron frame bed. On the wall was a framed picture of Lena Horne. Through his open closet door, I could see rows and rows of sneaker boxes and every other imaginable item neatly stacked. Even his hats were neatly hung up. Wil was definitely not sloppy.

He put my bag on the floor, sat down on the bed, and reached to turn on the TV. I sat next to him and started massaging his back, until I heard the front door open. It startled me. Then someone walked up the stairs. There was a light knock that cracked the door open a bit before it opened completely.

"Sorry, William. I didn't know you had company," an attractive, petite woman said.

Wil introduced me to his mother.

"Kayla. Oh, you're the reason I never get to see my son anymore," she said smiling at me.

I didn't know what to say, so I just laughed it off. Wil looked embarrassed.

"Where's dad at?" he said, trying to change the subject.

"Downstairs. Bring your friend down to meet him."

"Yeah, yeah. I'll be there."

His mom closed the door on her way out. I told Wil his mother looked young. He said she was young, and his dad had fifteen years on her. She had met him when she was 18 and he was 33.

"It must have been nice growing up with both your mom and dad. I wish my dad lived with me. I never even had a full conversation with him. That's fucked up. I don't see how a man can do that. But my mother is partially to blame 'cause she didn't really want me to deal with him."

"You're right. It is nice and I do feel blessed. That's why I don't want any kids yet. I want to be a good husband and father to my kids and to be with my kids and be with my kids' mother."

When I heard him say that, I smiled. Wil was such a good man. I walked in front of the TV and grabbed Wil's face. I kissed him and he kissed me back. I pushed him back on the bed and kissed him some more until he patted me and said, "Get up. Let's go meet my dad before he come up here."

After I smoothed my hair and tucked my blouse back in, we went downstairs and found his father in the dining room. With his gray hair, he looked like he could be Wil's grandfather instead of his dad.

"How are you?" he asked me sternly.

"Fine."

"Would you like something to eat?"

"No, that's OK."

I was starving, but I knew I would be too nervous to eat anything in front of this man.

"Don't be shy," he said, obviously trying to be gracious.

"No, thank-you. Well, nice meeting you," I said as I backed out of the room.

Wil was hungry. He headed off to the kitchen and I went back upstairs and called Yaz to see what she was doing. The phone kept clicking and then I was disconnected.

After jiggling the cord a bit, I managed to call Yaz back.

"Sorry, that was Wil's crazy phone. He needs to buy a cord. Guess what?"

"What?"

"I just met Wil's parents. He told them all about me. I have to whisper because he might be coming upstairs and I don't want him to hear me."

"And," she said sarcastically.

"And that's it. He told them about me and I met them."

"So, Kayla, that's not nothing. The first time I went out with Sam, I met his mother."

"Forget it. You don't understand, cause you're pissed at Sam. Forget it. What are the kids doing?"

"They sleep."

"I was just saying I'm happy he thought enough of me to introduce me to them," I said, still trying to get my point across. "So what's up for tomorrow?"

"I don't know. I might go to my mom's house. Why?"

"No reason. Wil just said it was going to be nice outside. I thought you might want to do something."

"I'll see. Well, Sam keep calling here, playing on your phone."

"How does he know where you are?"

"I called him to see when I could come and get the rest of my clothes. He must have dialed star sixty-nine. I got to get a ride over there, because he won't bring my shit to me."

"You shouldn't even see him. I'll go and get your clothes for you. You know me and Wil are supposed to get my car Saturday. We can go then."

"I got to go. Sam Jr. is trying to wake up. See you tomorrow."

I was just hanging up the phone as Wil returned upstairs carrying a plate of fried chicken and a glass of soda.

"Are you going to finish rubbing my back?" Wil asked.

"Yeah, I'll finish."

Wil sat on the floor eating off his overloaded plate while I sat on the edge of the bed and tried to massage all the stress out of his back. I tried to kiss him again, but he pushed me away. He was paying more attention to his food and the football game than to me and telling me to stop and have respect for his parents.

"Whatever," I said finally giving up.

I slipped into my nightgown and laid down in Wil's bed. I thought he would join me, but he didn't.

"Why you going to sleep so early?" he said, as he touched me on my shoulder and woke me from a light sleep.

"I have to go to school tomorrow."

"I'm going downstairs."

"For what?"

"We can't sleep in the same bed here. My parents won't go for that."

He was for real about that respect shit. He turned out the light and blew a kiss at me as he walked out of the room, closing the door behind him. When I woke up in the middle of the night, I was confused. I had forgotten where I was. Glancing at the clock, I saw it was 3 A.M.

I went to the hallway and peeped down the stairs. Wil had fallen asleep with the TV on. Silently, I slipped downstairs. Just as I was reaching to turn off the television, I felt Wil's hand on my leg, scaring me.

"Don't do that," I said, in a faint scream.

"Come here."

"Stop, Wil. What about your parents?" I said as his hands began to roam up and down my body.

"Sssh. Just don't be loud."

"But we don't have a condom."

"We're safe. It's just you and me."

I was skeptical at first. I couldn't remember the last time I had had sex without a condom, but Wil convinced me to relax as he undressed me. Then he placed my body gently on the floor and started kissing me and touching me all over. It felt so good that I grabbed my hair like I was about to pull it out and moaned in ecstasy. Before long, Wil had my back going back and forth on the hard oak floor. It was most definitely getting a polishing. Surely, it would shine in the morning. Wil was moaning my name, "Kayla, oh Kayla."

Then he did it. I couldn't believe it. In the middle of it all, he whispered, "I love you."

"I love you, too!" I said, as I hugged him even closer.

After two more sessions of wall-banging sex, we must have forgotten we weren't at my house, because we fell asleep right there in the middle of his parents' living room. I'm sure when his mother came downstairs for work she didn't appreciate seeing my bare ass sticking straight up in the air as I slept on top of her son.

"William, William! Get up and fix yourself before your father gets down here."

We jumped up and I pulled my nightgown over my head and ran into the bathroom to get ready for school. Not only was I embarrassed, but I was running late. Just what I needed, to be late again for history.

By the time I got to campus I was really late. Nobody else was walking to class. I tried to sneak into Anderson Lecture Hall. But the squeaking of the big green metal door announced my arrival. The entire class, which was roughly the size of an elementary school auditorium full of students, turned around to see who was late.

I hated being the late girl. I'm always the late girl. Every class no matter what time I get up, I somehow manage to be late. It's probably got something to do with Wil. I could hardly think about anything at all without also thinking about him. But that's another story.

It was now 9:53 and I was supposed to have been in class at 9:40 A.M. If I would have left Wil's house thirteen minutes earlier, I would have been on time. But no, there I was the late girl again.

I wanted to turn around and go home, but instead I opened the door the rest of the way. I walked my late ass in and grabbed the first seat I saw. I hoped somebody else would come in late so I wouldn't feel so bad.

My professor was passing out last week's quizzes. When he got to me, he placed my test on my desk facedown. Then he raised his hairy brown eyebrows at me and made an announcement about attendance being 15 percent of your grade. I was thinking *fuck you* as he was talking. When I unfolded my test, I saw a big fat 64 in red marker. What else could go wrong this morning? My study buddy, or the guy I always copied my notes from, pointed his fingers up, as if to say what's up.

"You got the notes?" I asked.

"Yeah."

"Can I see them?"

"Here you go."

"When is the test?" I whispered.

"Come to class and you'll find out," he said as he passed me his notes.

I copied them and tried to pay attention to the rest of the lecture, but all I could think about was Wil.

Later that evening after I came home from work, I went to the market. I wanted to pick the kids and Yaz some stuff up. I got the kids some cereal and me and Yaz junk food. I was standing in the twelve items or less aisle ready to pay for my stuff when I see that guy Samir in the other line. He spotted me soon as I turned my head. I'm thinking, *oh boy.*

He tapped me right on my shoulder and said, "Don't I know you?"

"No I don't think so," I said, playing along with his little game like I didn't know who he was, either.

"Yeah, I do think I know you. You're the girl I met at Karisma's who won't let me take her out, 'cause she keep saying she got a boyfriend."

"No that's not me."

"Yes, it is, Kayla," he said.

"What you doing in here anyway?" I asked.

"Picking something up for my mom. But they don't have it. So what's up? Can we go out right now?"

"No. I got to go home," I said as I turned around and paid the cashier. Samir started bagging my bags and said, "Why you got to go home? You on lockdown or something?"

"No, I ain't on lockdown, but I told you before I got somebody."

"Well I told you I don't care about dude. So you might as well call me."

"I'll think about it." I laughed as we were coming out of the market and about to catch a cab. I saw one, so I flagged it down but it went past.

"You getting in a cab?"

"Yeah."

"You don't have to do that. I'll give you a ride home."

"No, that's all right. I'm good."

"Come on, you know I'm good peoples. I'm going to get you home. I might want to kidnap you, but I wouldn't." With hesitation, I accepted his offer. I didn't see any other cabs anyway.

On the ride home I was real nervous. I thought about what if Wil saw me. He'd probably kill me.

I calmed down and began to notice how attractive Samir was. I kept staring at his smooth brown skin, bright eyes, and sexy hair and beard, which were still sharp. He was dressed down in a blue Dickey suit and black boots. He had a good boy thug quality to him.

I could tell he was one of those guys who knew about the streets but tried to stay out of them. If I wasn't with Wil, I would definitely take him up on his offer. He looked real good—but I still made him drop me off one block away from my house and told him I would try to call him.

When I got in the apartment, I found Yaz on the sofa.

"Guess who just gave me a ride home?" I said as I brought in the grocery bags.

"Who?"

"Samir."

"Where you see him at?"

"The market."

"For real? What was he talking about?"

"Nothing, trying to get with me."

"Uhm, that's nice."

"What's wrong with you?"

"Nothing," she answered. But I could tell something was wrong. So to cheer her up, I asked her if she wanted to go out or something. At first she said no, but I kept on until she gave in.

"I just got to see if my mom will watch the kids. How we going to get there?"

"I'm going to ask Wil if I can get the keys to the truck."

Yaz called her mom as I looked for something to wear. *Damn, where are my black pants?* I wondered as I looked around my closet. After pushing aside some hangers, I finally found them. Then Yaz walked back into my room and said her mom would watch the kids as long as they were asleep.

"I'm going to get in the shower. Beep Wil for me."

Yaz beeped him. I heard the phone ring moments later. Mia brought the cordless to me in the bathroom and said, "You booe-friend on the phone."

"Hello," I said as I leaned out of the shower to keep the phone from getting wet.

"What's up, Boo?" Wil said into the phone.

"Nuttin. What your mom say?"

"She didn't say anything, just why the living room. She already knew what was going on 'cause she heard us."

"Stop playing. Oh, my God, I'm never coming over there again."

"My mom is not thinking about you, girl. She's not like that. So what you doing?"

"Nothing. Uhm."

I was scared to ask him for the car. But I figured the worst thing he could say was no. He got a key to my house, I should be able to hold his car.

So I finally just asked him, "Boo, can I hold the car tonight?"

"For what? Where you going?"

"Uhm, well. Yaz has been kinda down and I wanted to take her out so she can stop worrying about her nut-ass boyfriend."

"I don't care if you hold the car, but where are y'all going on a Tuesday night?"

"You know the Mediterranean be doing it."

"Well, if it be doing it, you can't go. I don't want no niggas all in my girl face all night. I don't want you talking to no guys."

"Wil, I'm not going to be talking to anyone," I whined.

"You can hold it. I don't care. You just got to put some gas in it."

"I can do that. See you when you get here."

I jumped out of the shower, wrapped a towel around me, and ran shivering into my bedroom. I dried off, sat on the bed, and rubbed some pear glacé Victoria's Secret lotion on my body. I told Yaz he'd said yeah and asked if the kids were asleep yet.

"They on they way," she whispered back.

"Well, get in the shower. By the time you get out, they should be sleep."

I couldn't decide on which perfume to wear as I looked at my dresser, which was crowded with practically every fragrance ever made. I put on Tommy Girl. I turned my curling iron on so I could curl my hair a little. I had decided against the black pants and was instead dressed in a silver skirt, a black mock-neck sweater shirt and my new silver boots. Wil walked in, scaring me. I had forgotten he had his key.

"Y'all ready?" he said, taking off his jacket and tossing it on a chair.

"I am, but Yaz is still getting dressed."

"Where is she taking her kids?"

"We're taking them to her mom's house."

He looked down at Mia and Sam Jr., asleep on the sofa, and whispered, "Put them in your bed and they can stay here with me. Don't take them kids out. It's cold outside."

I didn't believe what I was hearing. Was this the same man who said he wouldn't stay in the same place with no bey beys?

"I'll ask Yaz if it's OK," I whispered back as I turned and walked into the bedroom, where Yaz was squeezing into a pair of red Gucci pants.

"Wil's here. He said the kids could stay here with him."

"Oh, that's what's up?" She was happy not having to haul the kids to her mom's.

"Finish getting dressed," I said as I shut the door behind me.

Wil was in the kitchen looking in the refrigerator. "Boo, you need to go shopping and do these dishes."

"I will when I get a chance," I snapped.

He better stop tripping before I take my key back, I thought to myself.

Finally, Yaz was ready. Wil told her not to let anything happen to me. Yaz thanked him for watching the kids and we walked out of the door.

"I can't believe he gave you the keys, Kay. I told you I could see you pushing that," she said as we headed outside.

"I told you he was a sweetheart. I don't believe it, either. And I really can't believe he's watching your kids. Wil don't like kids."

"That's 'cause they sleep."

"You right."

As we approached the truck, I hit the remote alarm button and we got in. I turned the radio on immediately.

"What CDs he got?" Yaz asked.

"I don't know. Look."

We needed some ride pass music for when we rode past guys. We had to make sure we had the hottest song playing so everybody would look at us. Sometimes we would ride all night with the same song playing. Yaz was looking all over the car for some CDs.

"Look in the glove compartment," I said.

As soon as Yaz opened it up, all these CDs and papers fell out, including his car registration.

"Pick those papers up."

"I will. First, let me tell you what he got. He got Jay Z, Major Figgas, Eve or 2 Pac. What you want to hear?"

"Put on Jay Z and pick those papers off the floor before they get lost."

"Who's Carmen Carson?" Yaz asked.

"Who? Oh, that's Wil's cousin. I saw her picture yesterday when I was at his house."

"Why he got his car in his cousin's name?"

"I guess for insurance. She's older," I told Yaz.

But I really didn't know or care. I just wanted to hurry up and get this over with so I could get back to the apartment with my baby.

* * *

The Mediterranean was off the hook. The smoky little club was filled to capacity, probably breaking the fire code. Yaz danced a lot and drank her usual Long Island iced teas.

I just stood next to the mirrored wall. A couple guys asked me to dance, but I didn't really feel like it. Over and over again, I said "No, thank-you," "No, my feet hurt," and "Sorry, I'm tired."

Honestly, the only reason I came out was for Yaz. I had a man lying in my bed waiting for me and I couldn't wait to get back home to him.

Two o'clock did not come soon enough. As we exited the club, there was a parade going on outside. That was the only way to explain why 400 people were outside at 2 A.M. on a Tuesday in the cold. This time of morning is called "the let out," meaning people who didn't go into the club come up to see the people who did and cause a massive traffic jam. Everybody loved just showing their car off and being seen. Traffic was jammed for at least five blocks. People were standing outside their cars. Me and Yaz got in Wil's car to participate in the car show.

"Oh, Kayla, look. There go Kevin." Yaz was leaning out the window, letting all the cold air come in.

"Kevin who?" I looked over to where she was pointing

"The one who live on my mom block. You said you used to go with him."

"Yeah," I said, taking a look at the guy trying to profile on the corner. "That sure is him."

"I'm going to call him over here."

"Don't do that. Stop trying to play me, Yaz." I snapped.

"Watch me, Kevin, Kevin, come here for a minute."

He came strolling over.

"You know me?" he said.

"Yeah, she know you. Kayla." Yaz said as she pointed to me.

"Little Kayla from Central High School. Damn girl, you look different." He started smiling at me.

I wanted to say "So do you," but it would have come out too sarcastically. He smelled like weed. Gross. He looked like he'd become a blunt master. His pants were hanging down and his lips were purplish brown where they used to be pink. He had his cap slanted over one eye like he was DMX or somebody, and he was wearing an old army fatigue jacket.

I don't know why Yaz invited him over. She played too much. He was so embarrassing.

I couldn't believe I used to be crazy about him. I went with him from ninth grade until the eleventh, when he went away to college and started messing with Gina. That was my first and last real boyfriend until Wil. Everyone else had just been someone to occupy my time.

"All right. I was just saying 'hi,'" I said, hoping he would get the hell away from the truck.

"Oh, all right. Can I get that number?" he said as he flashed his butter-colored teeth.

"No! I'm married," I said with an attitude.

"I don't see no ring."

"I'm about to get married."

"Well, until you get married, can I call you?"

"No, come on. Get away from the car," I said, by now annoyed.

"OK, Kayla. I see you rolling. Don't have time for a brother. Uhm, what year is this?" he asked as he eyed the truck up and down.

"It's a double O. Does it matter? Bye, Kevin," I said.

I was tired of smelling his weeded breath. I rolled the window up right in his face and pulled off. Yaz was saying, "Don't front on your boyfriend," and laughing.

I didn't find anything funny. She played too much with her drunk ass.

"That's not my boyfriend," I snapped at her.

"Don't front. You used to love you some Kevy Kev. Now he's a corner blunt boy. That shit's got nigga tossed."

"I don't know what happened to him. He used to go to Cheyney. Now he is just a waste of potential." I shook my head in disgust. "I wonder what his parents are saying. I'm ready to go home. You ready?"

"Yeah."

I made a sharp U-turn and headed home. When we got in the house, Wil was on the sofa. Quietly, I told Yaz she could sleep in the bed with the kids.

I stayed in the living room and started running my fingers lightly up and down Wil's neck as he slept. It made him jump, as if he felt a bug or something. I kissed him on his neck. Then I slowly unbuttoned his jeans and licked his stomach and navel. I felt his pubic hair press against my face. The kisses I planted on his lower body were sloppy and wet. I was so turned on.

I decided to try something a little different, something I had heard about since high school but had never tried. Something I had heard that if it is done properly will make a grown man cry. Something extremely intimate and so personal. I had never done it before, but now, suddenly, I had the urge. Something about Wil just made me want to try new things. He was my baby, my boo. And I wanted to please him.

By the expression on his face, I could tell I was doing it right. He seemed so excited. And then he made love to me like he had never done before. First, we did it on the floor of the living room. Then he turned me around and entered my body from the back, exciting and vibrating every muscle, bone, and wall in me. I was on my knees bending over the sofa with my head down on the seat cushions. He went faster and faster, losing control, knocking me on the floor, pumping harder and harder. I thought I was going to get rug burns.

"Oh baby, oh baby, I love you. I love you. I love you, Wil."

Chapter 9

Saturday came quickly. I was so happy I was getting my first car that I got up about 8 A.M. so I could go to the bank, cash my check, and withdraw my money before Wil got there.

Wil hadn't been staying over all week, since Yaz was still staying with me. I took a withdrawal slip and got in line. I waited until I got to a teller to fill the form out. I'm one of those customers who can never remember their account number.

As usual, the teller had to get it for me. I got my money and was out the door in minutes. By the time I reached my house, Wil was outside beeping his horn and hollering, "Come on, girl."

"We still going to the auction?" I asked.

"No, we going to go to this car dealer Stevie told me about. But first I want to check some places down in Kensington."

Every dealer we went to was tripping. They wanted $3,000 for an eight- or nine-year-old car. Please. At one dealership, I was looking at an '87 black Ford Taurus when Wil called me over to look at a 1990 Nissan Maxima.

"You like this, Boo?"

"It's all right."

"It's only $3,800. You want to take it for a drive?"

"All right," I said, reluctantly.

We got in, Wil in the back and Larry of Larry Auto Sales in the front with me. It rode good and was respectable. The car was growing on me.

"You like it?" Wil asked as he interrupted Larry's little speech about how great a value the car was.

After we got back to the sales office, Wil was able to talk old Larry down a few hundred dollars, and before long he was handing me the keys. I was so happy. I couldn't wait to show my mom and Yaz that finally I had a car. No more waiting for somebody to come and get me.

As we were heading off the car lot, Wil told me he was going to call me later. He gave me a kiss and said he had things to do.

It was strange driving down the street passing people on the corner waiting for the bus. *That used to be me,* I thought as I rode by. I wished I could pick everyone up and give them a ride. I turned my music up and proceeded home.

When I arrived home, Yaz was getting the kids dressed.

"You ready to pick up your stuff?"

"Yeah. Mia, come put your shoes on," Yaz shouted.

"Then we can stop past my mom's house so I can show her my car."

"I forgot you got your car today. I don't know how I thought we were going to get there. How much did he put to it?"

"Eighteen hundred." I noticed Mia was struggling to put her Nikes on. "Mia, come over here so I can help you," I said, kneeling down to her level.

I put her sneaker on and asked Yaz if she was ready.

"Yeah, I'm ready. Just let me call him and tell him we are on our way."

"For what? Fuck him. You got your key, don't you? Just get your shit. We don't need any contact with him. Let's go."

I grabbed Mia's hand and Yaz locked the door behind us as we headed downstairs.

"I like this. It's cute for you, Kay," Yaz said as she walked around admiring my new car.

"It's not a Lexus, but we riding."

"Fuck a Lexus. At least you don't have to worry about nobody taking it away from you."

When we pulled up at Yaz's apartment, we noticed Sam's Lex was parked outside.

"Do you want me to come in with you or wait out here?" I asked.

"No, come in with me."

Yaz pulled out her key and went to open the door but the key wouldn't work. "I know this is the key," she mumbled over and over again. So she tried another key, then another. Five keys later, she realized Sam had changed the locks.

"How the fuck is he going to change the locks on me when I left him? Motherfucker," she screamed, as she balled up her fists and started banging on the door. "Open this door, Sam. Open the fucking door."

Maybe Yaz thought it wasn't really over or maybe she just didn't want to believe it. Maybe she wanted to move back home. I didn't know. I never asked her. But the tears that ran down her cheeks explained it all. The kids just looked confused.

Finally, we heard the locks turning. Sam opened the door with his robe on and said, "What do you want?"

"My clothes," Yaz yelled.

"You don't have anything here."

"What?" Yaz said as she pushed past him with me and the kids following.

She ran straight into the bedroom, and of course I followed.

Sam tried to stop her.

All I heard was, "I don't believe this shit! I don't believe this shit!"

After I sat the kids down, I ran in the room behind her.

I couldn't believe what I saw, either. Sonya was naked in my girl Yaz's bed and so was her friend, the one who was on the subway with her. They were sitting there like we had interrupted something. Sam didn't say anything.

Yaz smacked the shit out of him and just started grabbing her clothes out of the closet. She pushed whatever was in her way on the floor. The CD player crashed with a loud bam!

I thought Sam was about to hit her but instead he grabbed Yaz and pushed her against the wall. Meanwhile, Sonya and her friend were fumbling around trying to find their clothes.

"Yazmine, do you think I want these dyke-ass, freak-ass bitches? You think I don't miss you and my kids? I do miss y'all. I love you, Yaz. Why you got to be jumping to conclusions like that? You left me."

"I was going to give you another chance, but you already locked me out," Yaz said as she struggled to break free of his grip. Then she stopped, realizing she wasn't as strong as him. She and Sam stood there staring at each other as if no one else was in the room until he finally eased up on his grip and let her go. I walked back into the living room as the freaks got dressed in the bathroom. Then Yaz started up again.

"How you going to be having a ménage à trois shit in our bed? Huh? How you going to do that? No, Sam, I can't forgive you."

"Yaz, I'm sorry. I was going crazy without you. Fuck all this. I want to be with you. I want to be with you and my kids again."

"No, I'm sorry, Sam. It's over. Enjoy your freak rendezvous."

We walked out of the building with Sam following, still in his robe. There was nothing he could say. I felt sorry for my friend and even for Sam. But most of all, I felt sorry for Sam Jr. He was waving and saying, "Bye, daddy," as we rode off.

"Are you all right, girl? You want to go home?"

"I'm cool. No, we can still go see your mother." Yaz stared straight ahead, not bothering to brush away the tears still rolling down her face.

I just drove. Nothing I could say would make her feel better. Nothing at all.

When we arrived at my mother's house, Leslie was in the living room. Her face lit up when she saw Yaz and her kids. My mom loved the kids. Nikki ran downstairs.

"Hi, Sam Jr. Hey, Mia. What's up, Yaz?"

"Hi, Nikki," Yaz said.

"Can you come here for a minute?" Nikki asked me.

I walked her in the kitchen to see what she wanted.

"What's up?"

"When are we going to the doctor's office?"

"What's today?"

"Today's November 5."

"Our appointment is tomorrow. I'll pick you up."

I walked back over to my mother and said "Leslie, go outside and look at my car."

"You bought a car," Leslie said as she jumped up and walked outside. I was right behind her.

"This is nice, Kayla. How much did you pay for this?"

"Thirty-three hundred. He wanted $3,800, but I talked him down."

"That wasn't bad. Where did you get the rest of the money?"

"I saved it," I lied.

"I'm proud of you, Kayla. You bought yourself a car. How does it ride?"

"Pretty good."

After walking all around the car and even sitting inside it, we went back into the house. Yaz was on the phone in the kitchen. When she saw me, she got a guilty look on her face.

"Who you talking to?" I asked suspiciously.

"Nobody."

Nobody—which really meant somebody, and that somebody was probably Sam.

"I know you're not talking on the phone with that sorry-ass Sam. I don't believe you. You're better than that, Yaz."

Yaz hung up the phone, wiping away tears. "Kay, can you take me to your house to get my stuff, then to my mother's house? I'll give you gas money."

"If that's what you want," I said, not bothering to hide the disgust in my voice. "Mom, we leaving. I'll see you tomorrow, Nikki."

At the apartment, Yaz was heated. She just grabbed all of the kids' and her stuff and packed them into a big green trash bag, forgetting about her luggage.

"You ready?" she asked.

"I know what you're doing. You're going back to Sam. You are such a nut," I yelled at her

"I'm not no nut," she hollered back.

"Well, that's what you're acting like! Go back to Sam. You can go backward, but I'm not going to help you."

Yaz began yelling and throwing her arms all up in the air. "Fine, Kayla. I'll catch a cab! You can't judge my situation. You're not in it. My kids need their father and I need my man. We are a family. Don't you understand?"

"You are weak, Yazmine. Weak!" I screamed at my best friend. "He is sitting there disrespecting you to your face. You always get on me about my relationship, and now you're going to turn around and let him get away with this. I'll take you to your mom's house, but I got to tell you, you're playing yourself. He had two women in your bed and you're going back to him?"

Yaz just stood there. I couldn't get through to her, so I just took her home. Whatever she did next was on her.

The next day, I woke up with a pain in my stomach. It had been hurting off and on for a while and my period hadn't come on yet. It was a week late, so I figured I probably had cramps.

Plus, I was still upset about Yazmine going back to Sam. But if she wanted to be a dumb bitch, I knew I could not stop her.

Besides, my stomach was killing me. I was glad I had an appointment at Planned Parenthood that day. I had called out from work, and my classes were canceled due to a meeting or something. I thought I'd hang out with Nikki after we got back.

When Nikki and I walked into the Planned Parenthood office, I noticed it had the same beige wallpaper on the wall that had been there when Leslie first brought me there when I was like sixteen, trying to get me on birth control. We sat down and Nikki started thumbing through the *Philadelphia Weekly*. It wasn't long before her name was called.

As I waited, I continued filling out a form requesting information that had no business being in your doctor's file. For instance, the form asked how many sexual partners you had had; how old you were when you first had sex, and how old were you when your period first came on. I always lied. Nobody needs to know my business, OK?

"Kayla Johnson," I heard a woman's voice say.

I stood up, grabbed my bag, and followed the counselor to the examining room. She instructed me to take all of my clothes off so I could get a full exam.

Yuck. I hated full exams. It's bad enough they stick that speculum in you. Then they want to press and feel on your breasts. Oh, and don't let it be a lady GYN, because you will feel funny and think she is a dyke. If it's a male doctor, you'll think he is a pervert.

I sat on the examining table and read the pamphlets on safe sex, sexually transmitted diseases, and contraceptives. I found myself wondering why sex was so dangerous. Why couldn't it be like the fifties or sixties, when none of this hot shit was around? Why can't the men be more like the guys back then? They had respect for you and asked you out on a date like a week in advance. They rang the bell and met your parents.

Not now. Guys beeped the horn outside your door and you only have one parent 'cause your parents are divorced, dead, deadbeat, or incarcerated. Guys take you nowhere but to their house, then ask you "What's up?" They got kids two months apart by different baby moms. Men today make me sick with that shit. My thoughts were interrupted by a knock at the door.

"Is it all right to come in?"

I answered "Yes," and Dr. Green came in.

"I haven't seen you in a while, Kayla. How have you been doing?"

"I'm fine."

"What seems to be the problem?"

"No problem. Just here for my annual visit, plus I had to bring my sister."

But what I really wanted to say was, "Why is my stomach hurting?" and "What's up with this pain when I pee?"

Now, I knew I didn't have anything to worry about. Wil was seeing only me, and I knew I wasn't pregnant. I was just jumping to conclusions. So I decided not to even mention my symptoms to Dr. Green.

But what if I was wrong and I was pregnant? Oh my God. What would I do? Leslie would kill me, and what would Wil say? I knew he loved me, but we weren't ready for a baby. Then I decided that I was being silly.

I decided to go ahead and tell Dr. Green what had been happening. That way, maybe he could find out what was going on with me.

"Dr. Green, I have been feeling real sick lately,"

"What kind of symptoms have you been having?"

"Well, I feel like I've got to throw up, I have pain when I urinate, and my period is late."

"I'll take a look and see what's going on and I'll give you a pregnancy test," Dr. Green said as he pulled on plastic gloves and pulled out the speculum. "Relax, relax," he said.

I'm thinking, *how can I relax when it feels like twenty inches of raw steel is being forced inside of me?*

"Lay your legs back," he said. Then he bent down, grabbed a cotton swab, and started scraping a little. "I'll be right back," he said, leaving the room.

Within a few moments, he was back with a little plastic cup. He instructed me to pee in it and place it on the counter when I was finished. I took the test and placed in on the counter when I was done.

He came back in the room, pulled up a chair next to me and said, "Well, Kayla, you're not pregnant. You have a yeast infection, which is nothing to really worry about. As far as your being nauseous, I would say you're probably coming down with the flu. That's going around. Nothing to worry about."

Thank God, I thought. I don't know what I would have done if I was pregnant. Maybe this was a sign for me to start protecting myself again, because I had been getting sloppy.

I got dressed and walked back out to the waiting room. Nikki was already there with a brown paper bag in her hand.

Dr. Green gave me a prescription. Nikki asked what it was for. I told her and was surprised to find out she didn't know what a yeast infection was. I explained exactly what it was and told her if she had any questions in the future to let me know. I really didn't know how uninformed she was about her body. I opened the car door, got in, and reached over and let Nikki in.

"You want to go get something to eat or go to the Gallery and get a shirt or something?" I asked as I started the engine. Nikki kept her eyes lowered as she spoke, but I could still see the sadness on her face.

"I'm not really hungry, but I wouldn't mind getting a shirt. Mommy don't buy me what I want without a speech about other nationalities not spending all their money and how black people are the only ones who waste their money on designer everything, while everybody else saves. She says that's why they have businesses and we have nothing, because all we do is spend money."

"Nikki, I know how Leslie is. Stop letting her go shopping with you and find a little job. I'll help you out, as long as you come to me when you have a problem. You don't have to be scared to talk to me. I won't criticize you. I meant to ask you about your abortion. Did you want to do it or did Leslie make you?"

"Mommy made me. I know I wasn't ready for a baby, but I could have given it up for adoption or something. I was scared. I think about that baby sometime, like what would it look like? Did I do the right thing? I could have told Mommy no, but she probably would have disowned me. I hope I don't go to hell."

I didn't know what to say.

"Uhm uhm, uh, Nikki, you did what was best for you at the time. You're only seventeen. You couldn't offer a child a good life right now. God will forgive you. Just pray and make sure it never happens again. I know we just came from getting your pills, but you know you don't have to have sex. Sex is not all that, trust me. It will always be there."

She promised me she would make better decisions in the future and I told her not to promise me, promise herself. We were one block away from the mall when I decided to take a yellow light. That's when five-0, I mean two of Philly's finest, flashed their lights behind me. Why were they pulling me over? A team of two women cops—one black, the other white—came up to the car, one on each side. I rolled down my window.

"Yes, what did I do?"

"You just ran a red light," the white cop said. "May I see your license and registration?"

"What? The light may have been red when you reached it, but it was yellow when I went through it."

"License and registration, please," she said again. After I pulled out my license, the black lady cop walked back to the car and called my tags in.

"I need your insurance card," the other one said.

"Uhm, I don't have my insurance card on me."

I knew I should have listened to Leslie when she told me to get insurance, but I wasn't about to pay $4,000 a year for a car that was only worth $3,000. The cops had us sitting there drawn as hell.

I was beginning to get mad and a crowd was forming. Everybody was laughing and making jokes. This one guy said, "Damn, sis, what they get you for?" He was not funny. The red and blue lights were still flashing. I became more and more impatient and the red and blue lights flashing were glowing brighter, because it was becoming dark.

"How long is this going to take?" I demanded.

"As long as it takes to write this ticket," the white cop said.

"What am I'm getting a ticket for?"

"One, you ran a red light. Two, you don't have any insurance."

I couldn't say anything. I was busted. A few minutes later, the cop handed me the tickets and told me to have a nice day. The whole scenario took about an hour.

I was not in the mood for shopping anymore. All I wanted to do was go home and rest. I dropped Nikki off and ran through some more yellow lights. When I got home, I was surprised to see Wil had placed lighted candles everywhere.

"Oh, Boo," I said, kissing him. "How did you know?"

"Nikki called here to see if you were OK and told me everything. I even cooked."

"No, you didn't."

"You right, I didn't. But I got some shrimp fried rice in the kitchen for you and your bubble bath is running. When you get out, I'm going to give you a full body massage."

My boo knew exactly what I needed. He apologized for not being able to spend a lot of time with me. He said it was partially because he hadn't felt comfortable around Yazmine and her kids. They made him feel like an intruder.

I told him I understood and thanked him for being so sweet. I got undressed and just soaked in my favorite Victoria Secret pear glacé bubble bath as the Isley Brothers greatest hits played on the stereo. Wil came in behind me and knelt on the bathroom floor and massaged my feet. That's when he started saying we needed to move.

"This is a cute apartment, but we need more room," he complained.

I told him I had to think about it and talk it over with my mom. This was kind of fast, even for me.

"Well, I just suggested it so we didn't have to semi-live together. I wouldn't stay some nights and not others. I would be with you every night. Think it over and call your mom and ask her what she thinks."

Wil was saying everything I wanted to hear. But I didn't know how Leslie would react to me officially living with a man.

"What do you think my mom is going to say when I call her and say, 'Hi, mom, I met a man in August and now I want to get an apartment with him after three months of knowing him. He's really nice and cute. Mom, what do you think?' I think my mom would say 'Girl, why would a man buy the cow when he can get the milk for free?' But if you really want to meet my mom and family, come to Thanksgiving at my grandmom's house."

"I'll be there," he promised.

Chapter 10

Wil didn't show up for Thanksgiving dinner. I was so embarrassed. I'd told all my family he was coming.

All night, everybody kept asking me where he was: "I thought your boyfriend was coming, Kayla." "What time is your man coming?"

I beeped him like three times and he didn't call me back. I decided to page him one more time. If he didn't call me back this time, fuck him.

My Aunt Lydia came in the room, rubbing it in. "So where's your friend?"

"I don't know. He said he might stop past. He had to stop at his family's house first. Then he has to pick up his cousin."

I was going crazy. It was eight. He supposed to have been here at six. The only thing that relaxed me a little was seeing Leslie so happy with Mr. Charlie. He was a nice man. I hoped everything would work out between them. Then my mind drifted from Leslie back to Wil. I called Yaz and told her Wil hadn't shown up yet.

"He'll be there. Don't worry."

"I hope so."

"When he gets there, call me, so you and him can stop past my mom's house. Everybody is here. All my sisters and even Little Man is home from the army this Thanksgiving."

"If he don't come, I'll still be there," I said, then hung up.

Even though I was upset about Wil, it didn't hurt my appetite. I tried to wait for him. But eventually, my resistance wore down. I piled macaroni and cheese, turkey, chicken, string beans, stuffing, and mashed potatoes all up on my plate and was digging in when I heard the doorbell ringing. Dropping my fork, I ran out of the kitchen to answer it. It was Karim.

"Hi, Kayla, where's Nikki?"

"She's in the kitchen with Grandmom Ronnie."

"Can you make me a plate?"

"No! What do I look like? Your girl?" I said, irritated, as I rolled my eyes.

"What's up with the attitude?" he asked.

I ignored him as Nikki walked in, saying, "Don't worry about her. She just mad 'cause her little Thanksgiving date stood her up."

"Nikki, shut up 'cause you don't know what you're talking about."

"Look, Kayla, we already ate dinner. He ain't coming," she teased.

My little sister's boyfriend had shown up and my man hadn't. I couldn't believe it. Wil was making me so mad. I had walked back into the kitchen when I heard a knock at the door.

Uncle Bubbie yelled, "Kay-Kay, it's a guy at the door for you."

This time, I didn't get excited. I just walked to the door and there stood my man. I was so glad he made it, but all I could say was, "You're late. Where have you been?"

"I had to go get Stevie 'cause he wanted to hold the truck." He pointed behind him to Stevie, who was waiting in the Expedition.

"So why is Stevie still waiting? Are you coming in or what?"

Looking back at Stevie in the truck, Wil said "Yo, man, I'll beep you when I'm ready."

As Stevie drove away, I wondered what girl he was spending Thanksgiving with. Wil walked in the room and my whole family looked up. I introduced him to my Grandmom Ronnie first.

"Hi, baby," she said.

Then to my mom I whispered, "This is a good one." My mom just smiled as we all gathered in the living room.

My sister Nikki said "How you doin'?" Wil shook hands with Charlie, Uncle Bubbie, and Karim. Then I introduced him to Aunt Lydia.

"How you doing, baby? Nice of you to join us," she said as she looked down at her watch.

I ignored that. "You ready to eat?" I asked my man.

"What you got?"

"Everything. Mashed potatoes, candy yams, collard greens, turkey, chicken, string beans, duck, potato salad, stuffing, cabbage, and sweet potato pie."

"Then give me a little of everything."

Happily, I fixed his plate. I was so glad he'd finally made it that I didn't even get mad when he ignored me as he sat watching the football game with Uncle Bubbie, Mr. Charlie, and Karim. The Eagles were playing Dallas. The score was 14 to 0. Duce Staley had the ball and was about to make a touchdown. Everyone was screaming "Go, go, go!" Then he crossed the goal line.

"Yesss!" Uncle Bubbie screamed. "Eagles all the way," he said as he slapped high five with Karim and Charlie. The Eagles won, 14-7.

After a while, I noticed the game was over and Wil was sitting on the carpet doing nothing. So I decided to go ahead and ask Wil if he felt like going to Yaz's mom's house.

"I'm not driving," he responded.

"We can take my car."

"All right, come on," Wil said as he stood up.

"Leslie, we going to Yaz mom's house. See you," I said as I went around the room kissing everyone good-bye. Then I put my coat on. "I'll call you, Nikki. Bye, Uncle Bubbie. Bye, Grandmom. See ya, Charlie."

"Did you forget anyone?" Wil asked.

Yes. I had. My Aunt Lydia. She is such a bitch. She real crazy because she needs a man real bad. She's nosy and she's been married like four times. She is the exact opposite of mom. You would never believe they're twins, I told Wil as we walked out to my car.

"What, they fraternal?"

"Yeah."

"I thought it was something wrong with her when I saw her look down at her watch."

"Yeah, she be trippin'," I said.

"Hurry up and open the door 'cause I'm cold," Wil said. "Where's Yazmine's mom live anyway?"

"In Germantown."

"You taking the expressway?"

"Yeah."

Yaz's Thanksgiving was totally different from mine at Grandmom Ronnie's house. Her family was five times as big as ours, for one thing. There were her sisters, Rashidah, Carrey, Katrina, and the twins Najah and Nadirah, and her brother, Lil' Man Lamar, and all their kids.

And then she had her mom and dad, all her cousins—about fifteen in all—and everybody's baby mom and dad. And don't let me forget her grandfather and grandmother.

Mia and Sam Jr. were running around with their cousins, having a good time.

Yaz and her older sister Katrina were just now setting the tables for dinner. The kid's table was dressed with plastic everything, while the adult table was set with real china and sterling silver. Two huge golden brown turkeys served as centerpieces. I introduced Wil to everybody.

He already knew Carrey. I wasn't surprised. She gets around. Wil said Stevie used to talk to her.

Yaz grabbed me away from Wil. "He showed up, huh?"

I just nodded yeah. Wil shook Sam's hand and once again the men migrated to the living room while the women went back and forth putting the final touches on the food. *Soul Food* was playing on Showtime. When Yaz noticed, she was like, "How corny is my family to watch *Soul Food* on Thanksgiving? We are the *Soul Food* family."

"Well, we all know who would play the whore cousin," Lil' Man said.

Everybody looked at Carrey and started laughing.

"Fuck you, Lil' Man," she snapped at him.

"No, see, that's the problem exactly—your fucking," Little Man laughed.

Then Yaz's mother, Mrs. Yvette, said, "Both of y'all shut the fuck up. Can't you see we got company? And respect my mother-fucking grandkids."

Their family was so crazy. They were so tight, I loved it. Sometimes

I wished they were my family, all those brothers and sisters, and they had lived with their dad all their life. Mrs. Yvette was the captain and her kids were her soldiers. When it came to them, she didn't play.

And she was about getting money. She made sure all her daughters only dealt with men with money. She even had Carrey's men paying some of her bills. She was the kind of mom who would fight right alongside of her daughters. She would beat your ass and roll up some weed, and still had class.

Their father, Mr. Tony, was a hustler back in the day. They say he had North Philly on lock. That's why Mrs. Yvette married him. Now he had an honest gig as a supervisor for the Philadelphia Sanitation Department.

The only thing Mrs. Yvette hadn't taught her kids was how to use birth control, because there she was only forty-three and had twelve grandkids.

Yes, Yaz's family was crazy, but I loved it. Me and Wil enjoyed ourselves that night.

The next day, I beeped Wil. When he didn't call me back, I beeped him again. I wanted to tell him how much my family had liked him. The phone started ringing, but it turned out to be Yaz.

"I thought you were Wil. I just beeped him."

"No, sorry, it's just me. I know you don't like Sam no more, but he asked me to marry him."

"Are you serious?"

"Yes. He wants to do it as soon as possible. He said he's going to change and turn his life over to Allah. He's not going to sell drugs no more and he's going to get a job. He said when we left, he cried like a baby and got on his knees and prayed I would come back to him. He said this Muslim brother at the barbershop told him to leave it in Allah's hands and He would help him in his transformation."

"I don't know if I believe that," I said suspiciously. "He might be telling the truth, but there's only one way to find out. Hold on. I've got a call on the other line."

"Hello, yes, did someone call a beeper?" a woman's voice asked.

"Yes, I did, but I beeped my boyfriend. I must have dialed the wrong number, sorry."

I clicked back over and asked Yaz to beep Wil on the three-way. "Who was that?" she said.

"Some lady with the wrong number."

"Oh."

The line clicked again. I told Yaz to hold on. It was the same lady again.

"What number are you trying to dial?" she asked.

I repeated Wil's number to her then she said, "Yes, you have the right number. This is Wil's beeper. Can I help you?"

"Where's Wil?"

"Who is this?" she asked.

"This is his girlfriend. Who are you?" I snapped back.

"Girlfriend huh? Well, I'm his wife."

"Wife! No, no, there's been a mistake," I said in disbelief. "My Wil is not married!"

"My Wil is very married."

"Wil never said anything about being married."

"Probably because we have been separated for the last three months, but we're back together and that means you have no reason to call him," she said arrogantly.

"What do you mean, I don't have no reason to call him? That's my man. We are in a relationship." I was yelling into the phone by now.

"Honey, he told me about you. What you, like twenty, twenty-one? You are a little girl. I'm twenty-six. Wil likes young girls, but you mean nothing to him. He was on the rebound when he started fucking with you. Like I said, he don't need you no more, because he got me and his daughter again."

"Daughter? He got a daughter?" My mind flashed back to the picture in his parents' living room with the woman and the pretty little girl who looked just like him.

"I don't know what kind of relationship you have with Wil, but I'll tell you one thing, he's not your man. What, you knew him two or three months? Wil is a trick-a-ho. He gets what he wants, then steps. Wil don't care about nobody but himself. What? He gave you a couple of dollars? He give all his girls loot—or did he promise you a house or apartment? All he want you to do is get it in your name, like he do with everything. He got bad credit. He can't get shit in his name. That truck he drive is in my name."

When she said apartment, my heart hit the ground. He just was talking about us getting a place together. She continued telling me how Wil was spoiled and how money meant very little to him. His family had money, she said, and if he never had to work again, he wouldn't. And if I had been over at his parents' house, it was only because his parents didn't like her and weren't shit, either. And all he do is hang around his slimy ho cousin, Stevie, trying to be like him, she said.

"Let me tell you, honey, because I know you're young," she continued. "You want to mess with my husband? Go right ahead, but you won't last very long. None of you do, 'cause I'm the one that got a house, a Benz in the driveway, and every designer hanging up in my closet. I get the money and when he dies, I get everything."

By now, I had heard enough. I clicked back over to Yaz.

"About time you decided to click back over. Who was that?" Yaz asked.

"Wil's wife."

"What! Hold up. What are you talking about? Kayla, stop playing."

"Yaz, he never told me he had a wife, and she said him and Stevie are ho's," I said, crying.

"Girl, here I come," Yaz said.

I couldn't even put the phone on the receiver, I was so upset. Over my sobs, I heard the faint voice of the operator saying, "If you'd like to make a call, please hang up and try again." Then it made that irritating dat-dat-dat noise.

Suddenly, I felt nauseated. All I could think about was his wife and what was going on. I couldn't move. All I could do was stare at my burgundy carpet. I stared so long, the diamond shapes started twinkling at me. I was in the bathroom throwing up when I heard the door open. It was Wil.

"What's wrong, baby? Why you crying?"

"No reason," I said.

"Kayla, you're crying and spitting up. What's going on? Are you pregnant?"

"No. Where's your beeper?"

"I left it home."

"With your wife?"

"Wife? What are you talking about? I don't have no wife." He was so surprised he actually jumped back from me.

"She didn't say that just now when she called me back. She said she was your wife."

"What? I am going to kill Carmen! Boo, let me explain," he said as he came closer.

"Why Wil? Why? Why did you have to lie? You didn't tell me you had a daughter. Carmen. That's the name your car is in, ain't it? You said she was your cousin. I hate you!" I screamed at him. "You're a fucking liar."

Standing up, I tried to fight him, but I couldn't. I was too weak from crying. All I could do was sink back to the floor and cry.

He bent down and held me as he said, "Boo, I didn't mean it. I didn't think you could handle it. I'm not married. I was married. I'm divorced now. I didn't get married for all the right reasons. That's why it didn't work out. I married her 'cause I got her pregnant and we had been together for a year or two. My family was against it but, I did it anyway. I didn't want to be a 'baby father.' I wanted to raise my child with the mother by my side. I was twenty-one when it happened. I was too young to be married and tied down. The marriage lasted until the beginning of last summer. Then I left. I just couldn't take it anymore. I didn't tell you about my daughter or any of this 'cause I didn't think you would understand. Come on, baby, you got to believe me."

Me being me, I believed every word he said. Then I thought about before this he was exactly what I was looking for in a man. How it had taken me so long to find him and how long it would be before I met somebody like him? Did it really have to come to an end now?

"How your beeper get there?" I asked, as I wiped the tears away from my face.

"When I went to visit my daughter yesterday, she was playing with it. She called it her 'beep beep' and her stupid mother must have found it and started calling numbers back."

Grabbing a washcloth and wetting it, he wiped my face. The doorbell rang. Wil got up and answered it.

It was Yaz. She brushed past him and came into the bathroom where I was still huddled on the floor.

"What are you doing on the floor? Fuck him!!!! He got a wife . A w-i-f-e," she spelled out to me.

"He's not married no more."

"Girl, don't be no fool. Look at your face. Your eyes are red and swollen from crying. Do you want a man that bad? A man that's going to lie to you?"

Next thing I knew, Yaz had stomped out of the bathroom into the living room with Wil. All I heard was cussing and the door slam shut. The next thing I knew, my Wil was all gone, out of my life. Yaz had kicked him out. It was OK, though, because I could never have dealt with him again.

"Get yourself together," Yaz said as she helped me off the floor. "Fuck him. Go get in the bed."

She made me some tea and ordered me to stop crying because I was going to make myself sick. I staggered into the bedroom. I was dizzy, my head was pounding, and my eyes were all puffy and red. I was embarrassed my friend had seen me like this but, on the other hand, I knew Yaz could relate. She had been there herself many times. But she was on the other side of the fence this time. Usually, she was the woman calling back the numbers off of Sam's beeper.

"You going to be OK?" she asked as I sipped on my tea.

"I'm going to be fine."

She stayed for a while, plumping the pillows under me and handing me tissues. Then she told me she had to go and pick up her kids.

"I'll call you later on, and don't talk to that pussy. Don't listen to shit he got to say," Yaz said as she walked toward the door.

"Thank you, girl, for coming."

"You're always there when I need you, so it's only right that I be there for you. Don't let that nigga get you down. It's too many out there for that."

"Yaz, is it ever going to end?"

"Is what going to end?"

"You know, the search? The meeting that special person?"

"Probably not. I don't even believe in meeting that special person anymore. I think you get with somebody that's half decent and work it out with them and try to mold them."

Then she was gone and, once again, I was alone. I turned the answering machine on and the ringer off. Then I shuffled through my CDs and put on some Phyllis Hyman. I could relate to every song she sang, like the one that started off, "It used to be a time when we were lovers and we shared this apartment together just us two . . ." Or the one that went "When I give my love this time I'm going to make it last forever . . ."

All of her songs were about a love lost or found or picking up and starting all over again. After that CD, I played Mary J. Bilge's *My Life*. But I should have taken the next CD out, 'cause I was miserable singing along with Faith's and Mary J's "Love Don't Live Here Anymore."

Every song I played that night reminded me of Wil. *Why must my heart be beat, abused, stomped on, mangled, strangled, and tortured?* I thought. *Why?* I didn't have any answers. I turned off the lights and sipped the rest of the tea Yaz had made for me. Then I went to sleep.

The next morning, I was still thinking about what happened. No matter what I tried, I couldn't get my mind off of him. I tried to say "Fuck it."

Then I went into the bathroom to get cleaned up and saw his toothbrush and remembered all his things were here. But I decided that I wasn't *Waiting to Exhale*. Instead of burning his clothes like in the movie, I packed them up to give to the Salvation Army.

Looking in the mirror, I could see I looked a mess. My eyes were still red. I put my sunglasses on so I wouldn't have to deal with annoying *What's wrongs* all day.

I went to school, but I was just there. I went to every class, but didn't hear a word any of my instructors spoke. Everything was a blur. Every guy I passed looked just like Wil.

When I arrived at my job, the ladies were all smiling. I didn't understand why until I noticed a big bouquet of flowers on my desk and a note saying, "I'm very sorry. No matter what, I will always love you. William Carter Jr."

I had always dreamed of getting flowers from a man, but not like this. I threw them in the trash. For once, the ladies in my office were quiet. I didn't have to say anything for them to figure out Wil and me had broken up. They didn't complain when I didn't do much work that day.

I felt like a zombie. I started just going through the motions. I went to work only because I had to. School wasn't paying the bills, so I didn't go.

When some people get depressed, they can't eat or sleep. I'm the total opposite. All I could do was sleep, then eat, then go back to sleep.

One day I checked my messages and saw Wil had called like thirty times. I wasn't returning his calls. I reasoned if he had really cared about me, he wouldn't have lied. I didn't ask him to date me. I was minding my damn business. Why'd he have to fuck with me?

It took about three weeks for me to come back to life. I had to really make myself go on. I was beginning to feel like somebody had died and I was mourning them. I could not stop crying, but then I reminded myself Wil was not crying over me. He was probably out somewhere having a good time. And here I was being depressed about that nigga.

But I couldn't help it. I thought I loved him. He was my best friend. How was I supposed to move on without him?

I looked awful and felt worst. I had gained about ten pounds. As soon as my head cleared, I made a hair and nail appointment. I figured that would cheer me up. I also turned my ringer on and started listening to my messages.

The last one was from my mom, who she said she was getting married. That was good news. I was so happy for her. I picked up the phone and called her right way. She answered on the first ring.

"Congratulations," I said.

"About time you called me back. Baby, I was beginning to worry. You've been busy, huh? Uhm, how's that young man you brought to Thanksgiving?"

"He's fine." I didn't have the heart to tell her we had broken up.

"I want you to bring him to the wedding. It's going to be in January."

"That soon? Mom, are you sure about this?"

"Yup, I sure am. I'll call you later with more details. Bye, baby."

My hair appointment was for ten. Hopefully it wasn't crowded and I would get out early.

But what was I thinking? It was a Saturday, and you know how that goes. At least I had my car. I could go grab something to eat as I waited.

As I thought about it, I realized my car had been the only good thing that had come out of my relationship with Wil. Then again, there was all the money, the clothes, and, of course, the love and attention. But none of it had been worth all the pain I was feeling now.

Michelle was in her usual spot as I walked into the salon. "What you getting done today, Kayla? Ooh, you got fat, girl. What you been doing?"

"I know. Shut up. I don't know what I want done with my hair. Why don't you cut it?" I said to Michelle.

"Girl, I'm not cutting it. Leave it alone. It's trying to grow."

"Just do it regular then. Next week, I'm getting a rinse."

"So you going to start getting your hair done every week again?"

"Yeah, I just been busy. Before I was just wrapping my hair around since it got longer."

"Busy with that man, huh?"

"Yup, but that's over."

"Why? What happened?"

Michelle was so nosy. But I still told her everything that had happened with me and Wil. Why is it when you sit in the hairdresser's chair you just lose all control of your mouth? It was like I was in confession, and I wasn't even Catholic.

But talking to her was therapeutic. Like Yaz, Michelle told me to just live my life and don't worry about him. Just live. Then she started asking about Yaz.

"Who be doing Yaz hair now? What's up with her?"

"Nothing. She chilling. Her cousin be doing her hair."

I knew what Michelle was trying to do and that was get info from me on Yaz and Sam, but that was not going to happen. If she wanted to find out Yazmine's business, she would have to hear it from Yaz's mouth. From then on, I just kept my mouth shut until my hair was completed.

After leaving the hair salon, I went to get my nails done and eyebrows arched down 52nd Street. Of course, it was an Asian spot. They were all ready to help me as soon as I walked in.

"You want nail done?" the small Asian man said with a slight accent.

"Yeah."

"Be right with you. We have special today. Full set and pedicure, $35."

"OK, I'll get that."

I took a seat and looked around. Then I picked up the latest issue of *Honey* and read it until it was time to get serviced.

"I'm ready for you," the man said.

I sat down in the pedicure chair and placed my feet in the warm, soapy water. At first it was hot, but it cooled down and I felt so relaxed. One person started on my fingernails while the other worked on my feet.

Then it happened. I closed my eyes, and the pedicure was beginning to remind me of how Wil used to rub my feet. He used to love and care for me.

What am I going to do without him? I asked myself as I felt tears swelling up in my eyes. I loved him. I thought he loved me.

Oh, I missed Wil so very bad. I was getting pampered on the outside, but on the inside, I still felt overworked and tired. After the technicians finished with me, I walked out of the nailery, got back in my car, and tried to get myself together. I started up the car and went to get something to eat.

Then I saw him, Wil and a girl riding past. I couldn't imagine in a million years I would run into him. At the next light, I made a fast U-turn and followed him. He saw me, so he started driving faster at the yellow light. It was red by the time I reached it, but I still went through it and caught up with him at the next light. I pulled right up beside the car and looked over, and that's when I realized it wasn't him.

I felt like an asshole. I tried to play it off. After the fake Wil sighting, that truck kept going and I was at a red light when this guy started beeping his horn at me to get my attention. I rolled my window down to see what he wanted. When he said "What's up, baby girl? Can I go with you?"

"I'm going to get something to eat," I replied.

"Where at?" he asked.

"Uhm, down 41st Street, to Sea Heaven."

"I'm following you, baby girl."

Usually I wouldn't let anyone I didn't know follow me. *What the hell,* I thought. He looked safe. He looked normal. Why eat alone? Anyway, he followed me into the parking lot of the Sea Heaven on 41st Street. By the time I had parked, he was already at my door, waiting for me to get out. I could see he was handsome. He had this D'Angelo, Allen Iverson braid thing going on, with a glistening diamond medallion chain, blue jeans, tan Timberlands, and a black Avirex jacket. He looked kind of young, like twenty-one, twenty-two. I usually like men a little older, but what the hell, I figured.

"So what's your name, baby girl?" he asked.

"Kayla," I said, as we walked across the parking lot.

"They call me T.R.," he said, opening the restaurant door.

We walked in and I asked, "Do you want to just have a seat at the bar?"

"Yeah."

"What does T.R. stand for?" I asked as I sat down.

"Why you want to know? What you, the police?"

"No, I just asked." Dag. What was his problem? Was he America's most wanted or something?

"Nah, it stand for Terrell Raymond. I got tired of kids' saying I had two first names, so I became T to the motherfucking R. You dig, baby girl? So where your man at?"

"We broke up." I started feeling sad again, but I refused to let my eyes water up.

"Uhm, that's messed up. See, that's how me and my baby mom is. She be trippin'. See, me and her used to go together, but she want to be around me all the time. I ain't got no time for that 'cause I'm about this money, baby girl, ya heard?"

"How many kids do you have?"

"I got two sons. How many you got?"

"None."

"That's what's up. What, you work or something?"

"Yeah."

"You smoke weed?"

"No."

"Yeah, I'm trying to stop. So where you live at?"

"Seventeenth and Wallace."

"Really? My daughter's mom lived around that way."

"Oh, you got a daughter, too! I thought you had sons."

"Nah, I got two sons and a daughter, but my daughter mom don't let me see her 'cause when I went to jail she was cheating on me with my boy. So I left her alone. That's how I got with my second baby mom. So she be hatin' on me now. You dig, baby girl?"

"Uhm," I said. *A loser.*

The boah's baby mama drama stories were getting worser and worser and I had just about had it with the *baby girls.* From what I could see, T.R. was like a fake gangster. He didn't seem like a real thug, just a wannabe. You would have thought I was sitting at the bar with Mobb Deep, Capone, or Noriega the way he was reciting their rhymes. Acting like he wrote them: "Nigga, this nigga, that nigga, I got a gat." At least they shit was real. This boah was majorly fake.

At that point, I was like ready to end our little lunch before it even began. I wanted to go home and analyze why I kept running into all the fucking crazy bastards. Was I ever going to get it right? I didn't think so. It seemed like I was the loco magnet.

So I told him I wasn't really that hungry and that I had somewhere to go. I took his number and gave him Yaz's old number, instead of giving him mine. He had enough drama going on without adding me.

After the episode with T. R., I decided to go home and go to sleep, even though it was a beautiful day for December. Usually after I get my hair done, I would sleep like a princess so I wouldn't mess my hair up, but this time I laid right on it and didn't care.

But I couldn't get to sleep. I just laid there looking at the ceiling and listening to Sade. That girl has a pretty voice. Selection number 14 on her CD was the best—"Send Me Someone to Love Me." I think it was a remake. I don't know, but that song was talking about me.

I looked at the phone trying to figure who could I call. Samir came to mind. He should be home, since he said he comes every weekend. I dialed his number.

"Yo," he said as he answered the phone.

I could hear Wu Tang playing loudly in the back.

"Hello, may I speak to Samir?"

"Who dis?"

"This is Kayla."

I heard the music go down and his voice softened.

"How you doing?" he said, sounding surprised and happy all at once.

"I'm fine."

"What's up?"

"Nuttin. I just thought I'd call you."

"Oh, you were thinking about me. That's so sweet."

I wanted to say not really. Instead, I asked him what he was doing. He told me he was making beats.

"You rap?"

"Kinda."

By then, I was thinking, *Oh no, not another nigga that think they can rap, talking about they getting a record deal.* Then he asked if I wanted to go out. I contemplated for a minute or two, then said, "Why not?" It was a Saturday, I had had my hair and nails done, and I wasn't accomplishing anything by staying in the house.

"Yeah, I'll go. Where you trying to go?"

"You driving?"

"Yeah, meet me at Friday's on the Parkway."

"Give me twenty minutes."

I parked the car and walked in the restaurant and sat at the bar. Samir arrived a few minutes later. He looked good, but not as good as my Wil. The first thing he said was, "Your hair looks nice. Is it a weave?"

"No." I never thought the day would come that a guy would ask you with a straight face if your hair was a weave or not. He must have read my mind, because then he apologized.

"It's just that it look so nice. Did you order yet?"

"No. I think I'll have some chicken fingers and a strawberry daiquiri, though."

The boah had only been there for five minutes and already he was getting on my nerves. Then he started talking about how he was trying to get into the rap game and how he was down with all these New York guys. I was like, "Please."

"You like the Wu Tang Clan?"

"Yeah. I like rap but I'm into soul, soothing music like R. Kelly and Mary J. Blige," I said, as I tried to yawn.

"So, basically, you like just chilling music."

"Yeah."

When the waitress came by again to tell us our food would be ready soon, I ordered another daiquiri. The conversation was OK, but I was through with him after he told me he had only brought $30 out of the house, so don't get embarrassed by ordering a lot unless I wanted to be doing dishes. *What, you little nut,* I thought. He had looked all right when he first came in with his all black on, but he was becoming uglier by the minute.

I excused myself from the table, telling him I had to go to the bathroom. I really went to call Yazmine to tell her about the date from hell. I told her to start blowing my beeper up. That meant that she should beep me and keep beeping me to give me a reason to leave. I had just sat back down when the beeper went off. I acted like I was ignoring it, then I looked down and said, "Samir, this is my mom, she keep beeping me 911. I got to go. I'll call you later."

As I walked out of the restaurant, I felt like I was getting released from prison. I hoped he never called again, but I knew I probably wouldn't be that fortunate.

I went home, got in the bed and read the latest issue of *Essence.* I didn't bother calling Yaz again. She was preparing for her wedding, which was going to be an Islamic ceremony. Did I mention she was converting to Islam, too? I couldn't disagree with any religion that encouraged marriage, family, unity, modesty, and spirituality. Maybe Sam really was going to change, or already had.

That all led me to start thinking about Wil again. I missed him and wanted to call him so bad, but I couldn't. I picked up the phone, then hung it back up. I dialed half of his number, then put the phone down again. I was starting to feel like a fiend in a withdrawal state. But instead of my drug being a narcotic, my drug of choice was Wil. By now, I had finished with *Essence,* so I picked up *Sista 2 Sista.*

Now that I was coming out of my depression, I had discovered I couldn't sleep. At night, I would lie in bed for hours thinking about Wil and how I wished I could feel his warmth and his arms around me again. The uncertainty was killing me. I mean, was it really over?

I must have dozed off because when I woke up, Wil was on top of me, kissing all over me.

"How did you get in here?" I yelled while trying to push him away.

"Shhh, shh. Don't worry about that," he said. "Boo, I missed you. I love you, and I will never hurt you again."

He placed a metal object in my hand. I opened my hand and inside was a diamond baguette and cluster ring. It was at least two carats with the highest clarity, at least as far as I could see.

"Wil, what is this for?" I asked.

"You are my friend and I never want to lose you. It's a friendship ring for right now, but when I regain your trust, I'm going to get you a better one."

I went to put it on my right ring finger, but Wil told me to wear it on my left hand. He kissed me and carried me into the bathroom, where he undressed me and then himself. He turned on the shower and put me in. The hot water pounded against my skin. The bathroom was all hot and steamy. My hair was getting all messed up, but I didn't care. Wil washed my back. I felt the soap lathering up, then his hands between my legs, his fingers tickling my body and the bubbles caressing my breast. His body slipped inside of mine, pushing in and out, in and out. I felt what I was missing for the last three weeks.

"Baby, I've missed you so much. I never want us to be apart again," I said as I passionately kissed him on the neck.

Then, I woke up and looked down at my hand. There was no diamond, just the *Sista 2 Sista* magazine I had been reading through. I must have fallen asleep after all.

My dream made me realize how much I really did miss him. I decided I had to call him, because I was tripping so bad. I decided to beep him. He called me right back.

"Kayla, what's up, baby? I miss you."

"Nothing," I said.

"What are you doing?"

"Thinking."

"It's cold out here. I'm on a pay phone. Can I come think with you?"

"Yeah, you can come."

I know I should have told him no, but I couldn't make myself do it. I missed him. I hadn't seen my Boo in a while, so I went in the bathroom to freshen up. Then I put on a black sheer nightgown and waited by the door. The bell rang and I opened the door.

Wil walked in and hugged me, but I couldn't get too happy. The only thing I could think of was that I was giving in too easily. But on the other hand, maybe he had been telling the truth. Maybe he was about to get a divorce from her. He didn't have enough time to cheat, because he was always with me. Besides, if I let him go, she would win.

"I know I messed up, but I'm going to make it up to you, all right, Boo?"

We just laid on the sofa and held each other so close. It felt so good and so right to be with him again. After that night, I decided even though he had did me dirty, I didn't want to live without him.

Days passed, and it was like a honeymoon. It was as if nothing bad had ever happened between us, like we had never parted. We never talked about what had happened, but every day, Wil brought me home a gift—candy, a watch, a gold bracelet, even a ring. Not a two-carat diamond, but a one-carat cluster. Everything was going great until the day I got a reality check from Yazmine. I knew I was going to hear it. She called and Wil answered the phone.

"What's he doing there?" she said like she was my mom.

I caught an instant attitude. "Look, you got your own problems to worry about."

"What?"

"You heard me. Worry about Yazmine Harrison soon to be Mrs. Samuel ménage à trois Gerry. I got this. I'm handling 1752 Wallace Street, all right?"

"Kayla, I can't believe you would go there. He'll do it again. You're playing yourself."

"Yaz, I know you're not talking," I said as I slammed down the phone on her.

I didn't care. She needed to mind her own business. I knew I had a lot of nerve being mad at Yaz for going back to Sam. Look at me.

But I was happy again. I had my man back. I didn't care about Yaz or Carmen, Wil's so-called wife, right now. The only person I was looking out for was Kayla Simone Johnson. As long as she was happy, it was cool.

But was she really happy? Wasn't she scared? Didn't she think Wil might leave her again?

Every time he left, I worried that might be the night he chose not to return, or that he might be going to meet someone else. I didn't trust him anymore. A Gucci watch, a diamond tennis bracelet, and a diamond ring could not replace the trust that had been broken.

Chapter 11

Wil wanted to bring his daughter Ashley over to my apartment. I couldn't say no. At least this way, I would know where he was.

Ashley was a little kindergarten doll baby. She looked just like Wil, except she had sandy brown hair and eyes to match. She must have got that from her mother. And she was sweet as hell—yet I still despised her.

She represented lies and secrets to me. Sometimes when she came over, I just sat and stared at her. Wil caught me doing it one morning during breakfast.

"What we doing for New Year's?" he said, breaking the silence.

"I don't know. It doesn't matter to me."

"I was thinking about going to the Poconos with Stevie and his girl."

"What girl?"

"Oh, he got this Jamaican johne' he really likes. Her name is Angie. She got two-year-old twins. He's been asking about you, too."

"I thought he didn't like girls with kids."

"He doesn't usually. I think this girl got him sprung."

"I'll go. I never been skiing before. When we leaving?"

"Probably New Year's Eve."

Wil saw right through me that day. I was not worrying about a trip. I was staring at Ashley and thinking about us.

So, being Wil, money solves everything. He plopped a stack of twenties in front of me and told me to take myself and Ashley shopping.

Well, I love shopping and I always will, so I jumped at the chance. Even though I hated to say it, I hated Ashley.

Well, I didn't hate her—you can't hate a child, especially if the child is as well-mannered, sweet, and loving as this one. The entire day at the mall, she kept hugging me and kissing me and saying, "Thank you for taking me shopping, Ms. Kayla." She was only five and knew so much.

Then she told me, "My daddy left Mommy for you. He said she real fat and a whore. My mom was sad, but now she's better."

At that moment, I didn't know if I wanted to laugh or cry. I wanted to cry, because a child should not have to go through this shit. I wanted to laugh because at least my presence was known.

I spent the majority of the money Wil gave me on Ashley. I bought her this pretty pink-flowered jean jumper, sneakers, and bows out of Gap Kids. Then I took her to Toys "R" Us and let her pick out whatever she wanted. She got Barbies, a Ken doll, and a dollhouse. I felt like I was giving her an early Christmas.

As we walked out of the mall, I saw a picture stand, so I got me and Ashley's picture taken together for her dad's key chain. Then we loaded all the stuff into the car and went back to my apartment.

Wil wasn't home yet. Then I decided to surprise him by changing Ashley's hair and putting some of her new clothes on her. I thought Wil would be happy I had treated Ashley like she was mine.

"Why did you change her clothes and buy her all these toys?" he yelled angrily, as he looked through all the shopping bags I had brought home.

"What? You the one who told me to take her shopping," I said, starting to catch an attitude.

"No, I didn't. I said 'go shopping and take her with you,'" he said as he grabbed the bags and stomped into the bedroom.

He came back in the living room a few minutes later and told Ashley to put her coat on.

"I'm going to drop Ashley off at her grandmother's and I'll be right back," he said without looking at me.

"Bye, Miss Kayla," Ashley said as she walked out of the door holding Wil's hand.

Wil's right back turned into right long. He was taking forever to drop Ashley off. Wil was getting on my last nerve having me wait for him, so I paged him an ungodly number of times. He still didn't call me back.

I grew angrier and angrier. I started putting fake numbers in his pager, like straight sixes, fives, eights, or whatever came to mind. I knew he would say I was acting childish, but I didn't care. He should have called me back.

While he was gone, I sat and watched *Friday* for the tenth time, laughing at every part, like I had never seen it before. Chris Tucker was funny as shit.

When Wil finally came back to my apartment, he asked me why I had paged him like that.

"You should have called me back. It don't take two hours to drop Ashley off."

"I was talking to Ashley's grandmother. Then I stopped past Stevie's house. You don't have to page me like that, all right."

"Call me right back and I won't."

"If I don't call you right back, it must be important. Anyway, where did you put the rest of my clothes?" he said as he walked into the bedroom.

I jumped off of the sofa, laughing, and ran into the bathroom and locked the door behind me.

"You gonna be mad," I said from behind the bathroom door.

"Where are my clothes?"

"At the Salvation Army."

"The Salvation damn Army? Why the hell did you do that?" he yelled. There was a pause, and I thought he had walked away from the bathroom door, but then I heard him laugh quietly. "I must have got you really mad. That's how you gained all that weight, huh? Worrying about me."

I cracked open the door and said, "Nobody was worrying about you."

"That's what your mouth say, but as soon as I got back you was all up on me. 'Wil, I love you. I need love. Don't leave me'," he said, mimicking me.

I couldn't believe he was making fun of the way I felt about him. I was beginning to get angry. Reaching into the bathroom, he grabbed my arm and said he was only playing.

"No, you wasn't," I said, snatching my arm away.

"Say what you want, Kayla, but you do really need to lose weight."

"I only weigh one-sixty and I'm five four."

"Well you need to be weighing at least fifteen pounds less so you can be trim for me. You was a lot smaller when I met you."

I began to cry. My feelings were hurt, and I was scared that my man was not satisfied. He might leave me if I didn't lose weight. I had to lose weight.

I had to if I wanted to keep him. I didn't want him to leave me like he had left his wife because she was fat.

As soon as I woke the next morning, I looked in the yellow pages for a gym. I made an appointment to enroll. I wasn't going to lose my man over a couple of pounds.

Chapter 12

I spent Christmas over my Mom's house. It was no big deal. I was just glad fall semester was through. Somehow I managed to get one A, two Bs, and a C. Another semester was under my belt.

I gave Leslie a gold link bracelet, and I gave Nikki a gift certificate to Foot Locker, because she's so picky I never know what she likes. Leslie got me a VCR to replace the one stolen when I lived in the dorm. Nikki bought me some CDs I had wanted.

Wil spent the day with his parents. He told me he was going to pick up Ashley and bring her over there, too, and then stop over Leslie's when he dropped her home to her mom's around eight o'clock. I remembered Thanksgiving, how he took all day, I told him I didn't want to sit around waiting for him. He promised me he was going to be on time, so you know I was shocked when he was a little early.

"I didn't expect you until like midnight," I told him as I kissed him on the cheek.

"Why? I told you I'd be here at eight."

"Yeah, but you know how you get on holidays."

He shrugged. "Well, I'm here now. Where's my gift?"

"I ain't get you nothing," I joked as I walked to the tree to get his present. I had bought him some tan Timbs. He told me I had to wait to get my gift until we got home. I knew it was something good, so I told my mom and Nikki we were going home so I could get my gift.

When we got home I turned on the lights and waited by the door for Wil. He came inside with a bright red box with a white ribbon. I snatched the box from him. "What is it?"

"Open it up and see."

I did exactly what Wil said. I ripped the wrapping off and opened the box to find a black Coach shoulder bag.

"Thank you, Boo. This is nice."

"You're welcome. Now look inside."

I looked inside the bag and saw five big-face one hundred dollar bills. I gave him a hug. He said, "I couldn't figure out anything else to buy you. So just buy yourself something nice with that money."

"I will." I knew what I was going to do with the money, and that was buy myself a coat and a pair of boots for our Pocono trip.

It was supposed to take two hours to get from Philly to the Poconos, but we got lost somewhere on the Pennsylvania Turnpike. I had the map in my hand. Looking at it, I could see we were almost in Harrisburg.

"Wil, I think we're going the wrong way."

"Look, Kayla, I know where I'm going. We're near the turnpike."

Then Stevie interjected, "Uhm, brothaman, the sign we just passed said Turnpike NE extension."

"I told you so. You should have listened," I repeated to Wil, until I could tell he was tired of hearing it.

He wasn't listening to me anyway. He just got off at the next exit, stopped at a gas station, got some gas, and got back on the dark highway going in the opposite direction. A two-hour ride had turned into a three-and-a-half-hour journey.

"Why don't they have lights on this highway?" Angie asked.

"I don't know, but these roads make me think of Jason in *Friday the 13th* or something," I answered.

We finally reached the hotel, only to find out we had no reservations. Angie got so upset she started going berserk in a thick Jamaican accent. She got in that front desk agent's world and area code.

After that, they somehow managed to "find" our reservations. Wil and Stevie took our luggage to the rooms, while me and Angie finished the paperwork at the front desk. I carried the bag that was left.

The room was beautiful. It had a heart-shaped Jacuzzi, heart-shaped soap, and heart-shaped candles. Everything was in the shape of a heart. There were two private suites equipped with fireplaces. Because I was carrying that heavy bag, I was huffing and puffing.

Instead of Wil trying to help me, he started laughing. "Fatty, what, you can't breathe?"

"Shut up, Wil, I'm tired of your fat jokes. I'm losing weight."

"Not enough. Psyche, naw. Baby, come here. I'm only joking," he said as he kissed my forehead.

Wil was really starting to get on my nerves talking about my weight. He made me feel so self-conscious.

Later on that night, Wil and I sipped champagne and danced off of Seals "Kiss of a Rose" song and counted down the New Year. 10-9-8-7-6-5-4-3-2-1. "Happy New Year!" we screamed.

Wil kissed me. It was the longest, most intense kiss I had ever experienced. It was so sensual.

Then I realized this was the first new year of my life I wasn't at home watching Dick Clark in New York City drop the ball over Times Square. I was with my man.

You know what they say, whoever you're with on New Year's Eve you'll be with for the rest of the year. So I guessed I'd be with my Boo.

The entire stay, Wil and I never left the suite. I didn't want to ski. I couldn't see being cold for fun, plus Stevie and Angie were starting to get on my nerves. They kept knocking on our door and asking us to go out with them.

"No, no, no, no," was the answer. "Leave us the fuck alone. Don't you see we're trying to piece our relationship back together?"

We were putting in QT. For those of you who don't know, that's quality time. Plus, for real, Angie wasn't even that cute. She was plumper than me, with an irritating nasal voice. She didn't look half as good as Kia or even Lan'ique. I wondered why Stevie had chosen her.

The Poconos was the bomb. I had never brought the New Year in so right. And everything else in my life was going right for a change. My boo was back. A new semester was about to start. I was looking forward to going back to school. I had passed all of my classes by the grace of God. Leslie and Yaz were getting married.

Wil had moved all his stuff in. I was losing all the weight he wanted me to lose. I had gotten down to 149 pounds in about three weeks. I had begun eating less and exercising seven times a week. I even signed up at the gym in my neighborhood. It cost sixty dollars per month, even if you didn't go that month, but I didn't care. I signed the contract for twenty-four months. Nothing was going to stand in the way of my being Wil's all.

Chapter 13

"Hurry up and get dressed. I can't be late to my mom's wedding."

"I'm coming," Wil said as he tightened his black satin tie.

"Just hurry up, Wil. Whose car are we taking?"

"Need you ask? We taking the truck."

"Just hurry up and put your coat on."

Finally, Wil was ready. We raced down Broad Street, trying to make the 11 A.M. appointment. I don't know why anyone would want to get married in City Hall. How unromantic. But Leslie said she didn't feel like a big wedding. She said she was too old for that.

I do was all I heard as we entered the courtroom. My mom turned and smiled and kissed her new husband.

I ran over to her and Nikki and hugged them. There were tears running down my cheeks. I was so happy for Leslie. This day had taken a long time to come after David died.

I still remembered that horrible night like it was yesterday. The police had come to our house and banged on the door. Then all I heard was my mother screaming. She had not even been married that long. She was still enjoying being a new bride only to find out that she had become a widow. I never thought she would be happy again, but I'm glad I was wrong.

After Leslie's wedding, we all went to dinner at the Chart House on

Delaware Avenue. Then we drove Leslie and Mr. Charlie to the airport. They went to Las Vegas for their honeymoon. On our way home from the airport, I suggested we go to the movies.

What a bad idea. At the movies we ran into one of Wil's old girls. Her name was Sheila. You would have thought her name was "Food, eat me up" from the way Wil was looking at her. He gazed at her like she was a T-bone steak. He didn't even introduce us. He just kept complimenting her as I stood there.

"Your hair look nice. So does them pants."

"Thank you," Sheila said.

I couldn't believe it. He must have forgotten I was standing there. She was pretty, though, about a size six. She had nice skin and a short baldy kind of blonde haircut.

But who cares? Wil didn't have no business all up in her face like that. I felt like kicking him right in the mouth. As soon as she walked away, I turned around and asked him, "Why were you all in that girl's face right in front of me?"

"What are you talking about? All I said was hi."

" 'Oh, nice pants,' 'Oh your hair look so nice.' What was that all about?" I said as I got in his face.

"Man, come on, stop tripping. I love you. I'm with you. I don't want that girl. If I wanted her, I would be with her."

"I couldn't tell," I responded.

Needless to say, I didn't enjoy the movie. The rest of the night I didn't say anything to him, not in the car, not even when we got back to the apartment. I went straight to the bedroom, got in my night clothes, turned the lights out and got in the bed. Wil sensed my attitude and just got in the bed without saying anything, either. At times like this, I hated him. He was so disrespectful.

The day after, Saturday morning, I got up to use the bathroom and start my cleaning, when I almost fell in the toilet. I turned the light switch on to find Wil had left the toilet seat up again.

I started going off. I don't know why I got so upset about such a trivial thing. Maybe I was PMS-ing or was still mad about the previous night at the movies. At any rate, I had just told him about that shit the other day. Men are so fucking selfish. Why the fuck couldn't he have put the toilet seat down?

"Dumb motherfucker," I said aloud.

He was still sleep. At first I wasn't going to wake him, but I had to. He had to learn. I walked over to the bed and nudged him.

"Yo, Wil, get up."

He opened his eyes and asked what I wanted.

"I want you to stop leaving the toilet seat up."

"I know you're not waking me up for that bullshit," he said as he turned the other way and put the covers over his head.

"Yes, I am. I don't want to fall in the fucking toilet again like I just did," I yelled as I snatched the covers off of him.

He looked at me, sighed, then got up. I thought Wil was getting up to talk to me. Instead he looked at the clock, picked up the phone, and called Stevie.

"Stevie, yo man. You ready to go run some ball? All right, I'll meet you down there."

"Where are you going?" I asked, as I stood there.

"To run some ball."

"We're not finished talking."

"Yes, we are. I won't do it anymore. OK? You happy?"

I couldn't refuse Wil, so like an idiot I said, "Yes, I'm happy."

The next thing I knew he was out the door and I was back in the bathroom again cleaning the floor. I cleaned the kitchen, living room, and bedroom. Afterward, I was exhausted.

I flopped on the bed and was about to fall asleep when I heard a beeping noise. At first I thought it was my beeper. So I found my black Coach bag and dug it out. But it wasn't mine. And still I heard beeping. I began searching around the house, listening to the beep, beep, beep. I couldn't figure out where it was coming from. It kept going off every five minutes.

I finally found it in Wil's leather jacket. It had overflow on the screen. I wanted to know who and why someone was paging him so often. I thought I was the only one who did that. So I dialed the number and a familiar voice answered.

"Hello, did somebody beep Wil?"

"Yes I did. Who is this?"

"This is Kayla."

"Little girl, what are you doing with my husband's pager?"

Oh shit, I thought. *Carmen.*

For some reason, my first reaction was fear, but then I reasoned, why should I be scared? He was my man, and she wasn't scared when she called me that last time. *Let's see how she likes it now that the shoe is on the other foot.*

"I beeped him, not you. You don't call me the fuck back," she continued. "Who do you think you are? If you're calling me, he must be on his way to take us out like he does every Saturday."

"I don't think so. He plays ball with Stevie every Saturday."

"I told you my husband's back with me."

"Listen, one, he's not your husband. Two, Wil already told me it was something wrong with you and you be in la-la land fantasizing about how you're getting back together. But it's not going to happen, 'cause I'm here to stay. I'm not going anywhere. Plus, he lives with me, baby."

"You're lying. He just made love to me and is about to move back home. He doesn't stay here with me because his father wants him to get up in the morning so he can be on time for work, but he comes past every night."

"No, he doesn't."

"You're a lying little young girl. You're just a piece on the side. You know that, right?"

"Believe whatever you want, but ask your daughter if she has ever been to this piece-on-the-side's house."

I heard her call Ashley. "Did daddy ever take you over to his girlfriend's house?"

Then I heard Ashley's sweet little voice saying, "Yes. Daddy said it was our secret and don't tell you, Mommy. Daddy's girlfriend was pretty and nice. She bought me clothes and toys."

After that, I heard a click. I sat with the receiver next to my ear for a moment, trying to make sense of what I had just heard. After all the *I love yous,* Wil still was loving someone else.

Even though I was playing the big girl role with that bitch Carmen, I had believed every word she said. Wil was still cheating. I was pissed. Why did he keep doing this? Couldn't he have just left me alone if he had wanted to be with her?

I was going to kill him. Wil walked in around 4 P.M. like he had
played basketball all day. I just sat on the sofa waiting for him to act a
little different, like he knew what was going on.

"Why you sitting there looking all stupid?" he said.

"Probably 'cause Carmen been beeping you all day."

"What are you talking about, Kayla? You going to start that shit up
again?" he said angrily, opening the refrigerator door and taking out
orange juice.

"What shit?"

"Look, I told you, I want only you and she going to beep me. She
got my daughter," he said as he poured some juice into a glass.

"What? Stop lying, Wil. I called her back. She told me everything.
She didn't beep you for no fucking Ashley," I said as I jumped up in
his face.

"Look, I'm not having this conversation with you, Kayla. You
shouldn't have been checking my beeper anyway. You're acting inse-
cure, like a little young girl. I do everything for you and you don't appreciate it. You sitting here stressing over minor shit. All you should
be worried about is me taking care of you and being here with you
every night. What I do outside of that door you shouldn't care about."

"Fuck that shit. I'm going to concern myself with everything. I'm
not going to be no dumb bitch content with a nigga taking care of
me. I don't need you that bad. You can get the fuck out if that's the
case. You're not going to cheat on me, bitch. I don't need you!"

"I'm not cheating on you."

"I don't believe you even uttered that bullshit out of your mouth."
I felt like jabbing him right in the fucking eye. "You know what, get
out. Give me my key and get the fuck out now! You don't respect me
and I don't need you."

Wil stood there for a minute, then stepped back, took my key off
the key chain, and threw it at me. I ducked and reached for the first
thing I saw, which was a bunch of CDs. I threw them at him, but I
missed.

"Fine, Kayla, I'm out of here. When you get your shit together,
beep me or call me at Stevie's," Wil said as he slammed the door.

Who was he walking out on? I thought to myself. I was pissed. *He's not coming back this time, I swear. I'm getting the locks changed and my phone number changed, too.* It was definitely over. I didn't have time for him. He was a liar. I hated him. *He ain't shit, fuck him!*

The more I thought about it, the madder I got. I gathered all his belongings once again and drove them over to his mom's house. His truck wasn't outside, so I went to Stevie's and knocked on the door. He came to the door, "What's up, Dog?"

"Nothing. Where's your cousin?"

"I don't know, but I'll beep him for you."

"You got company tonight?"

"Naw."

"Let me get something." I walked straight to the car and gathered the trash bag I had put all of Wil's belongings in.

"What's that?"

"This is all your cousin's stuff. Tell him I'm not playing with him this time."

"What he do?" he asked.

"He still messing with his wife."

"No, he don't. For real, Kayla. She crazy. He don't mess with her. She be trippin' on him."

"I don't believe that."

"Just come in, Kayla. I'm going to beep him and y'all get this straightened out."

I went inside and had a seat as Stevie beeped Wil. I waited about a half an hour, but he never called back.

"I'm leaving, Stevie." I knew Wil must have been with someone else, because he always called Stevie right back.

"OK, when I see him I'll tell him you were here," Stevie said.

I went home mad, so mad at myself for allowing myself to go down the same road again. When I got home, I beeped him and beeped him. He never called back. I called his mother's house. I hung up on her like twelve times. I got tired of asking for him.

I was so upset I was about to call Yazmine, but then I thought of our last conversation, which hadn't been good. All she would say is, "I told you so." And I would deserve it.

I sat on my bed trying to figure out where I had gone wrong. How had this happened? I know we had only been together for five months, but he was still my man.

I refused to go to Yazmine's wedding alone. She would see all the envy written on my face. To be totally honest, I'd rather be in her situation than mine. I wished I had a boyfriend, the same one for years. I would love it. But no, I couldn't be so lucky. I needed the next best thing, a date. So I got on the phone and called Samir. First I called his 800 number, and once again he called back in like half a minute.

"What's up, Kay Kay?"

Ill, my mom calls me Kay Kay, I thought. "Hi, Samir. What are you doing?"

"I'm down at school."

"Oh, I just called to see if you were going to Yaz and Sam wedding."

"Yeah, I'm going. You going?"

"Yeah."

"Oh, who you going with?"

"Nobody." I wished he hurry up and ask me so I could get the hell off the phone.

"Dag, I would ask you to go but I'm taking this johne'."

I couldn't believe I had beeped my nut johne' and he had a date already. My stomach was hitting the floor.

Then he said, "Psyche, I ain't going with nobody. Damn, Kayla, I can't even get you mad. You didn't care if I had a date or not. That's fucked up. I been chasing you since September. Here it is almost February. When you going to give me a chance?"

I wanted to say, *I gave you a chance, but you didn't tap an ATM before you took me to dinner at Friday's.*

"Well, it's next Saturday. When are you coming home?"

"I'll be there Friday afternoon. I'll call you then."

"Bye, Samir."

I hung up the phone and studied myself in the mirror. I was looking for just a trace of gray hair. They say stress brings gray out at an early age. If that really were true, I figured I should have a full head.

Chapter 14

My girl, Yazmine Harrison—now Yazmine Gerry—cut no corner on her wedding. She said since she was only doing it once, she might as well do it right.

Leslie asked, "Isn't that girl too young to be getting married?" I had to remind her me and Yaz were not the same age. Yaz was twenty-four years old and she already was playing house, so why not be a wife, too?

I still harbored some negative feelings toward Sam for that whole Sonya apartment incident, but if his wife could forgive him, so could I, I guess.

He claimed to have changed, and it had been almost two months since Sam had gotten out of the game. I admired his strength to walk away from the money and glitz, but then again, that shit don't last. You get locked up, all your shit gets repossessed, your girl or mom gets everything that's left, and the next nigga takes over your corner. He's the man now and you're a has-been. A legend behind bars.

Maybe Sam really did wake up. He'd gotten a job at the University of Pennsylvania Hospital. He was making nice money and Yaz had a job at this day care that was going to pay her to go to night school to study early childhood education. *Yup, maybe it'll work out for them after all.*

Back to the wedding. It was da bomb, do you hear me? Da bomb. Me and Samir arrived about ten minutes before the wedding started.

Yaz's mom had saved me a seat up front and Samir just sat in the back with his boys. I had forgotten Yaz was about to marry one of the biggest ex-drug dealers in the city. Everybody was there.

After the vows were read by the imam, that's what Muslims call their minister, they sat down across from one another during the ceremony. There were no bridesmaids or none of that because of Muslim tradition.

Yaz didn't need anybody else to look good anyhow. She was doing it all by herself. She had on a cream-colored long satin and lace dress and a lace kemar. Sam had on a black suit with a cream-colored tie. They were introduced as Mr. and Mrs. Samuel Gerry, as Kenny G played in the background.

The reception was at the Four Caesars, a banquet hall on City Line Avenue. There was an ice sculpture of a couple holding hands and shrimp everywhere. The buffet tables held chicken, salmon, steak, rice pilaf, and different kinds of salad. There was also a live band and a deejay for when the band took breaks.

Everyone was crowding around Yaz. I didn't get an opportunity to give my congrats until after the traditional black wedding and get-together song went off. Yes, you guessed right, "The Electric Slide."

Everybody got up and did the slide, even Samir. I was happy I had come with him. He was a nut, but I thought about cracking him. He was so silly, he made me laugh all night. He had me doing old dances like the Whop, the Cabbage Patch, and the Running Man. When he started acting like James Brown, a crowd gathered around him. That boy could really dance. At one point, Yaz came over to the table.

"Hey, girl," I said, hugging her.

"Look at this," she said, placing her hand in front of my face.

"Damn, Zsa Zsa, how can I be down?" I said, as I looked at the stunning ring.

The diamond was the size of a nickel, with a glistening diamond band.

"Just have a few kids and put up with some shit."

"You know, this is the playa's ball," I said, looking around at all the boys dressed in tuxedoes and shit.

"Yeah, this is my player's last ball. Sam's friends all paid for this. We didn't have to pay for anything. Not even our honeymoon. We leave for Hawaii tomorrow."

"Damn, Yaz, I'm jealous."

"I know you'll be here one day, too," she said and laughed. "All I want to know is how you come here with Samir?"

"I don't know. I didn't have anybody else to come with."

"What's up with Wil?"

"Girl, you don't want to know. I don't want to ruin your day. I'll tell you some other time." I hugged my friend once more and said, "I'm so happy for you."

"Thank-you," she whispered.

Yaz walked around the floor speaking to everyone, taking pictures and accepting gifts. Darryl walked over to the table and was like, "You finally gave in to my little brother."

"No, I didn't," I shot back.

"Well, Kayla, if you didn't, you ought to. My brother really likes you. He's a good guy. He doin' shit with his life. That's why Sam and I wanted y'all to hook up so bad, 'cause you know I don't be sweating no ho's."

"Dag, for a minute I was about to have a little respect for you."

"Naw, don't respect me," he laughed. "I'm not the respectable type, but Samir is for real. Treat that brother right."

After Darryl left the table, I thought about what he had just said. It had to be some truth to it. Samir had been chasing me and I hadn't been very open minded.

Was what they say true? Do we treat the good guys like shit and the bad ones like princes? Did I have a good man under my nose and not realize it?

Maybe I should give him a chance, I thought. Besides, Wil was most definitely out of the picture and Samir was nice looking. He was cheap, though, and I don't like that shit. But I probably could change him.

This Luther Vandross song came on and all these older people got up and danced. Samir was dancing with Yaz's mom. They were doing something called the Bop. It looked decent.

When they finished, I got Samir to teach me, and then we went outside to the lobby bar to get drinks, because now that Sam was claiming to be a changed man he didn't want any alcohol around him, and all they had to drink at the wedding was sparkling cider.

At the bar, me and Samir played a drinking game to see who could take the most shots of Hennessey. I got so drunk Samir had to take me home. I didn't know how he figured out which key was the correct one to get in the apartment.

When I awoke, I realized I still had my dress on from the night before and there was a bottle of aspirin and some ginger ale on my nightstand. Samir must have known I was going to have a headache. When I got up, I felt dizzy. I looked around and noticed Samir asleep on the floor with no blanket or pillow. He just had his balled up jacket under his head.

"Samir, get up and get in the bed."

"Huh?"

Samir crawled up on the opposite end of the bed and fell back asleep. The next day was a lazy Sunday, the kind of day when you wake up, get something to eat, then go back to sleep again. When I awoke, I smelled bacon and eggs. Samir had went and got us breakfast.

"You finally up?"

"Yeah, I was tired."

"You must have smelled the food. I went to this place called the New Deal on 16th and Fairmont," he said as he sprinkled salt and pepper onto his food.

"What you get me?"

"Eggs, pancakes, and bacon."

"Thank-you for breakfast," I said as I grabbed the platter out of the plastic bag.

Then I noticed Samir staring at me. "What are you looking at?" I asked.

"You. You know, you're so cute."

"Really?" I said, laughing his compliment off.

I wasn't really that hungry, so I ate only half of the food. Then I climbed back in the bed and nodded back off to sleep.

When I awoke, Samir was in my living room watching football. I thought he would have went home by now.

"What time is it?" I asked.

"Like three. You been asleep all day. I was waiting for you to get up so you could lock your door."

Then Samir came closer. He caressed the back of my neck and touched my hair gently. The next thing I knew, Samir was kissing me.

I stopped him and looked at him as if he was crazy, as if to say, *What are you doing?* It didn't bother him, because he kept kissing me and kissing me. Then our clothes came off and we were doing it.

All I know is that it felt like a dog was humping on me. If Wil was a man, Samir was definitely a boy. On a scale of one to ten, his sex skills were a five. I couldn't even get excited. I don't even know why I let him keep doing it. I thought about making him stop, but then I thought that maybe I wasn't giving him a chance. Maybe it was just so bad because it wasn't Wil. No one could ever replace Wil.

Afterward, I felt like the roles were reversed, because Samir wanted to snuggle all on me and I just wanted him to get out. He thought he had just had the best sex ever. I knew I had just had the worst. He kept kissing on me and complimenting me, but I was not impressed. I wanted him out of my apartment, but didn't know how to say "Get out!"

Finally, Samir announced he had to head back to school. I told him to call me as soon as he got home, but I really didn't mean it. Deep down inside, I hoped he'd never call me again.

OK, how this happened I don't know, but me and Samir started talking on the phone every day. I now looked forward to his calls. I waited by the phone for his calls.

Before he was a bugaboo. But he was slowly but surely filling the void that Wil left behind. We talked about everything from who our first grade teacher was to the first person we ever kissed. I was beginning to dig the shit out of Samir.

One night on the phone, I even told him how at first I didn't like him because he was so cheap that night at Friday's. He apologized and attributed his being cheap to growing up really poor and never having had anything. Then I had to ask him why Darryl wasn't cheap.

"Because Darryl gambles and hustles. Money comes and goes to him. So he don't mind spending it. Me, I just don't ever want to know how it feels to be broke again. It was a fucked-up feeling, Kay. We was poor as shit."

"Well, I understand that, but you only live once. I buy myself whatever I want, whatever makes me happy."

"Yeah, but why should I make some other people richer, spending money like a fool?"

"You're right," I said.

Then the phone went silent for a minute.

"Kayla, where is your man?"

I hadn't thought he had noticed. Well, I guess we had been talking every day and I hadn't been dissing him anymore, so I might as well tell him the truth.

"We broke up. He was putting me through a lot of shit."

"When did y'all break up?"

"A while ago. I mean, he was trying to get back for a minute, but I'm done with him. I got tired of the lying."

"Yeah, I used to go through that same lying shit with my ex."

"It's sickening, I mean."

"But, Kayla, I wouldn't hurt you or lie to you. So now you can come down Maryland and visit me, right?"

"I guess."

A trip to Baltimore. I guess that's what's up. I needed something to make me stop thinking about Wil. At least I wasn't thinking about him every day now. I could go a day and think, *I didn't think about Wil today.*

So I made arrangements to go see Samir. At first I was going to drive, but I didn't want to take the Maxima out of the city limits. Plus it might break down, and I wasn't trying to get stranded on Interstate 95 South.

The day I was leaving, traffic was a mess on Broad Street, so I missed my bus and I had to catch the train. I called Amtrak to find out the schedule. The next and last train was leaving at 4:30 P.M. Glancing at my watch, I saw it was 3:45. I hung up the phone and called a cab.

Then I called Samir and left a message on his pager that my plans had changed and to meet me at the train station around 6 P.M. The cab dropped me off at 30th Street Station at 4:20. After buying my ticket, I couldn't find the right track, so I asked the attendant and he pointed me in the right direction.

I ran down the stairs, walked on board, found a seat, and put my bag on the rack above my head. I caught my breath and relaxed. The train seemed like it was moving slow, but actually it was doing like 100 miles per hour. All I could see was trees out my window, and that was beginning to bore me, so I got up and walked around. I grabbed a bag of cookies and a soda from the café car and it came to like $4.00. If I had been at the corner store, this would have been $2.00. Oh well.

Walking back down the aisle, I was knocked off balance by the swaying of the train. I almost fell into this guy typing on his laptop.

"Sorry," I said.

"That's quite OK. If you wanted to sit with me, all you had to do was ask. But then again, I do have that kind of magnetic pull on women."

I looked up stunned, as this incredible-looking white man smiled at me. Yes, I said white man. I'm not really into the interracial thing, but this guy, Chris, had it going on. Even though he was sitting down, I could see he was short and he had dark hair and green eyes. He was wearing tan khakis and a blue Polo-styled shirt and seemed nice as hell.

I sat down and talked with him. He showed me pictures of his wife and two kids and talked about his job as a reporter for *The New York Times*. We just basically kicked it. He said he was on his way to Atlanta to cover a story.

"Why are you traveling by train?" I asked, as I finished eating my cookies.

"I'm scared of flying," he said.

"Oh, I see."

An hour had passed and my stop was approaching. I told Chris it was nice falling into him. He asked if we could meet again. He offered to pay for me to fly out to wherever I wanted and he would meet me for the weekend.

Excuse me, was this an indecent proposal? Didn't he say he had a wife who was pregnant? Here her husband was on the Amtrak train heading south trying to put the moves on a sistah from Philly. I couldn't believe Chris, especially after the long story he just got finished telling me about all Carolyn had done for him, how she had forgotten about her career to raise the kids and put him through his last year of school.

Boy, I tell you, black men, white men, they are all the same. They ain't shit. How could he even look me in the eyes and ask me if I'd meet him somewhere? But I did take his number. I was scared not to because I didn't want him to find me and kill me.

He wasn't the only one who had been running his mouth. I had told him about Wil and Samir and school and Tuesday and Sherm, and what school I went to and what my major was. He might track me down and try to murder me if I didn't call him. He could be a psycho.

On the way back to my seat, I threw his number into the trash receptacle. The train stopped and I reached up and grabbed my bag. Samir was waiting when I came off the escalator.

"Hi, Kay-Kay," he said, as he hugged me and kissed me on the cheek.

"Stop calling me Kay-Kay. You make me feel like a little kid when you call me that," I said as I handed him my bag.

"I'm sorry. I'm just happy you made it down. How was your ride?"

"Well, I met this crazy white man who worked for *The New York Times* and he wanted to meet me again in any city I wanted."

"Kayla, don't you know better than to talk to strangers? He probably was a weirdo."

"So where we going?" I said, annoyed. I didn't need him telling me what to do.

"To my apartment. But first I got to stop past my boah, Gerald's, dorm."

"How far are we from there? 'Cause I got to pee."

"Not far."

We drove up to Blount Towers and double-parked in front of the stone building. His friend came downstairs to meet us.

"Which way is the ladies' room?" I asked.

"Right down the hall."

"We'll be in room 307. The bathroom is to your right."

The bathroom had about eight stalls, a dim light and smelled like cigarettes. As soon as I walked in, I noticed these girls talking in the bathroom. I ignored them and walked into the stall, but before I could close the door completely, I heard my name being called. I re-opened the door, surprised by the fact that I was in a ladies' bathroom in Maryland and somebody knew me. I came out and saw no one other than Gina, the chick from the club who I didn't like, that used to fuck with Samir. I closed the door as she began minding my business.

"Who you down here with?" she asked, like we was cool.

"My friend," I answered.

"Your friend. Is it a guy or girl? I might know them," she said as I flushed the toilet and came out of the stall.

Her girlfriend said something to her, but she brushed it off.

I fixed my clothes in the mirror as I caught a jealous glance. She asked me again who I was down here for. I don't know why I was scared to tell this whore I was here at Morgan to see her old johne', Samir. Finally, I confessed.

"I'm here with my boyfriend, Samir."

Her mouth dropped wide open. "Samir Braxton?"

"Yes, do you know him?"

"Yes, I know him. Kayla, Samir is my old boyfriend, as a matter of fact. From one sister to another, we're trying to work out our differences. Right now we are separated."

"Well, he never mentioned you, and we have been dealing with each other for a minute," I said with a devilish grin.

"He didn't!" she looked shocked.

"No, he didn't. So see you later," I said as I turned and exited the bathroom.

"Kayla, wait. Look, please leave Samir alone. We've been together off and on for about three years and he doesn't need to jump right back into a relationship."

I was beginning to feel like I was a part of a bad soap opera. So I just turned around and told Ms. Thang, "If you can get him, you can have him. All I can tell you is, what goes around comes around. Remember Kevin? You started this. You're the one who likes walking in the back of people's trails."

I walked out of the bathroom feeling like I finally got that bitch back for stealing Kevin back in high school. The only way she got him was because she was fucking and I wasn't. Who was laughing now? I found room 307. Samir was sitting on the top bunk talking to Gerald when I came in. Samir jumped off the bunk and said, "Gerald, this is my girl, Kayla."

"Nice to meet you, Kayla."

"How you doing?" I said as I thought, *Who told Samir I was his girl?*

"Well, Joe, we about to get out of here," Samir said as he grabbed his jacket.

"I thought you said his name was Gerald."

"It is. Joe is like 'boah' down here. Like they say 'country' down here. That means corny and bamma means nut."

"So you my bamma," I said and giggled.

He pushed me out the door as we said our good-byes.

"So where are we going now?" I quizzed him as we got back into the car.

"To my apartment."

"Oh, guess who I just saw?"

"Who?"

"Gina."

"Did she know you were down here for me?"

"Yeah, I told her. I hate her. She made me and my first boyfriend break up in high school. She always was a little slut. She said y'all getting back together."

"What? You know she is lying. I keep telling that girl to leave me alone."

Once in the house, Samir turned into Romeo. I don't know if I forgot my lines or if I just didn't want to play the part of Juliet just yet. Didn't I still love Wil? Why was I here? I questioned myself over and over.

Still, I couldn't get up and say I'm going home. I was stuck miles away from home. I turned around and saw balloons were waiting in the living room. There were about three extra large ones and five smaller ones. They all had different messages, "Thinking of you," "Miss you, and "My special friend." It was obvious what Samir wanted. A relationship.

"Thank-you. But how am I going to get them home on the train?"

"I'll drive you home. You don't have to take the train. My brother wants to switch cars anyway."

"So what you trying to get into?" I asked.

"You," he said as he walked closer to me.

He picked me up off the ground and sat me on top of his kitchen countertop. He opened my legs and nestled his face between them. "Samir, stop. Stop," I said, as he unbuttoned my pants. "Samir, stop." "You really want me to stop? You know you don't, 'cause if you did, you wouldn't be sitting here with your legs wide open. Come on," he said, reaching for my hand and walking me into his bedroom.

The lights were out, but I still could see posters of Tupac and Foxy Brown and his cream-colored, mirrored bedroom set.

"Lay down, Kayla," he said as he kissed me.

I did what he said. I was beginning to like Samir, but I couldn't help looking up at the mini blinds and thinking I shouldn't be here. If he could read minds, he would have known my body was there with him but my mind was two states away with Wil.

But then the words of that oldies song went through my head, "If you can't be with the one you love, love the one you're with." So I did. And you know what? It was nothing like the first time at my apartment. This time around, it was ten times better.

Damn, I'd been letting this get away, not just the sex but this nice man. This man that really wanted to be with me. Here I was tripping over someone who wasn't even concerned about me. Maybe that little light that peeked through the blinds was waking me up or maybe I was just lonely, missing Wil so much I allowed Samir to be Wil. Not Wil, but he was doing everything Wil did. He was even wearing the same cologne, Issey Miyake.

After it was over, I stared at myself in the mirror on the headboard. *What am I doing?* I asked myself. Then Samir asked me "Kayla, how many partners have you had?"

"What?"

Leave it to Samir to ask a stupid question and spoil a good time. I was shocked by his question. I was embarrassed, too. Let's just say I had not been the poster girl for chastity over the last year, but it wasn't my fault. I mean I know I'm the one who opened my legs. If only Emar would have acted right, I would have still been with him. Instead, I was still out here searching. But I was afraid if I told Samir the truth, he might think less of me, so I just got smart with him.

"Does it matter?" I asked, raising my eyebrows.

"I just wanted to know."

"I don't know."

"Kayla, how could you not know?"

"Samir, if it matters so much, why didn't you ask me a half hour ago?"

He was dumbfounded because he knew I was right.

"You right, Kayla. It doesn't make a difference. I just want to know everything about you. You really know how to treat me, Kayla. Gina used to dog me. She used to have me chase her. I mean, I had to chase you too, but I know that's over, right? I mean, I just want us to be together. Can we work on that?" he said, as he slipped out of bed and got on his knees next to the bed.

"Samir, I just came out of a relationship," I said as I stroked his facial hair.

"Kayla, I want you. I want to be with you," he begged, still kneeling on the floor.

I paused because I didn't know what to say.

"We can work on it," I finally said.

"Bey, I just want to make you happy," Samir stated as he gazed into my eyes.

"Aaah, Bey," I murmured as I kissed Samir.

Samir was so sweet—*but what the hell am I going to do with him?* I thought to myself.

"So what you want to do tomorrow?" he asked me.

"I want to go shopping."

"Your last boyfriend must have spoiled you. You don't look like you need to go shopping. You got rings and earrings all glistening, but that's what's up. I guess I have to spoil you, too. How much I need to take you to the mall?"

"This much," I said as I put my hand in a C form.

"How much is that? What, you think I got money?"

"You got money. You just cheap. So when are you going to give me my money back from the train?"

"Girl, I got you."

"Yeah, all right."

"You hungry?" Samir asked.

"A little."

"Well, I'm going to order a pizza. What you want on it?"

"Uhm, mushrooms and green peppers."

"Yeah, that's cool. Now I just got to find the cordless phone. You seen it, Bey?"

Samir walked into the other room in search of the phone.

"Bey, I think I saw it in the living room. Why don't you just press the page button on the phone?"

Seconds later I heard Samir on the phone ordering the pizza. I walked to the bathroom to freshen up when I heard Samir whispering something like, "Don't call me no more" and "Don't worry about that or her" and "Yeah, that's my girl." Then he said, "Look, I'm hanging up. Bye, Gina."

I had just heard it all. I wanted to laugh out loud, but I couldn't let Samir know that I was listening, so I flushed the toilet and walked back into the bedroom. When Samir entered the room again, I asked him if the pizza was on its way.

"Yeah, and guess who just called here?"

"Who?"

"Gina."

"What she say?"

"Nothing, really, she just sickening," he said as he laid his head on my stomach looking up at me, like an affectionate puppy dog in love with its master.

The pizza came. It was hot and delicious. We ate, drank, and watched *Goodfellas*. That movie was funny as hell. I leaned on my bey, Samir. This was different, very different.

Life in Philly was back to normal. I was going to school and work, then coming home to my empty apartment and calling Samir every night, talking for at least two hours. My phone bill was $300, but Samir Western Union'ed me the money to pay for it. I had to ask him. He didn't do shit automatically like Wil. I decided to start buying some of those prepaid calling cards. Sammie Sam is what I now called my bey. I had to call him.

"Bey, what you doing?" I asked.

"Missing you."

"I miss you, too!"

"I miss you more, but I have to study, so I'll call you back."

"All right, Bey."

"See you. I'll be home this weekend."

It had been a while since I had spoken to Wil. Valentine's Day was approaching. I thought about sending him something like some dead roses, but I had started thinking about him less and less. He had been replaced by Samir.

Samir was the sweetest ever. For Valentine's Day, he gave me a dozen pink roses, a strawberry shortcake, and he cooked me dinner, too! He made some crab imperial dish with pasta. Then we went to Dave and Busters and played pool. Rather, he taught me how to play pool.

Samir was so different from Wil. He was so patient and understanding. With him I was in charge, and he would do anything I asked. Samir would not mind massaging my back all day if I asked, whereas Wil would rub my back for two minutes, say he's done, then ask me to do him. I am so glad I realized Wil is not the one and Samir is.

Chapter 15

Samir called me from his cell phone to tell me he was around the corner and to come outside because he would be there shortly. I went out and took in the very mild May-like weather in March. A gentle breeze lifted my hair off my shoulders as I waited for Samir. Mrs. Franklin's boys were playing touch football. I was suddenly distracted by the rhm, rhm, rhm sound of roaring motorcycles. Samir.

"What's up, bey? You want to go for a ride?" he asked.

"On that?" I asked, as I raised my eyebrows at the neon green Kawasaki Ninja ZX6.

"Yeah, on this," he said.

"Naw, I'm cool," I replied.

Mrs. Franklin's kids gathered around, screaming, "That's decent. That's the kind of bike I want when I grow up." Then their mother came down the steps saying, "Boys, come in the house, it's time to eat. How you doing, Kayla?"

"I'm fine."

"Well, be careful. Don't get on the back of that thing."

"I won't."

Mrs. Franklin stood out on the steps for a minute, then went back into the house. As soon as she left, Samir started pressuring me again to get on that bike.

"So are you going or what?" he demanded.

I hesitated. I'd never been on the back of a motorcycle before. But I didn't want Samir to think I was a nut, so I gave in even though I was scared. Trying to play it cool, I swung my leg over the back of the bike and held on tight to his waist.

Samir took off so fast my neck snapped. He was going fast as shit. "Samir, stop. Samir, please stop."

He didn't pay me any attention. He just rode faster. Then he popped a wheelie—you know, like when the front end of the bike goes up. Finally, he stopped at a red light. As soon as we stopped, I punched him in the arm and told him to stop going so fast. He promised to stop playing. That's when I heard a familiar voice coming from the car behind us.

"Oh, Kayla, you a rider now?"

It was Stevie, Wil's cousin. And that Jamaican girl, Angie, was with him.

"What's up?" I said, trying to act like riding a motorcycle was no big thing for me.

"Nuttin. I just got to tell my cousin you're a rider."

"So tell your cousin whatever you want. I don't care," I said.

I turned away from him and wrapped my arms even tighter around Samir's waist. *Tell your cousin that,* I thought to myself. Out of the corner of my eye, I snuck a peek to see if he was watching. He was.

"Don't front," Stevie said as he sped off after the light changed.

Samir, racing for male pride, sped off, too.

The machine went booooop, boooooop, booooop. I could barely open my eyes. And my head hurt so bad. I turned my head and saw a gray room and my mother and sister. I could hardly speak.

"What's going on?" I whispered.

"You fell off of a motorcycle."

"Huh?"

"Yeah, baby, you and some boy, but he didn't make it. You've been in a coma for about two weeks. That nice boy, Wil's cousin, called me and Nikki. It's going to be OK. I notified your school and job. You can stay with me when you come home. We saw the ambulance people bring in the guy you was with. They put a white blanket over his body."

"No, no, no. Not Samir. Oh, God, no."

"Calm down, Kayla," my mother said as tears flowed down her face. I couldn't take it anymore. I closed my eyes. I heard the monitor noise start boop, boop, booping even louder than before. My mother started screaming. Nikki was holding on to me.

"Don't go, Kayla. Don't go. Don't leave me," she said, grabbing me by the shoulders and shaking my limp body.

There was nothing I could do. I couldn't open my eyes, even though I tried and tried. I tried lifting my arms to part my eyes open, but they wouldn't move either. It was over, as simple as that.

Please let me go on, God. Please don't take me and Samir. Please, not yet.

Then I heard the boop, boop noise again. Only this time the room was bright white and Nikki, my mom, Charlie, Wil, and Yaz were all in my hospital room.

Nicole came over to me, saying, "Hi, sis. How you feel?"

"I feel fine."

Leslie leaned over me and gave me a big hug.

"You had us so worried. You've been out of it for a couple hours. Do you remember falling?"

"No. Where's Samir?"

"Right here, bey," he said as he approached the bed, looking ashamed. He had bandages covering his head.

"I do remember telling you to slow down and you kept going, Samir." I was still groggy, but everything was beginning to come back to me.

"Bey, I know. I'm sorry," Samir whined.

"You're sorry. You almost killed my daughter!" Leslie shouted.

Samir tried to defend himself, but everyone just started ganging up on him.

"Young man, you just don't play with someone's life like that. You just can't," Charlie scolded him.

Samir looked again at me and turned and said, "Kayla, I'll just talk to you later."

I screamed as loud as I could for him to come back, but he didn't even turn around.

Wil, looking fine as ever, walked over and asked, "Are you OK?"

"Uhm, how did you get here?" He was the last person I expected to see.

"Remember? Your little boyfriend was trying to race my cousin. He crashed into a car and you fell across the street and bumped your head. You're lucky you're talking."

"Yes, Kayla, you are lucky. Why didn't you have a helmet on? And what were you doing with that boy?" Leslie asked.

Charlie grabbed my mother and said, "Let's all get something to eat and let her rest. Would you like anything, Kayla?"

"No," I said. Nikki, Leslie, and Charlie left. Wil came closer and gave me a soft, sweet kiss on the cheek.

"Boo, how you been?" he asked gently.

"I've been fine."

"I've missed you."

"I can't tell."

"Well, I did. I'll let you get some rest and I'll come through later on."

"Uhmm," is all I said as Wil walked out the room. The only one left now was Yaz.

"Bitch, you scared the shit out of me."

"For real? What's going on?"

"Girrrrl, Samir and Wil been going at it all day. Wil's been trying to intimidate that poor boy. Samir wouldn't even look at him. He just stared at the ground."

"So what exactly happened and when am I getting out of here?"

"Well, Samir was going too fast and crashed into a car. You fell and bumped your head. You've got a couple of bruises on your arms and legs, and a slight concussion, too. But you'll be all right. You'll probably be out of here tomorrow."

"Really? I don't remember anything. I still can't believe Samir and Wil were in the same room together."

"You're awake." A lively, gray-haired nurse entered the room. "How are you feeling, Miss Johnson?" she said as she checked my blood pressure.

"I'm a little hungry."

"OK, what do you want?"

"Buffalo wings."

"No, we don't have any of those. How about some pasta?"

"OK," I replied as she took my temperature and changed the bandages on my head.

"Well, Miss Johnson, I'll have them bring you something up," she said as she jotted something down on her clipboard. "The doctor will be in to see you shortly."

After she left the room, Yaz started talking again.

"Uhm, did I tell you we moving? We found a house right outside of Philly in Yeadon. You know Mia started school. She goes where I work at. You know Sam's cousin, Kelly, got me the job. I'm going to put Sam Jr. in there, too. Sam is doing real good at his job. Things are really going well for us. They really are."

I guess Yaz was rambling on and on 'cause we hadn't talked in a while. But after a while, she said she had to go see about the kids.

"Yo, Yaz," I said as she picked up her brown bag and made her way to the door. "We've been through some shit. But you always there when I needed you. We just got to stop cursing each other out about our relationships. I just had this dream that I died. It was real strange. And you know what else? I realize that Samir is the best thing for me now. Fuck Wil."

"Really," Yaz said as if she didn't believe me.

She left and I tried to go back to sleep. But my eyes hadn't been closed long before the nurse arrived with the spaghetti. Leslie, Charlie, and Nikki showed back up around the same time, too. They saw my eyes were closed and whispered, "She's sleep. Let's let her rest."

Good, I thought. *I have a lot to think about.*

I was so happy when they released me the next day. Lying there in bed was boring as shit. The food was nasty. There was no cable, and the phone stopped accepting incoming calls after 9 P.M.

I wasn't thrilled that Charlie came and picked me up, but Leslie was at work and Nikki was at her new part-time job. And I hadn't heard from Samir. When we reached my house, Mrs. Franklin was sitting on the steps smoking a cigarette.

"Sorry to hear what happened to you. I told you not to get on the back of that thing," she said as she exhaled a puff of smoke.

"Thank-you," I said. But what I really wanted to say was, *Ain't nobody ask you anything.*

"Yeah, well. You know me and the boys are always here. If you need us, just stomp on the floor and I'll come right up."

"OK," I said, then proceeded into the apartment. Charlie asked if there was anything he could do.

"Just continue to take care of my mother."

"I will," he said as he smiled.

He was a nice man. And really growing on me, I thought as I locked the door behind him.

Alone at last, the first thing I did was take a hot bath. I wasn't due back to work for another week, so I was just going to relax. The ladies had called me while I was in the hospital. People had been so nice to me.

Except for Samir. I hadn't heard from him since the day before when he ran out of my hospital room. I decided to call him again and let him know I wasn't mad at him. I tried all three of his numbers, but got no response. On his cell and his 800 beeper, I said "Samir, I'm not mad at you. I miss you, bey. Call me so we can talk. I'm home from the hospital now. Call me."

Two days passed and Samir hadn't called me back. Wil kept calling, but I screened his calls with my caller ID box. I didn't answer the calls from his mom's house, the office, or from Stevie's. There was nothing I had to say to him. He was a liar and a cheat. I thought if he treated his wife like shit, why would he treat me any different? I hated him.

Meanwhile, Samir's not calling was starting to make me mad. He was going overboard with this. I know he felt guilty but, God. I called him and apologized for everything I could possibly think of. Then I even got Yaz to get Sam to tell Darryl, Samir's brother, to tell him I wasn't mad at him and for him to call me. But he still didn't call.

Then I started to think about the accident. Maybe it was his fault. Maybe that's why he wouldn't call me back, because he was wrong and he knew it.

No, it wasn't really his fault. It was really Stevie's and Angie's fault, trying to play my baby. He was only trying to defend his pride.

Chapter 16

A week went by and still no Samir. But Mr. Wil had been very persistent. He kept calling and I kept checking my caller ID box and not answering the phone.

Then one day he caught me. The caller ID box read phone booth, so I answered, hoping it was Samir.

"Hello," I answered, smiling from ear to ear.

"Please, Kayla. Don't hang up. We need to talk."

I recognized the voice immediately.

"What do we have to talk about, huh? The fact that you're married or how you're a liar and a cheating dog?"

"Kayla, come on now. I signed my divorce papers weeks ago. Kayla, that's what I've been trying to tell you. I'm free, Kay. We can start our life together. Can you give me one more chance, Boo? I promise you it'll be just you and me this time."

Me and Wil. Wil and me. The notion of our getting back together sounded kind of good to me. Actually, it sounded real good. Pleasant memories started drifting through my mind—all the good times we had had, the intimate late night talks, the love, the sex.

Then my thoughts turned to less pleasant times, like when I found out he was married and all the hurt and pain I went through. Just recalling those times made me feel like I'd been kicked in the stomach.

I took a deep breath as Wil anticipated my response to his million-dol-lar question.

"Wil, I can't take another one of your promises. I'm going to ask you nicely: Don't call here anymore."

I hung up on him, and it felt so good. Then I called the phone company and requested to get my telephone number changed. The operator asked what the reason was and I told her I was being ha-rassed. She told me my number would be changed by the end of the day.

Then she proceeded to give me my new telephone number. I wrote it down and then called Leslie's answering machine and Yaz's beeper, to let them know I had gotten the number changed. I could only imagine Wil's expression when he called my old number and he got the recording that my number had been changed. He would be so salty. He would probably try to just show up on my doorstep. I de-cided if he started playing that game, I would just move.

In my dream in the hospital, I had prayed to God to give me life, so I wasn't going to waste any time on a messed-up person like Wil. But I should have known Wil wasn't the give-up type. A few days later he was at my door banging, flowers in hand. I opened the door, pissed as shit.

"I thought I made myself clear that I don't want to be bothered with you anymore. It's over. Leave me the hell alone," I said.

"Kayla, let's talk," he said as he tried to brush past me into the apartment.

"Get out! Wil, don't play yourself. I will call the cops on you."

"Stop tripping," he said as he pushed past me.

He grabbed my arm, and began dragging me over to the sofa. Then he pushed me so hard that I fell back on the sofa. I wanted him out, but he was too strong for me. The only thing I could think of doing to get him out of my apartment was to bang on the floor with my foot like Mrs. Franklin had told me to. I did it.

Wil looked at me like I was crazy, but it worked. Within seconds, Mrs. Franklin and her three sons were running through my door, which Wil had left open, bat in hand.

"Is there a problem?" she asked looking like she was about to go up side Wil's head. All she needed was a signal.

"No, we're all right. We're just going through something right now, Miss," Wil answered in a respectable tone.

"You need me to call the cops or anything, baby?"

I thought about it for a minute. I wasn't really trying to get Wil in trouble, so I decided to let him say what he had to say and then hopefully he'd leave.

"No, thank-you, Mrs. Franklin. We're OK," I said.

"OK, baby. Stomp again if you need me. I'll be right downstairs," she replied as she lowered the bat and turned and headed out of the apartment. Then I heard her and her little boys charging back down the stairs.

Smoothing down my hair, which had gotten all wild during our scuffle, I crossed my legs and folded my arms across my chest as I waited to hear Wil out. He sat down next to me and sighed.

"Look, let's not go through this. You love me and I love you. We want to be with each other. I know I can't live without you and I definitely don't want to see you with anyone else."

"So this is what this is about. You can't stand the fact I was with someone else."

"No!"

"Yes, it is. And to think you almost had me going for a minute. I'm not going for that I-changed-in-a-day bullshit you're kicking."

I stood up, pointed toward the door, and asked him once more to leave. Wil got up off the sofa and walked toward the door, but before he reached it, he grabbed me and hugged me good-bye. He held me so tightly that I was inhaling his cologne. It triggered feelings and emotions I thought I had forgotten.

Then he pulled away from me and gently tilted my face up so our eyes met. Then he kissed me.

I tried hard not to kiss him back even as I felt his warm tongue next to mine. But my body had a mind of its own. Every cell in my brain was saying no, but I couldn't help it. Wil had the power.

My arms slowly crept up Wil's back until they were around his neck. I had become a team player in this game of Wil's. I was kissing him back. I was holding him, loving him, feeling him. *This is getting good,* I thought.

Then I thought about Samir. *If I get back with Wil, what about Samir?*

Well, what about him? He hasn't even called me to make sure I was OK and Wil has. As my skirt was being lowered over my hips, I looked up at Wil and asked him what this meant.

"This means I love you. We're together in our circle and we won't let anyone else in. We don't have to rush. I won't move back in. I got me an apartment. This time it will be different."

So by now you must have guessed me and Wil got back together. I know what you're saying. You think I'm dumb, but I don't care, 'cause I got my Wil. We vowed to give each other 100 percent this time.

But after our sexual escapade of the other day, Wil did something he never did before. He left. Usually, after we make love he would stay and hold me. But this time, I didn't really mind.

After he left, I jumped in the shower and put my nightclothes on, ready to fall asleep, when I heard a knock at the door. I figured it was Wil again, so I opened the door without asking who it was only to find Samir standing in the entrance of my apartment.

"Samir. What are you doing here?" I said, surprised.

"Kayla, you have to understand how I felt. I thought you were going to be mad at me, so I kept my distance, you understand, right?" He could barely look at me as he stood in the doorway

"Samir, why didn't you call me when I was beeping you and calling your cell phone leaving messages?" *And why would you pick now of all times to show up?* I thought.

"You got to understand, bey, your family made me feel real bad. I was playing with your life. I was showing off 'cause I knew that the boah in the car was your ex's cousin. I wanted him to know you were happy without him. Instead I almost killed you."

He looked so pitiful standing there, like he was about to cry.

"Bey, come in," I said gently as I reached for his hand.

I felt sorry for him. But if only he knew Wil had just left, that I still loved Wil and only liked him. Or did I love him, too? I didn't know.

Samir sat on the sofa me and Wil had just made love on. I wondered if he could tell. Nervously, I sat down next to him. He started holding me. Then he tried to kiss me.

I couldn't kiss him. Well, at least I tried not to. Samir's lips were kissing the same two lips Wil just got finished suckling. Oh, my God, but Samir was so much of a better kisser.

Then he tried to take it further, but I couldn't allow it to happen. I had never been with two people closer than a month apart, and I surely wasn't going to be with two men in one evening.

After a few more minutes of "No, no, no, Samir," he got the point and said he would call me tomorrow. He walked out of the door, and then I lost my mind. *What was I going to do? Samir or Wil? Wil or Samir? They both want me and I want both of them. Where the hell were either of them when I didn't have anyone?*

I needed to talk with someone. But I figured calling Yaz about the Wil/Samir situation was not a wise choice. One, she favored Samir because he never hurt me like Wil, and two, she just didn't like Wil. But I decided to call her anyway. The fact that I couldn't make up my mind was wreckin' my brain.

So I was shocked when she said "Be with both of them. Fuck it, men do it all the time. They have their cake and eat it, too. Ya know they always play us."

"You right, but I really care about both of them."

"And you can still care about both of them. Just live your life."

Yazmine was right. Wil was doing his thang on me before, and after all I didn't know exactly what Samir was doing down at school. I decided I would talk to them both. I wouldn't get caught.

Chapter 17

OK, so I was living a lie. I was performing a miraculous juggling act. When Samir was in town, I would kick it with him as soon as I got off work until around twelve. Then I would send him home and Wil would be finished running the streets and chill with me on the late night.

I called Samir *bey* and I called Wil *boo*. To make it easy on me, I started calling both of them babe.

Don't get me wrong, it wasn't all hard work. It was a lot of fun. I felt like a secret agent getting away with selling secrets to the enemy, because I was getting away with murder.

One day, Wil spent the night and Samir called me and asked me if I wanted to go to breakfast. I looked over at Wil. He was still asleep, so I decided what the hell and went and met Samir while Wil unknowingly laid in my bed knocked out.

Another time, Samir had literally just pulled off when Wil pulled up. Wil asked me what I was doing outside. I told him I was waiting for him.

It was tiring. How men do it, I don't know. But I could see why they do it. I mean, why have just one person love you when you can have two people loving you?

But things were getting out of control. I mean, Samir wanted to be around me every second of the day. "I need to make up for the way I treated you," was his favorite line.

I couldn't take it. He got mad when the other line clicked and wanted to know who I was hanging up on him for. Usually I'd lie and say Yaz and she having problems with Sam and she needs someone to talk to and I would call him right back. The last time I did it, he said something about "They are sure having a lot of problems lately. Huh?" I guess he was catching on. I don't know.

Meanwhile, Wil would be on the other line asking me why it took so long for me to hang up on Yaz. They both was stressing me. Yaz was always my alibi. I made sure she could always back my story up. I think that's the difference between men and women. Men just lie without thinking. When women lie, we already got a backup lie for the first lie just in case we get caught.

The funniest thing about the whole situation was that seeing both of them at the same time, I thought I would begin to like one better than the other. That wasn't the case. I now was totally confused about who I really loved, and I was starting to see how you could love two people at the same time.

The only thing I hate more than a man screaming at a football game is seeing a grown man play football on Sega Dreamcast as if it was the real thing. I can't stand it.

"Wil, Wil," I said into the phone.

"Huh?"

"What are you doing?"

"Playing a game."

"What? That Steven Madden bullshit?"

"It's not bullshit and it's John Madden. I got $100 on this game against Stevie."

"Well, you're supposed to be listening to me."

"I am."

"No, you're not. The game is more important."

"Nigga, what, ha ha. I'm the man. Give me my money," was all I heard.

"Wil, you heard me?"

"Yeah, I heard you."

"What did I say?"

"I forgot."

All I heard was the music from the stupid video game and somebody yelling, "Interception!" That stupid game gets on my nerves.

"You know what? Bye. I'm hanging up because I didn't say anything," I said, irritated.

I only did this 'cause I knew I could and he loved me and I wanted him to pay attention to me. Then my line clicked. "Hold on, all right?"

"Un huh." He didn't even hear me.

I clicked over. "Hello."

"Kayla?"

"Yeah."

"Kayla Johnson?"

"Yeah, who this?"

"Kayla, it's me, Tuesday."

"Tuesday. Oh, my God, girl, how you doing? How have you been? How long has it been? What are you doing with yourself now?" I couldn't believe it was my old roommate Tuesday calling me.

"Chilling. I'm back in Mississippi."

"Y'all got married and moved. Oh, that's so nice."

"No, I said I'm back. Prepare yourself girl. Me and Sherm broke up."

"What?"

"We got to Arizona and he started tripping. Sherm started telling me what I was going to do and what time to be home, what to wear and to have dinner ready. Then one day I was in the market with this list he wrote for the food he wanted cooked by six.

"I started thinking, 'What am I doing this for?' Then I asked myself a question I had never asked myself before—did I even love him? And no kept popping up in my head over and over again. I felt tied down, like I was closed in. I felt like I would never go back to school, like my purpose in life would be to serve Sherm. So one day when he left for work, I started packing my clothes and was out."

"I can't believe you. So what about school? What made you leave like that in the first place?"

"Well, when I took Sherm home to meet my parents, they hated him. So I guess I was just rebelling. But it's a lesson learned. I'm going to the community college down here, and just sitting back relaxing."

"Uhm uhmmm," I murmured.

Then Tuesday said in her country drawl, "Fuck that. I got to live my life, you know what I'm saying? For the last three years I've been letting a man rule me, and I'm only twenty-one."

"Did you say fuck that?"

"Shut up girl, you heard what I said. I'm making Tuesday happy now."

"OK, so you living for you now. I still can't get over that. So how'd you get my number anyway?"

"From your mom. Some man answered the phone. Who was that? He acted like he didn't want to give me your number."

"Girl, my mom got married. So did Yaz."

"That's nice. So what up with your life?"

"You wouldn't believe it if I told you."

"I got all night."

I told Tuesday everything, from Emar to Wil and even back to stalker Jay.

"You know, so what do you think?" I said, tired after talking so long.

"All I can say is, go with your heart. Go with whatever makes you happy. Don't live for money or fame or just for love. Love somebody that loves you as much as you love them."

"Well, you most certainly have grown up. Damn girl, I forgot I was on the other line with my boyfriend. I got to call him back before he get mad."

"Which boyfriend?" Tuesday asked as she started laughing. "Well, whichever one, just go ahead call him back. Girl, we been on the phone too long. My bill going to be high. Take my number down and call me. I'll probably call you again sometime next week."

I called Wil back. The first thing he asked was, "Who was that?"

"My old roommate, Tuesday."

"So you couldn't click over and tell me that?" he said with an attitude.

"No, sorry, babe."

"It's OK. Just don't let it happen anymore. What my boo doing anyway?"

"Waiting for her boo to come home."

"Why? What you going to do to your boo?"

"He'll find out when he gets here."

"I'll be there. Love you, baby," Wil said, happily.

"Love you, too."

I hung up the phone and called Samir.

"Babe. What you doing? "

"Talking to this boah. Why, what's up?"

"Nothing. I was just calling to tell you I was going to bed. I got a lot of stuff to do tomorrow," I said between fake yawns. "So I'll talk to you tomorrow, OK."

"OK. I love you Kayla," he said while blowing kisses.

"I love you, too! Bye," I said as I put down the phone. I didn't want him calling in the middle of the night, because he was good for that, and I didn't need Wil questioning me about who was calling so late.

I sat on the sofa and began to think about the whole Samir and Wil scenario, because it was really getting complicated. I didn't know what I was going to do.

Then my thoughts wandered back to Tuesday and Sherman. I had thought they were the perfect couple. I had always figured one day I would be going to their 50th anniversary party.

At least I'm not the only one with issues. I guess in life nothing is promised, not even love.

It was easy to jump back into a relationship with Wil because I was still in love with him. But at the same time I needed my space and he needed his, too. So we started out slowly. It was great. He had his own apartment in Darby, right outside of Philadelphia. It was really nice. It had a man's touch, but didn't resemble Stevie's bachelor pad. Wil's apartment looked lived in, with a little flavor. I stayed over there sometimes, but then when I wanted, I still went home and laid in my bed by myself or was with Samir somewhere. We took our time getting reacquainted.

For my birthday, Wil and I decided to go to South Street and celebrate my turning twenty-one. We went into an erotic bookstore, where we laughed at all the sex toys and ended up buying some fragrant massage oils and candles. Afterward, we strolled down the street, kissing and holding hands. I was tipsy from the three margaritas he bought me at the Copabanana.

On our way back to the car, Wil was holding me up for support when we passed a tattoo parlor. Wil looked in the window and said, "Come on. Let's go in." He already had enough tattoos. He had Ashley's name on his right arm, his name on his left and a Chinese good luck symbol on his chest.

"For what? You getting another tattoo?" I asked, trying not to slur my words.

"No, but you are. For your birthday."

"What? I'm not getting no tattoo."

"What? You scared?" he asked.

"No, but what you want me to get?" I asked.

"I want you to get my name."

"What, you tripping?"

"No, I'm serious."

"I don't know, Wil. Would it hurt?"

"No, it won't."

A man covered with tattoos approached us, saying, "Can I help youse?"

Wil responded by telling him I wanted *Wil* on my arm as he pulled up my shirtsleeve. I don't know what I was thinking. I just sat down and let the tattoo man sketch what the tattoo was going to look like with a pen. Then I felt a needle on my arm, scraping the shit out of me. I was ready to cry, and then the pain faded.

Once I saw my boo's smile, it didn't hurt any more. I would do anything to make him happy. It took just a half hour, and my arm was forever engraved with Wil's name. I was cool about it, until I got on the phone and called Yaz. She told me I was a nut and then asked me did he have my name on him? I started thinking, and said, "I didn't ask him to, but if I did he would."

"Are you sure about that, Kayla?" she asked, sounding sarcastic.

I didn't tell her I was drunk when this all happened, 'cause she would have had something to say about that, too. Plus, I was the only one now, so it didn't matter if he had my name on his body or not.

When I got my tattoo, I was thinking all about Wil and not at all about Samir. I was so stupid. The next day I almost forgot about the tattoo. But luckily, I remembered it in time and threw on a long shirt to cover it when I went over Samir's house.

Ms. Robin, Samir's mom, was in the kitchen saying, "Is that my future daughter-in-law who's going to give me some more grandbabies?" I was thinking, *Didn't Darryl give you enough? He got like four kids.*

Ms. Robin only knew me from over the telephone, yet she really did like me and told me I was the one for her son, and that I was the best girlfriend he'd ever had. When Samir came downstairs, he smiled at me, then tried to hug me, wrapping his arm around where my tattoo was.

"Ow, you're hurting my arm!" I whined as I pulled away from him.

"Your arm. What's wrong with your arm?"

"I got a tattoo yesterday," I said without thinking.

"You did? Let me see."

"Psyche, I don't have no tattoo. Where we going?"

"I don't know, bey. It's all about you."

"Well, let's just go back to my house and chill. We can rent some movies or something."

"That's a plan."

We drove to Blockbuster, where we rented *CB4*, a funny Chris Rock flick, and *Heat*, which was intriguing 'cause you don't know what's going to happen until the end, and *The Water Boy*, another comedy.

The evening was going smoothly. Wil didn't come by and to make sure he didn't call while Samir was there, I turned my ringer off and relaxed. Samir began rubbing my back with the oil Wil had just bought on South Street. It felt so good.

I took my shirt off so he could oil me down all over. *Mmm*, I thought. *I could get used to this.*

Then I noticed that Samir had stopped caressing me. And suddenly I remembered the tattoo. I was busted. There was nothing I could say or do. I just grabbed my shirt and looked at Samir. He looked as if he wanted to hit me, but of course he didn't. I didn't know what to say.

"Samir, I know what you're thinking. I was drunk," I said, trying to explain myself.

Samir wasn't trying to hear it. He got up, grabbed his things, and walked out without saying a word. I didn't try to chase him down, because I knew I was wrong, very wrong. I started thinking maybe I hadn't been that drunk after all when I got my tattoo. Maybe I had subconsciously planned the whole scenario on purpose 'cause I was tired of putting Samir on ice while I defrosted Wil.

My mind kept replaying how Samir had looked at me with disgust and then walked out on me. *Fuck him,* I thought.

But I couldn't say fuck Samir. I hadn't meant to hurt him. I was sorry. I had been greedy. Although I had only wanted one man, I had been given two and I couldn't say no.

For days, I beeped Samir, but he never called me back. Meanwhile, Wil would be over my apartment and Samir would be on my mind. What a change of events. Sometimes, I would hear a motorcycle riding past and hope it was him. It never was. I had lost a good man. But maybe it was for the best. Who knows?

I went to Samir's house to try to get him back. His mother let me in, but he wouldn't come downstairs.

"I'll try to talk to him for you, Kayla, because I like you," Mrs. Robin promised as she headed to his room.

I got a little hopeful that Samir might at least come downstairs and listen to me, but a few moments later Ms. Robin returned to tell me she told Samir I was sorry and he had said I *was* sorry.

So I just ran past her and up the stairs and opened his door. Samir was laying on the bed in his boxers with a wife beater T-shirt on, watching television.

I walked in and said "Samir, let's talk."

He turned around and gave me the angriest look I had ever seen. Then he turned back toward the television.

"Samir, Samir," I kept saying.

But he didn't even turn around to look at me. He just stared right into the television at some football game that was on. I stepped in front of the TV, blocking his view.

"Samir, you know I want to be with you."

Samir jumped up from his bed and got in my face.

"Kayla, look. You was playing with me. You went and got some other nigga's name on your arm while I was ready to make plans to spend my life with you like a nut. You don't care about me. Please, Kayla. It's over."

He started pushing me toward the door. "You don't want a nice guy like me. You want a nigga that's gonna treat you like shit and disrespect you like the one you got. Now get out!" He slammed the bedroom door after me.

Finally, I just gave up, because I still didn't know who it was I really wanted. Samir was right. Maybe one day I would get it right.

Chapter 18

It had been about a month since Samir had seen my tattoo, and Wil was not showing any signs of his old personality, so I slowly let my guard down and started giving my all to Wil.

One night we were at the Laff House, this comedy place on South Street, having a nice time laughing and joking. All the fun we had made me realize what I really wanted was to be back with him. So later that night when we were back at his place, I started talking to him about how I thought we should get back together into a one-on-one relationship, even though I had just told him I was cool and I needed some time.

You know what he said? He said he was happy with the current circumstances. He said we both were free agents who could sign to any team we liked and he wasn't sure if he wanted to renew his contract with me.

"You know, Kayla, I've been thinking. I do want to see other people."

I couldn't believe my ears. I thought about it for a minute and decided Wil was just trying to upset me. "You know what? That's what's up! There are a couple of niggas trying to holler at me," I said casually.

That's when Mr. Big Boy said, "Kayla, please don't make me fuck you up."

"What you mean, fuck me up? You want to deal with other people, but you want me to just wait for you? Please, I'm outta here." I jumped up from the sofa.

"No, you're not," he said. He jumped up after me and grabbed me and began shaking me so hard my neck was snapping.

Crying, I bit him on his neck and ran from the bedroom. He chased me, saying, "Sit down, Kayla!"

"No! You don't know what you want."

I wasn't really going anywhere. I just wanted to make Wil mad, and it was working, 'cause he beat me to the door and grabbed me so tight. He wiped my fake tears away, and said, "Baby, we are going to work on this."

That night, I tried to go to sleep, but couldn't. Every other minute, the phone was ringing. He usually turned the ringer off when I came over. He must have forgot. He claimed all the girls that call are girls he met when we was broke up. He could sleep through anything. So I answered the phone and told all his little girlfriends where to go. But they kept calling.

Finally, I woke Wil up and he picked up the phone and said, "Whoever this is, stop calling here. My girl here."

That satisfied me momentarily. However, I wondered why, if he wanted me so bad, did he have all these bitches calling him? When I looked at the clock again, it was 6 A.M. I wasn't going to get any sleep. So I told Wil it was time for him to go to work and I was about to leave. I gave him a kiss on his cheek and asked, "Could we go to dinner tonight?"

Wil agreed.

"All right, Boo. I'll see you around six," I said.

"That's what up. We going to discuss everything and make this thing work, all right?" he said as he tilted my head and gave me a kiss on my cheek. As I walked out the door, Wil said, "Kayla."

"Yes, Boo?"

"I love you."

"I love you, too!" I replied.

That's when I just knew everything was going to be OK. If I could put up with this situation a little longer, things would go back to the way they were.

That day, I went to work with a smile on my face. The day went by so fast because all I could think about was Wil and our future, the good times, the old times, just everything. I couldn't wait to see him that night.

As soon as I got in the house, I beeped him. I ate some ice cream as I waited for him to call back. I must have dozed off while watching TV, 'cause next thing I knew, I woke up and it was 3 o'clock in the morning. Damn, I didn't believe I had slept for all that time.

The first thing I did was look at the caller ID box. No one had called. *Where the fuck was Wil and why hadn't he called me back yet?* I wondered. I hoped he was OK.

I beeped him again and then just dialed his number. He answered on the first ring.

"Wil, what happened? I thought we were going out. I miss you. Can I come over?"

"No!" he said, sounding annoyed.

"Why? Wil, I miss you."

"No, I'll call you back."

Then he hung up the phone. I sat there for a minute and thought about how I wasn't gonna fuck with him anymore. Then I decided to call him back so I could find out what was up with him.

"Wil, what's up with you? Why are you tripping? Why can't I come over?"

"Something came up. I'm going to call you back."

"Who is that?" I heard a female voice say in the background.

"Wil, what is going on? You got company?"

"Something like that. I'll call you back."

"What you mean something like that? Pussy! I will fuck you up. No, you gonna tell me now!" I demanded.

Then he hung up in my ear.

I was so furious.

"It's that Carmen bitch at his house," I muttered to myself. "I know he better stop playing with me or I'm going to fuck him up."

I pressed redial. Someone answered but hung up without saying anything. Tears ran down my face.

For some reason I just started thinking about Emar and everyone who had ever hurt me and everyone I had ever hurt. I cried and cried.

The tears that ran down my cheeks, the sting in my eyes, the uncontrollable shake were all too familiar. It was my reaction of a man doing me wrong again.

I called Wil again. Someone answered the phone, and I heard, "Tell her. Tell her. Tell her you love me and your daughter. Tell her, William. I'm not playing with you."

Then the phone hung up. I called back again, and this time Carmen answered the telephone.

"Let me speak to Wil," I demanded.

"Look, little girl, I told you not to call my husband. If I got to tell you again, you're going to be sorry."

"Bitch, who the fuck are you talking to? I will come up there right now and make your ass nonexistent," I shouted into the phone.

"Do it," she had the nerve to shout back.

"Wait right there."

"Bring it on."

Who was this bitch talking to? Didn't she know I would kill her? Wil must have snatched the phone from her.

"Kayla, don't come up here," he said "It's over between us. This is my wife. I love her, and this is who I'm going to be with."

"Wil, what are you talking about? I thought you loved me!" I cried.

"I do, but I got to go. Calm down and get yourself together. I'm sorry."

Then I heard a lot of movement as if people were tussling. I could hear Ashley crying in the background. Then I heard the straw that broke the camel's back. I heard it with my own two ears.

"I love you and only you. Fuck her. She's nobody. We got to worry about us and get our life together."

Then he must have started kissing her, 'cause I heard kissing noises. Then the phone clicked. Someone had hung up.

"No, he didn't! No, he fucking didn't," I said out loud. "Who is he playing with? Oh, God!"

I was shaking with rage. I thought to myself I was going to kill him. It wasn't that he had somebody else. No, that wasn't why I was going to kill him. I was going to kill that black bitch, Carmen. I lost control and began talking out loud.

"I asked you, Wil. I asked you. I asked you. I begged you. And you want to play? Oh I'm going to show you," I hollered at the ceiling.

I pulled the phone out of the wall. I ran to the mirror and smacked myself.

"I hate you, you dumb bitch," I yelled as loud as I could. "I hate you for being so dumb."

I screamed and jumped up and down. I ran into the kitchen. I threw the toaster at the microwave, took all the canned goods out of the cabinet and threw them at the refrigerator. I punched and kicked the walls. Then, exhausted, I took a deep breath. I found the cordless phone and dialed Yaz's number.

"Hello," Sam answered as if he was asleep.

"Can I speak to Yaz?" I asked between sobs.

"Yazmine is sleep and I got to go to work. Don't call here this late."

"I need to talk to her," I begged.

I heard Sam in the background tell Yazmine to get the phone. She said hello and I burst out crying.

"What is it, Kayla?"

"I'm going to kill Wil," was the only thing I could get out.

"What he do?"

I was too choked up to talk. All I could do was keep repeating, "I'm going to kill him."

"Kayla, are you home?"

"Yes."

"Here I come."

"No, I'm coming to get you. That wife bitch is over at Wil's house. I'm going to kill her, too."

"I'm getting dressed."

"I'll be there."

I was on my way out of the door when I realized I didn't have my keys. I searched all over. *Where the fuck are my keys?* I thought. I looked everywhere, on top of the refrigerator, in the bathroom, on my dresser.

Then I remembered I had come into the house and fallen asleep on the sofa. So I took the sofa pillows out, and sure enough my keys were there between the cushions. I grabbed them, got in my car, and pulled off like a bat out of hell. I went through every stop sign and light. If the cops wanted me, they had to catch me.

"You want to play, lie, and cheat? I got something for you," I muttered as I drove.

I pulled up to Yaz's house and beeped the horn. It was 4 o'clock in the morning, so, of course, it sounded loud. Yaz came running out of her house with a black hooded sweatshirt on and jumped inside of the car.

I began driving as Yaz pushed back the hood of her sweatshirt and asked, "What the fuck is going on? Are you losing your mind? You letting a nigga drive you crazy? Huh?"

"No!"

"Tell me what is going on."

I took a deep breath. Then, with tears and snot running all down my face, I said, "Wil gonna tell me first he love me, then I found out he got a wife. He said he got a divorce and he left her alone. Then I find out he still seeing her. Then I leave him and found Mr. Right, but I left my Mr. Right alone to mess back with him, Mr. Wrong. Then tonight I called him 'cause we suppose to go out. I beep him and beep him but he never called me back. I woke up at 3 in the morning and started worrying about him. Then I call him and he said he'll call me back, then he says it's over, he loves his wife and don't call him no more, after I gave him everything and got his name tattooed on my body. Is he fuckin' crazy?" I started sobbing again.

"So what are you going over there to do?" Yaz asked, clutching her seat as I took a wide turn.

"I'm going to kick in the door and stab the shit out of him, scalp the bitch, and cut off his dick."

By the time I had explained everything to Yaz, we had arrived at Wil's apartment. I jumped out of the car. That's when I remembered we needed a code to get in the front door. Luckily, somebody was coming out right at that moment and I grabbed the door open before it shut. I pressed the button for the elevator, but it was taking too long, so I took the stairs two at a time with Yaz following close behind me.

When I saw his apartment door, I felt rage enter and exit my body at the same time. I knocked on the door. No one answered, so I knocked again. And again, no answer. Before I realized what I was doing, I was kicking the door. I knew them two bitches were in there. Fury and madness took over then. It had me running down the hall, and trying to fly-kick at the door to bust it down. No luck.

"Bitch, come out now," I screamed. "Come out! Answer the fucking door, you bitch!"

Wil's neighbors started coming to their doors and I figured I'd better cool out. They might call the Po Po on us, and I didn't want to go to jail. So I kicked at the door once more and yelled, "Wil, you are a fucking coward. When I see you, you're done," I yelled. Yaz just looked at me.

"Maybe he's not in there," she said.

But I knew she knew full well he was.

"He's in there. It's cool, though, 'cause when I catch him, he's done," I said, loud enough for him to hear me.

"Just leave it alone." Yaz started pulling on my arm.

"What? I'm not leaving shit alone. He has to learn," I said as we exited the apartment building. Then I saw my evidence Wil was definitely home. His truck.

"Yaz, look, there go his truck." I pointed. "He's home."

I just shook my head and held back the tears as I started climbing in my car. Then I saw the steering wheel club. I don't know what came over me. All I know is that I grabbed the club and raced to Wil's truck and busted out the front window. The broken glass shimmered and sparkled like crushed diamonds as it cascaded to the ground.

Then I took care of the two right side windows, then the left side front and back window.

Yaz picked up a rock and smashed in the back one for me.

Then I remembered the little pen knife that was on my key chain. I pulled it out and tried to slash his tires but the blade wasn't sharp enough. So I keyed the car up and down and all around and engraved "Don't fuck with me" on the hood.

Then I heard a male voice say, "Hey, what are you doing?"

Me and Yaz ran back to my car and pulled off. As soon as we got around the corner we looked at each other and started laughing hysterically and gave each other high fives.

"That's what that nigga get," she said with satisfaction.

"You right, that's what they all get. All he had to do was tell the truth. That's what I don't understand. Why can't men stop lying?"

"Yeah, ain't no man that fucking good. If Sam do something while we married, I'm out." Then she looked down and gasped. "Yo, Kay, you fucked up your hand."

It was bleeding—bad. I must have cut it while I was breaking out Wil's windows. I hadn't even felt it. I wrapped some napkins around it that I found in my glove compartment.

"You know I got to explain to Sam why I had to leave my house at four in the morning to go somewhere with you."

"Man, tell that nigga, 'Fuck him.'"

"Yeah, I'm hype. If he asks me anything, I'm going to say, 'Nigga, shut up and go the fuck back to sleep.'" We laughed again.

By the time I dropped Yaz off and reached home, I was exhausted and surprised to see Mrs. Franklin sitting on the steps puffing on a cigarette at five-thirty in the morning.

"How you doing?" she asked as she looked me up and down.

"Fine," I answered.

"I can't tell. Why your hand bleeding, baby?"

I was caught off guard with that one. Then she just looked into space as she dragged her cigarette.

"You know my husband?" she finally asked me.

"Yeah."

"I just had to get him locked up. He pulled a gun on me."

"Are you serious?" I said with real concern.

"This is not the first time, either. See, honey, I see y'all young girls out here looking nice, having fun, with guys driving those big cars. That used to be me. I used to be a fly girl. Yup, that's until I met my husband and had all these babies and got stuck."

She took another drag off of her cigarette, then stared off into space as she continued to talk. "I love my babies. Don't get me wrong, but I wished I would have listened to my mother when she said don't get tied down. See, men have baby after baby and can get up and move on. Women can't do that. They got to take them babies with them, you know. No other man don't want to raise nobody else's baby. I didn't listen. But I'm going to give you the same advice my mom gave me. The only difference is, I hope you listen. One, once a man hit you, you get out. Don't stay, 'cause it's not going to get better. Two, once a cheater always a cheater. Three, don't let a man buy you, 'cause you're not for sale. Whatever a man can buy you, you can buy yourself. Four, don't get stuck. Don't get stuck, baby. Why keep trying to make it work? You know how many times in the last twelve years I tried to make it work? Hundreds. That's all I got to say, baby."

Then Mrs. Franklin put out her cigarette and flicked it into the darkness.

"Thank-you," I mumbled, but she didn't hear me, so I just walked past her and into the building. She had her demons to deal with and I damn sure had my own. I unlocked my door and stepped over the mess I made earlier. I took off my clothes and laid in the bed.

That's when I saw the red button flashing on my answering machine. I pressed play and saw one of the stones in my ring was gone. It was the same hand that was bleeding. Oh well, what else could go wrong?

Then I heard Wil say "Damn, Boo. I got you that mad? It don't matter though. My car will be fixed tomorrow, but will you? So I guess you think I owe you an explanation. Well, here you go. I can't be with one woman right now. Not you or Carmen. I just said that so she could get the fuck out, too. Ya know I killed two birds with one stone. Don't think I don't love you, 'cause I do. Honestly, it wasn't supposed to turn out this way. When I first met you, I was just going to fuck you, but then I started to dig you a little. You were so sweet and innocent. I had just left my wife when I met you. Me and Stevie was in the mall when he dared me that I couldn't get your number 'cause I had lost my skills from being married. So I came over to you with some game. You took the bait. I won the bet and here we are."

He rambled on, saying all types of shit I couldn't believe, like he wish I understood and how I would be the right one a couple of years from now, but today he's not the man he should be for me and maybe we can work it out in the future when he's ready to settle down. I listened again and again to the message.

I could not believe I had loved that man. He was a nut, a real fucking nut. I couldn't sleep. All I could think about was that it was going to take true will and strength not to really kill him.

By now, the morning sun was flooding through my window, but it didn't make any difference. The light was still on from the night before and so was my anger. So I got a pen and pad and wrote down a list of all the ways I could rid my life of William Carter Jr.

1. Get rid of tattoo.
2. Sell the ring he gave me.
3. Get my number changed again.

There it was. My plan was all together. I was going to rid him from my life completely.

I laid in the bed for a few hours reflecting on our entire relationship, from the beginning to end. All the good and bad times were replayed in my head.

After I cried one more time, I got up, yawned, and began running some bathwater. I looked through the yellow pages for a laser surgeon. I called one and he wanted too much money, so I decided to get another tattoo over his name instead.

My next mission was to get rid of the ring he had given me. After I soaked and washed, I got out and dried myself off and threw on my gray sweat suit and Nike sneakers and headed for Center City, where I walked into a jewelry store and looked around. The jeweler was helping someone else. She said she would be right with me, so I passed the time by looking in the display case. Then another woman with a heavy Middle Eastern accent came out of the back and said, "May I help?"

"Yes, I want to sell this ring," I declared as I took the ring off of my finger. She took the ring, put it up to the light and weighed it, and said, "I'll give you $70."

"What? That is a diamond ring."

"It's a good copy of a diamond ring. But it still is a cubic zirconia." She barely tried to hide her smile.

"You're joking, right?"

"No, I see this every day. It looks like a diamond, feels like a diamond, but it is not one."

"Thank-you, but no thank-you," I said as I exited the jewelry store. I wanted to sell the ring, but I wasn't going to sell for that little bit of money. I couldn't get mad. I couldn't even cry. I was just so fed up, I had to talk to somebody. But who?

I didn't have Tuesday's number with me, my mother wouldn't understand, and Nikki was too young. I thought about it some more. I could call Samir.

I found a phone booth and dug around in my purse for an old prepaid calling card. Praying I still had some time left on the card, I started dialing. Luckily, my call went through. But guess who picked up the phone? Gina.

"Can I speak to Samir?"

"Hold on," she said, sounding annoyed.

I was waiting for her to get smart or say something, but she didn't. She just gave him the phone.

"Hello," he answered.

"What's up? Please don't hang up."

"I'm not mad at you. I'm past all that. How are you doing?" He sounded as if he was in a good mood.

"I'm OK. I needed someone to talk to and I thought about you, but I see you got company."

"Yeah, something like that."

"I don't know why. She don't know how to treat you."

"And you do?"

"She only wants you because you was dealing with me."

"Kayla, I got to go. I'll give you a call later and we'll talk."

"All right, I'll let you go, but first I got to tell you something."

"What?"

"I love you, Samir."

"We'll talk, Kayla. We will talk."

I hung up the phone. For a minute, I just stood there lost in thought. Then I began walking back to my car and evaluating my life.

Why had I been such a fool for love? Why was it none of my relationships had worked out? I had messed up with Samir. I had gotten played by Wil. Reese only wanted me to be his side johne'. Terry just wanted some ass. Jay was a stalker. Emar was a dog.

Maybe I deserved everything that had happened to me, because when I had Samir, I didn't treat him right. I tried to play him. What we had was good, but not good enough to keep me from messing with Wil. And then when I found out Wil was married, I should have just let him go, but I got caught up in the competition game. I wasn't going to let Carmen take my man away from me, but in reality he was never really my man. The reality was he was her husband.

I continued to look back on all my fucked-up relationships as I put the key in the ignition and took off.

Tears stung my cheek and my mind continued to ramble over countless bad episodes of my love life. I began to ask myself, *Out of all this bullshit, what did I learn?* I mean, why did I always end up with a no good nigga that be trying to play me?

The more I thought about it, the angrier I got. But I had to admit my own actions got me in fucked-up predicaments. Me wanting to be somebody's girl, me wanting to have it all by any means necessary. I was the one who put myself out there, being nice and shit.

Huh, not no more, fuck that, I'm cool. I don't need a relationship. I refuse to go through anything else. I mean, it's not worth it. I'm right where I started from. Which is nowhere. I can just chill by myself. It's less drama, you know. Maybe it wasn't meant for me to be in a relationship, or maybe I just have to really sit back and wait my turn.

And after all, Samir did promise to give me a call.

About the Author

Daaimah S. Poole is currently completing her degree in journalism at Temple University of Philadelphia. She resides in Philadelphia with her son Hamid Poole. She is working on her second book, tentatively titled *You Don't Understand.*

You may visit her website at *www.daaimahspoole.com*

YO YO LOVE

DAAIMAH S. POOLE

ABOUT THIS GUIDE

The suggested questions are intended to enhance your group's
reading of Daaimah Poole's YO YO LOVE.

Discussion Questions

1. Where do you think Kayla went wrong with Emar? Did you feel sorry for her when she realized Emar wasn't coming back, or did she set herself up for failure?

2. What kind of advice would you give Kayla about men if she were your friend? Should she take her time, or should she keep trying until she gets it right?

3. Was Kayla suffering from the "I need a man" syndrome? Why do you think that is so? Was she in love with love?

4. Do you think it was appropriate for Kayla to accept Wil buying her boots? Why or why not? Was Wil trying to buy her?

5. When Wil's wife called Kayla, did she handle herself properly?

6. Did Kayla really love Samir, or was he a Wil substitute?

7. In your opinion, was Kayla justified in destroying Wil's truck? Would you have done the same?

8. Was Wil the perfect man after all, or is there no such thing?